Readers love *Happy Independence Day* by MICHAEL RUPURED

"Rupured is onto something, and I am glad he's writing a third novel. I want to see where these people go next. And you will, too."
　—Prism Book Alliance

"I have a serious love for this series by Michael Rupured. Reading his books is like peeling back the pages of history to get an honest, upfront view at the events that shaped LGBT history."
　—3 Chicks After Dark

"There was a lot going on in *Happy Independence Day*, all of it well written and entertaining."
　　　—The Novel Approach

By MICHAEL RUPURED

A Taste of Honey (Dreamspinner Anthology)
Whippersnapper

HOLIDAY TALES
Until Thanksgiving
Happy Independence Day

Published by DREAMSPINNER PRESS
www.dreamspinnerpress.com

Whippersnapper

MICHAEL RUPURED

DREAMSPINNER PRESS

Published by
Dreamspinner Press

5032 Capital Circle SW, Suite 2, PMB# 279, Tallahassee, FL 32305-7886 USA
www.dreamspinnerpress.com

Whippersnapper
© 2016 Michael Rupured.

Cover Art
© 2016 Maria Fanning.
Cover content is for illustrative purposes only and any person depicted on the cover is a model.

ISBN: 978-1-61372-934-2
Digital ISBN: 978-1-61372-940-3
Library of Congress Control Number: 2015950140
Published January 2016
v. 1.0

Printed in the United States of America
(∞)

This paper meets the requirements of
ANSI/NISO Z39.48-1992 (Permanence of Paper).

For Junie Rupured, my mother, best friend, and biggest fan.

Chapter One: Snowmageddon

WHERE ARE they? Tellumo Magnamater checked his smartphone for the twentieth time in as many minutes and peeked out between the blinds again. Ice and snow melted from car hoods and rooftops in a cacophony of splashes and trickling water. Sooty ridges of snow the same shade of gray as the late morning sky edged the glistening asphalt.

He hadn't seen his mothers since August, when they'd helped him move to Fallisville for his first teaching job, three days before the first day of school. He'd planned to visit Cincinnati for Christmas until Snowmageddon—thirty inches of snow in a week's time—had brought Northern Kentucky to a standstill, putting the kibosh on his holiday plans. Everyone else's too. Churches canceled Christmas services, and bars remained closed on New Year's Eve. Until yesterday's warm front had pushed the temperature into the lower fifties, the mercury hadn't climbed more than a degree or two above freezing since before Christmas, when the flurries had begun.

As Tellumo checked his smartphone for messages again, a white panel truck with Amazon Home Repair on the side in bright blue letters came into view—sporting noticeably more bumper stickers than the last time he'd seen it. He returned the device to his pocket and glanced around his efficiency apartment once more. Everything looked ready for company.

He ran out to greet his guests. Before the truck had come to a complete stop, the passenger side door opened and Trish bounded toward him, her camel coat unbuttoned to reveal the red-and-green plaid pants and gaudy Santa sweater she'd worn on Christmas for as long as he could remember.

"I've missed you so much!" She flung her arms around his neck, kissed his cheek, and held him tight.

He hugged her back, surprised by the tears in his eyes. "I've missed you too." He kissed her cheek, released her, and then turned to Jules, waiting beside them.

"Sorry we're late." Jules squeezed him hard. "Roads haven't been this clear since before Christmas. Everyone and her sister was out." She let go of him and folded her arms across her chest. The creases in her khaki pants and the long sleeves of the oxford cloth shirt she wore were sharp enough to cut hair. "We made good time once we got out of Cincinnati."

"I was starting to worry—you're never late." Tellumo kissed her cheek. "Need me to help you carry anything in?"

"Nah." Jules shook her head. "Sorry to disappoint you, but there's not much to carry." She gave him a grin and a wink. "I'll unload the car. You guys go on inside and catch up."

"If you insist." Trish grabbed Tellumo by the hand and pulled him toward his apartment. "Give her a few minutes to calm down," she whispered. "We've been arguing since we got off of I-75."

"About what?" Jules hadn't seemed the least bit agitated or annoyed. Tellumo hung Trish's coat on a hook on the back of his front door, leaving it ajar so Jules could get in with her hands full. "The car thing again?"

Trish nodded, plopped onto the sofa, and pushed her glasses up the bridge of her nose. "We've argued about it for weeks. She wanted your Christmas present from us to be the money for a down payment." She patted the sofa cushion and motioned for him to sit. "Don't get me wrong. I've missed you too, and having a car would make visits home easier, but if you don't want the responsibility…."

"I don't." He sat down beside her and smiled. Though he still sometimes wondered, he'd long ago stopped trying to figure out which woman was his biological mother. Trish and Jules weren't telling and looked enough alike to make guessing difficult. Knowing when he'd been younger might have made a difference but after all these years was unlikely to alter his feelings for either parent. "I thought about getting a car, but I really don't want the added expense."

"Makes sense to me." Trish ran her fingers through her curly brown hair and looked around. "This place can't cost much. What do you do with your money?"

"Save it—like you've drilled into me since I could walk." The furnished apartment had come with everything but dishes and linens. His additional needs were few—a smartphone, a laptop, Internet access with Wi-Fi, and a decent video gaming system. He lived on a fraction of his income and banked the rest. "Do we need to have a family meeting about the car thing… again?"

"No." She shrugged. "Your mind is made up, and I'm not changing my vote." She looped her arm over his shoulder and pulled him close. "Voting again would be pointless."

"Thanks, Trish." He kissed her cheek. His mothers had almost always presented a united front—especially in family meetings. On the rare occasion when they disagreed, his had been the deciding vote.

"Still struggling to keep your head above water at work?"

He shook his head. "The break gave me a chance to work ahead. I'm much more prepared for the second half of the year." He'd started the school year behind and had never caught up. Except for the occasional grocery run and daily trips to the gym to preserve his sanity, Tellumo had needed every waking moment for grading papers, preparing lesson plans, and otherwise tending to his teaching responsibilities. "Getting home should be easier this term."

"Good." She patted his leg. "Not seeing you since we dropped you off in August was hard, but we knew you'd be home for Christmas." Trish shrugged. "The first without you was rough—especially since we'd been expecting to see you."

"I really wanted to come home. Snowmageddon messed with everyone's holiday plans."

"Yell when you're ready. Taking a break from work is rarely a problem, and we like getting out of the city, so driving down to visit or pick you up isn't a problem." She squeezed his shoulder and pecked him on the cheek. "Jules thinks you'd be better off with a car and is mad because I won't take her side." She ruffled his hair and kissed his forehead. "You're a grown man—I trust you to make your own decisions."

"I do too." Jules stood in the doorway with a shopping bag in each hand. "And I'm not mad at anyone, I just think Tellumo's life would be a lot easier with a car."

"What about my carbon footprint?" Tellumo smiled. Keeping up with the causes his mothers supported was a full-time job, made only a little easier by the array of bumper stickers covering their van. "The shopping center behind my apartment has everything I need, and the bus gets me back and forth to work or anyplace else in town I need to go."

"You could still walk or take the bus," Jules said, dropping the bags in the kitchen. "A car would give you the freedom to take weekend road trips."

"Like to Cincinnati?" Tellumo had been ready for a change of scenery. Fallisville was close—about an hour from Cincinnati by car—and the principal of his school, Mr. Wyrick, hadn't lied. Teaching at Salt Lick County High was the job of his dreams.

"Melody misses you and sends her love," Trish said. "We almost invited her to come with us, but your place is so small." She glanced around his apartment. His double bed was visible behind the overstuffed sofa that divided the space into living and sleeping areas. "I was afraid one more might be one too many."

"Mel and I video chat a couple of times a week." Tellumo smiled. Trish and Jules had been disappointed he hadn't sprung for a larger apartment, with room for overnight guests.

On the other side of a counter with two stools where he ate his meals and graded papers, Jules unpacked the bags she'd carried in from the car. "What needs to go in the refrigerator and what goes in the oven?"

Trish rose from the sofa and joined her partner in the kitchen. "When do you guys want to eat?"

"It's almost noon now," Tellumo said. "Is one o'clock too soon?"

"Yeah—the tofurkey needs to bake for seventy-five minutes," Trish said, turning on the oven. "Will you starve before one thirty?"

He shook his head. "I think I'll live. Anything I can do to help?"

Jules folded the empty bags and placed them on top of the refrigerator. "Wait." She looked at Trish. "Seems like we're missing something."

Trish furrowed her brow and examined the items spread out on the counter before her. "Gluten-free rolls, edamame, quinoa stuffing...." She scanned the foil packets and plastic containers before turning to Jules. "No, looks like everything is here."

They looked at each other and then at Tellumo.

He folded his arms across his chest and shook his head. "I can't believe you're making me do this again. I'm twenty-three years old!"

"Humor me," Jules said. "See if I left anything in the van, will you?"

"If you insist." He took her keys and headed for the vehicle. At five, he'd stumbled upon a cache of not-yet-wrapped gifts intended for him for the upcoming winter solstice. Ever since, his mothers had found hiding places away from the two-bedroom townhome he'd called home from the day he'd arrived from the hospital to August of last year. They'd act like they'd forgotten about buying presents and then send him on a random errand, leading him to discover what they'd bought for him.

A pair of beautifully wrapped, oversized shirt boxes sat in the back seat. The nearest, obviously from Jules, sported thin black stripes against a shiny silver background, topped with a silver bowtie. Trish's featured a brightly colored tie-dye pattern beneath a riotous mass of thin, loosely curled ribbon in a rainbow of cheerful colors. He placed one under each arm and returned to his apartment.

"Well what do you know?" Jules beamed. "Go ahead—open them."

"Wait," Tellumo said. "If we're opening presents now...." He dropped the boxes on the coffee table, retrieved his gifts from the walk-in closet, and handed one to each of them. "You aren't the easiest people in the world to buy for, you know."

Jules ripped hers open and gasped. "A Gladys Bentley CD? Where on earth did you find it?"

Tellumo smiled. "I put it together with everything I could find about her on the Internet—including a couple of videos of her performing."

"Very cool!" She hugged him.

Trish held up the book he'd given her. "A first edition of *All Passion Spent*, signed by Vita Sackville-West." She looked at Tellumo. "How…?"

"Great deal on eBay," he lied. No point telling her Eduardo Clemente— an older man he'd gone out with a couple of times—had given the book to Tellumo after he'd mentioned her fascination with the author.

"Your turn," Trish said.

Tellumo opened the silver-and-black box first. Inside, he found a short-cut gray corduroy blazer with black patches on the elbows. In the other box was the same blazer, only in camel with brown patches.

"We couldn't make up our mind, so we got both." Jules furrowed her brow. "You like them, don't you?"

Tellumo shook his head. "Nope." Their faces fell, but before they could say anything, he added, "I love them!" He slid into the gray coat and twirled around. "Now I feel like a real teacher."

PEGGY TUCKER couldn't remember when she'd last washed and set her own hair. Professionals at Holy Snips had tended to her hairdressing needs for a long time. For the last four years, Giorgio Mancini had done the job.

"Look at you!" Giorgio stopped in front of Peggy, placed his hands on his hips, and looked her up and down. "Girl, you're looking good!" His high heels clicked on the tiled floor as he circled her, whistling like a construction worker several times. "We doing the makeover we've been talking about today?"

"No." Peggy's face grew hot. "Not until I'm ready for my after photo." His fawning tickled her. She'd quit wondering if he meant what he said or was buttering her up for a bigger tip. Like the good book says, better not to look a gift horse in the mouth. "You ready for me? My scalp is itching me to death."

"I'm sorry." He clasped his hands in front of him. "Please forgive me. Yesterday was the first day we've been open since before Christmas." He waved his hand toward half a dozen women sitting under hairdryers. "I'm running a little behind." He turned toward the back and yelled. "Ernesto! Can you wash Miss Peggy?"

A skinny young man with pale skin, spiky blue hair, big plugs in his earlobes, and tattoo-covered arms approached them. "Sure, Papi."

Giorgio cupped Ernesto's chin in his palm. "Thank you. Ti amo, amore mio."

"I love you too, Papi," Ernesto said, and then he turned to Peggy. "You ready, hon?"

Peggy nodded. "Past ready. Snowmageddon caused me to miss my last appointment."

"You and half of Fallisville." Ernesto pointed to the changing room door. "Slip into a smock, hon, and I'll shampoo you."

The changing room also served as the storage area for supplies and overstock of the products Holy Snips sold to customers. Peggy loved them all, but since she never washed her own hair, she only bought the Heavenly Cloud hairspray. She put on one of the lavender smocks hanging on hooks and found Ernesto waiting for her in front of a washing basin.

"Okay, hon, lean back for me."

She scooted up in the chair a bit until her neck fell into place on the edge of the basin. Ernesto sprayed water against his palm for a moment before turning the flow to her head. "Too hot, hon?"

"Just right," Peggy said, closing her eyes. "So Giorgio's your father?"

The water stopped. Ernesto stepped back and looked at her. "Excuse me?"

"You called him Papi." She met his gaze. "Is he your daddy?"

He looked at her for a long moment and then nodded. "Yes, he's my daddy."

"Lord have mercy! I didn't even know he was married." She studied his face. "You must favor your momma because you don't look a thing like Giorgio." He pushed her head down and cool glops of Halo shampoo hit her scalp as the familiar citrus fragrance reached her nose. "I didn't know he had children. Do you have any brothers or sisters?"

The young man washing someone's hair in the next basin over giggled. "Giorgio is my daddy too."

Peggy gasped and tilted her head toward him. "Really?" As far as she could tell, they were close to the same age. Giorgio was either older than he looked or had fathered the boys in his teen years. "What's your name?"

"Derrious."

"I'm Peggy. Nice to meet you." Ernesto had fair skin rather than his father's olive complexion. Derrious was as black as the ace of spades. "I'd never guess you two were brothers."

Ernesto snorted then redoubled his efforts to scrub and massage her itching scalp. "We have different mothers."

"Yeah." Derrious snickered. "That's it."

Good grief! She'd seen Giorgio every other week all this time and had no idea he'd ever been married or had children. As Ernesto rinsed the Angel Wing conditioner from her hair, she decided asking if his mother was the current wife would be insensitive. She'd wait and ask Giorgio.

"Perfect timing," Giorgio said. He held his elbow out. "Shall we?"

Peggy hooked her elbow into his. "Oh Giorgio—always such a gentleman." He escorted her to his chair. She sat down and he pumped the pedal, raising her several inches higher. "Wish I was thin enough to wear heels like those."

He lifted his leg and hitched up his slacks. "These?" He beamed. "I got them for Christmas and haven't taken them off except to sleep." He turned around and lifted his foot up again. "See the red bottoms? They're Louboutins."

The good Lord hadn't blessed Giorgio with height. Seeing him in women's high heels the first time had been a shock. "When men's shoes come with five-inch heels," he'd said, "I'll wear them. Until then, I need all the help I can get." Who was she to judge? She felt the same way about Spanx.

"Giorgio, you sly devil, you. I had no idea Ernesto and Derrious were your boys. For half brothers, they sure do get along well."

His scissors fell to the floor. "Oh, clumsy me!" He swapped them for a pair he pulled from a comb-filled jar of blue sanitizer. "What did they tell you?"

"Ernesto said you were his daddy. Derrious overheard our conversation and said you were his daddy too." She beamed. "Fine-looking boys."

"Thank you." The scissors whizzed around her head and wisps of hair fell to the floor.

"Which boy's mother is your current wife?"

He dropped the scissors again. When he stood, his face was beet red. "Uh, neither one, actually. We're, uh… not together."

"Oh, I see," Peggy said. "But the boys live with you?"

He nodded. "We didn't spend much time together when they were younger."

"How wonderful, then, for them to want to live with you now." Peggy wished she had sons or daughters who wanted to spend time with her, but alas, her childbearing years were behind her.

The hot air whooshing from the helmet over her head prevented her from hearing anything. She flipped through the pages of *Modern Bride*, replacing the faces of the happy couple with herself and Mr. Crumbly, the handsome man who motivated her participation in the grueling Boot Steppin' classes. She'd overheard the receptionist at the gym greeting him, but didn't know his first name, what he did for a living, or where he went to church.

He paid her no attention, but then she'd never seen him give so much as a second glance to another person. Besides, except for Walter Addison, whose wife, Virginia, showed no signs of kicking the bucket anytime soon, Mr. Crumbly was her only prospect. His ring finger was bare, and the absence of any telltale tan lines or imprints suggested he'd been single for a while. When she lost a few more pounds, she'd say hello or something.

OLIVER CRUMBLY watched the Salt Lick County snowplow scrape the street in front of his house with a mixture of satisfaction and relief. Ten days of complaining had finally paid off. Two feet of snow had fallen in the day or two leading up to Christmas. A week later, before plows or salt trucks had reached Thoroughbred Acres, another six inches had fallen.

He'd been trapped at home since Christmas Eve. Worn treads had kept his Taurus from getting any traction on the flat street in front of his house. Driving out of the hilly subdivision would have been impossible.

Bill Pinkley, head meteorologist for local Channel 13, said El Niño or La Niña had caused the winter storm. Oliver couldn't remember which, or why what happened so far away made a difference in the weather in Northern Kentucky, but if Bill Pinkley said so, it must be true. Heeding his advice to stock up on groceries ahead of the first flurries had kept Oliver from running out of food.

Thirty inches was a lot of snow to have fallen in a week's time, and Calumet Circle was in the back of Thoroughbred Acres. Still, ten days was too long to wait for snow removal. Calls to the county road department had fallen on deaf ears. The surly customer service representative had hung up on him—four times. Miss Bethany Williams, Customer Service Representative II, was about to learn messing with Oliver Crumbly was a mistake. He'd mailed a lengthy letter detailing her incompetence and rude behavior to the director of the county road department with copies to the mayor, Oliver's representative on the city council, and the Kentucky and U.S. Departments of Transportation.

Too bad Kevin Leonard had missed the blizzard. For eight years, Oliver's ex had complained about the lack of winter snow. But then, nothing in Kentucky had suited Kevin. He'd grown up in the upper Midwest, where life was better in every way. Eight years of Kevin's delusions of grandeur, condescending attitude, and manufactured facts had been a good four too many.

Oliver didn't miss him one little bit. Not anymore. He dropped into his recliner, turned on the television, and flipped to the TV's channel guide. His forty-eight-year-old ex had returned to North Dakota last February to live with his parents and, according to a mutual friend, was still unemployed. Because Mr. and Mrs. Leonard had often driven their camper down to Kentucky for weeklong visits, Oliver knew them a lot better than he'd have preferred. In his opinion, the sorry son and his parents deserved each other.

The viewing options scrolling on the screen at a snail's pace failed to keep his attention, and his mind wandered. Falling for the wrong guys was Oliver's gift. The first time his heart had been broken, he'd believed he would die. But he'd lived to love again… and again… and again… and again. Five times he'd survived a broken heart and the end of yet another relationship gone bad. Getting over kicking men out of his life had grown easier with experience. After Kevin left, Oliver's battle-scarred heart had healed in record-breaking time.

He settled on a home renovation show on HGTV. Considering how badly he'd been fooled this last time—not to mention for how long—Oliver had given up on a love life. His malfunctioning picker was either defective or damaged beyond repair. He'd wasted years trying to put broken, needy men back together—years he'd never get back. No more fixer-uppers. Unless a move-in-ready man came along, he was better off living out his golden years as a bachelor.

The lights had flickered a few times during the storm, but he'd never lost power. Foregoing his annual pilgrimage to Dayton, Ohio, to spend Christmas with Letty and Sid Dawson had been a disappointment. Spending the holiday alone for the first time in his life hadn't been easy, but he'd survived.

Cabin fever had set in days ago. Had the neighbors heeded the city ordinance and cleared the snow from the sidewalk in front of their houses, he'd have gone for walks. But they hadn't. As with requirements to clean up after one's pet and to park in the same direction as traffic, the ordinance wasn't worth the paper it was written on. Countless letters over the years to the mayor, city council members, the editor of the *Fallisville Gazette*, and agencies responsible for enforcement of the various ordinances had had no impact. When the book he was writing hit the *New York Times* best sellers list, he'd hire an attorney and sue someone.

If he had the money, he'd sue a lot of people. Nobody did what they were supposed to do anymore. Oliver blamed technology. The silly Internet was bad enough. The ability to access the time-sucking World Wide Web by telephone was the beginning of the end. He'd have none of it, thank you very much.

The television screen blurred into an abstract image comprised of little blinking boxes in various colors. More bad technology, although he had to admit, when the damn thing worked, HD was a big improvement over the black-and-white television he'd had when Kevin moved in. But needing cable to watch television totally pissed him off. Having to watch commercials *and* pay for television was infuriating. To make matters worse, he'd had nothing but problems since installation. Dealing with the local cable monopoly gave him a headache. Letters to the cable company, copied to the Federal Communications Commission, his representative on the city council, and the Kentucky Public Service Commission, had gone unanswered.

The world had changed, and not in a good way. Nobody cared anymore—about anything or anyone but themselves. Instead of engaging with the world around them, people stared at telephones and tuned out with earphones. Memorable events weren't experienced, but watched through the lens of a camera. Whizzes with technology couldn't read or write cursive. Soon, the average third grader would have no problem forging notes from Mom or Dad to the teacher. The thought of future presidents block printing signatures to turn bills into law turned his stomach.

He turned off the television and dropped the remote control on the coffee table. Jumping on the bandwagon for new technology wasn't his style. The eight-track tapes, the cassette tapes that had replaced them, and the compact discs he'd refused to buy were all obsolete. A few of his albums were a little scratched or skipped here and there, but the record collection he'd assembled in the seventies and eighties otherwise sounded as good as it had forty years ago.

Nope, high tech didn't interest him a bit. The old technology worked fine. He'd lived this long without computers, cell phones, and the Internet and saw no good reason to change.

Solitude wasn't so bad. Skipping the holiday decorations, parties, and elaborate dinners had freed up a lot of time—time he'd devoted to the book he was writing and clearing the house of any remnants of Kevin. Boxes of his junk filled the garage, leaving barely enough room to park the Taurus.

Shipping the lot of them to North Dakota would cost a fortune. Kevin would say to ship everything, promise to drop a check in the mail, and never send the money. Oliver had already paid for boxes and wasn't willing to spend another dime on his freeloading ex. If the junk had been important or at all valuable, Kevin wouldn't have left it behind. The dispatcher at Goodwill said she'd send a truck out when the roads cleared off.

The snowplow finally getting to his neighborhood was a good sign. Maybe this week, Goodwill would come. If not, he'd give them another call.

Chapter Two: Fit as a Fiddle

PEGGY TUCKER blew into Fit as a Fiddle fifteen minutes earlier than usual—half an hour before Boot Steppin' class. Arriving early guaranteed a spot on the back row right behind Mr. Crumbly's usual spot on the front row. The new workout ensemble she had on—a Christmas present to herself—motivated her to get to the gym especially early.

Jumping around in class sometimes made her pee her pants. Pads helped but were uncomfortable. An empty bladder made a bigger difference. Getting in and out of the leotard and yoga pants could be tricky. The extra fifteen minutes allowed plenty of time to go to the bathroom before class.

Despite her having lost seventeen and two-thirds pounds, the spandex covering everything but her head, feet, and hands wasn't nearly as flattering as she'd expected. The black stretchy fabric chafed her skin and emphasized bulges and curves nobody needed to see. At the last minute, she'd slid the colorful active-wear jacket and slacks she'd ordered from Lane Bryant over her new leotard and yoga pants.

She strode across the gym, wincing at the loud music blaring from the speakers. She and several women from the church had joined Body By God in October. The devilishly handsome Vic Hunter had come by Wednesday night prayer meeting to explain the gym's biblical approach to fitness and exercise. Vic had promised to transform her into a worship-worthy temple. His words had ignited a spark of hope and given her reason to believe—even at fifty-nine and three quarters—another marriage might still be in the cards.

The double doors to the Garden of Gethsemane, now called the Corral, closed behind her. The beautiful mural of Jesus surrounded by his apostles in an olive grove had been painted over and covered with posters of shirtless cowboys and half-naked cowgirls. She placed a step platform and a set of risers she knew she'd never use a couple of feet from the back wall, spreading across the step one of the Jesus Saves towels she embroidered and sold online.

Peggy didn't approve of the changes the new owners had made to the gym, not one iota. She would quit, but her prepaid membership didn't run out until April. Like the Bible says, waste not, want not. Besides, if she was ever going to get Mr. Crumbly to notice her on the back row, she needed to lose at least twenty more pounds. Thirty, if she were being honest with herself, but twenty would make a difference.

More than the music and décor suffered under the new owners. The place was going downhill, fast. The immodest workout attire some women wore was atrocious. Peggy shuddered. What was this world coming to? She counted at least a dozen girls wearing obscenely short cutoff blue jeans with pockets poking out from underneath—a few even wore cowboy hats, and boots instead of tennis shoes.

She glanced at her watch. Twenty minutes until class started. She smiled at a young, heavily tattooed woman beside her who was tapping away on one of those telephones young people stared at all the time. The phone-obsessed blonde was showing almost as much flesh as the girls pictured in the centerfolds of the magazines Peggy's last husband, Earl—God rest his soul—liked to sneak into the bathroom.

"Would you mind keeping an eye on my stuff?" Peggy asked.

The girl looked up long enough to respond, "Sure. No problem."

Peggy hurried out of the Corral and beelined for the women's locker room. A woman in a bright yellow jumpsuit caught her eye—Gladys Honeycutt, chair of the altar society at Trinity Baptist Church and the biggest gossip in Fallisville. Her strategic location overlooked the most direct route from the gym's entrance to the locker room. Given the chance, the gossipy woman would talk Peggy's right arm off and start on her left.

Keeping an eye on the back of the yellow jumpsuit, Peggy ducked her head and darted behind a row of treadmills as she snuck toward the locker room. She passed Tellumo, the handsome young man with chestnut hair and dazzling green eyes she'd befriended since joining the gym. He was a nice boy—like a pierced and tattooed version of Jesus, without the beard. He smiled at her and nodded in her direction.

Peggy raised a finger to her lips. "Shhh!" She jerked her head toward Gladys. He glanced in the direction of the yellow jumpsuit and then gave Peggy a thumbs-up.

She slipped into the locker room, striding with purpose through the changing area to a bathroom with a large mirror over a trio of sinks opposite a row of stalls. The handicapped stalls on either end were occupied. If she waited for one to open up, someone would think she needed the extra room. Peggy stepped into a smaller stall in the middle of the row and closed the door behind her.

She slipped out of the sweat suit, banging her head against the door and gouging her hip with the toilet paper dispenser in the process. She hung the loose-fitting slacks with the matching jacket on a hook on the stall door, dabbed her face and neck with a few squares of toilet paper, and fell onto the seat.

She stood and took a few deep breaths before grasping the high waistband of her yoga pants to push and wiggle until she'd maneuvered the clingy fabric over her hips. She dropped onto the toilet seat again and, without stopping to catch her breath, maneuvered the yoga pants past ample thighs to dimpled knees.

A toilet flushed and Peggy froze. A nasty aroma saturated the air she breathed. A moment later, she heard someone washing up. Sweat streamed from her face, cascading in rivulets down her neck, back, and chest. She yanked a swatch of paper from the roll and swabbed up what perspiration she could.

When she'd ordered her leotard, snaps in the crotch had sounded like a feature for women of easy virtue. The practical value had since become obvious. Future leotards would have them, but until then, wrestling her way through the neck of the tight-fitting garment was her only option.

As she struggled to free her arms from the long sleeves, she struck her funny bone against the stall. "Ouch!" She stood again, opening and closing her tingling fist and rubbing her elbow for a moment before mopping her face and torso with another big wad of toilet tissue. Success was within reach. She pushed the leotard over her hips to her knees, yanked her granny panties down, and collapsed—exhausted—onto the toilet seat.

She pulled a yard or so from the roll and sponged her body as her bladder emptied. After a deep, cleansing breath of stale farts, Peggy wiped with more of the scratchy paper, stood, and flushed. As she reached for her panties, she noticed something wasn't right.

Yellow water and toilet paper swirled around the bowl, drawing ever closer to the seat. She yanked her white cotton underpants into place as the water continued to rise. Then she grabbed the leotard and stretch pants knotted together around her ankles, lifting them from the floor as the water crested the bowl.

Peggy's heart rate soared. She sorted through the black fabric coiled around her calves until she found a sleeve. She yanked hard and the leotard broke free from the spandex yoga pants clasped between her knees.

Water cascaded over the rim, spreading beyond her stall across the tiled floor. She thought she was alone but wasn't sure. She thrust her hands into the sleeves of the leotard and raised her arms, ignoring the sharp pain in her sides from the effort, pushing and straining as the garment moved up her body until her fingers poked through the other end of the sleeves. She adjusted the snug fabric with a few well-placed tugs and the leotard was on. Gripping the waistband of the stretchy pants, she unclenched her knees and then tugged and yanked with all her might, grunting with effort as she maneuvered the yoga pants over her hips to her waist.

Compared to her battle with the spandex garments, slipping into her activewear jacket and slacks was a piece of cake. She opened the stall door and tiptoed across the wet tile, reaching the carpeted changing area at the same time as the ever-expanding puddle from the overflowing toilet.

The changing area was empty. Nobody had noticed the flood yet, but they would, and given the volume of water pouring from the toilet, sooner rather than later. If she hurried, nobody would know the flood had been her fault. She quickened her pace and headed for the gym.

OLIVER WAS never late, ever, but unexpected traffic and long lights had burned up the extra time he'd allowed for the trip across town. He scanned the rearview mirror and the road ahead before nudging his Taurus up four miles over the speed limit. Unless the police pulled him over or he ran into trouble parking, he might still be on time for his three o'clock step class.

Conditions had improved since his trip to the grocery the day before. The sun remained behind the clouds, but the temperature had climbed several degrees. Dirty gray ridges of snow remained in parking lots and along side streets across Fallisville, but roads were mostly clear and dry. Nonetheless, he watched for patches of black ice. Better safe than sorry.

His ex had followed a different philosophy. Oliver could almost hear Kevin berating him for driving so slow. "They're not allowed to pull you over unless you're going more than seven miles over the speed limit. It's in the Constitution. I swear!"

Letty O'Mara Dawson had warned him about Kevin, but Oliver had paid no attention. As always, he should have listened to his best friend. She'd never steered him wrong before, but he hadn't wanted to hear the truth. After he'd come home early from the gym and caught Kevin in bed with that trampy little blue-haired houseboy of Giorgio's, Letty had driven down from Dayton and stayed with him for a couple of days. Not once did she ever say, "I told you so," even when Oliver had acknowledged she'd been right.

Snowmageddon ruined their annual get-together and completely disrupted his fitness regimen. Jane Fonda workout videos were a fair replacement for the cardio classes he missed, but sit-ups, push-ups, and planks were no substitute for the strength-training equipment at the gym. Losing forty-five pounds hadn't been easy. Keeping the weight off was a challenge—especially this time of year. Retiring didn't mean he could let himself go. He'd worked too hard and come too far to backslide now.

Oliver pulled into the shopping center as the digits on the First Bank & Trust sign switched from 55° to 2:54. Seven years ago, he and Kevin had joined what was then known as Epic Fitness. Among the gyms they'd considered, the spacious new facility had state-of-the-art equipment and offered the widest variety of classes.

The place had changed hands and names several times in the intervening years. Since retiring from Salt Lick County High, Oliver had considered joining one closer to home—especially during the Body By God era. Stepping for Jesus to hymns and Christian pop tunes with big-haired women in full makeup had been entertaining, but the Reach for the Lord replacements for yoga classes had been too much.

Oliver couldn't prove anything, but was certain Kevin had fooled around with Vic Hunter, the owner of Body by God, in his office at the gym. Oliver had planned to drop his membership when his contract ran out in February, but the gym had again changed hands in November, reopening after a weeklong renovation as Fit as a Fiddle. The country-western theme appealed to rednecks of both genders and, by far, was the gym's most successful iteration. For Oliver, however, the jury was still out.

He grumbled under his breath about the pickup trucks of various hues, sizes, and distances from the ground filling the parking lot as he searched for a space one of the big gas-guzzlers hadn't encroached upon. Few in Fallisville needed a monster pickup truck, and they had little time for the gym. Oliver wondered when pickup trucks had become cool. He was about to park under a rusty red Chevrolet with eight-foot tires when he found an open space.

He stashed his wallet under the seat, grabbed his towel, and locked the door. The air was cool enough for a jacket, but he left his in the car. Lockers were an option, but unless he really had to pee, he avoided the locker room. Straight men in various stages of undress made him uncomfortable.

The gym's pretty blonde receptionist called to mind a Dallas Cowboys Cheerleader. The slim, athletic young woman wore western boots, tight-fitting jeans, a cropped top, and a ten-gallon hat. The white hat and shirt bore the Fit as a Fiddle logo, with red letters made to look like planks ripped from an old barn sandwiched between very fit, updated versions of Li'l Abner and Daisy Mae. The receptionist scanned the card on Oliver's key ring, furrowed her brow as she studied the computer screen for a few seconds, and then smiled. "Have a great workout, Mr. Crumbly."

Oliver headed toward the Corral for his Boot Steppin' class, searching for familiar faces as he made his way through the crowded facility. January was always busy at the gym, but Oliver suspected cabin fever had more to do with today's mob than New Year's resolutions. He saw the Yeller checking himself out in the mirror, and a few other guys he didn't care to meet who often worked out when Oliver did. He wondered if they had a nickname for him, like the Loner, Old Dude, or maybe Dances with Women.

Nine times out of ten, Oliver was the only man in the classes he attended. A quick glance around the room confirmed today's Boot Steppin' class would be no exception. He tossed his keys and towel on the floor, grabbed a step platform and two sets of risers from the shelves along the wall, and set up in his usual spot, right of center on the front row for unobstructed views of the instructor and Oliver's reflection in the mirrored front wall.

As the instructor made her way to the front of the room, Oliver warmed up with a few deep-knee bends and leg stretches. He glanced at his watch. Exactly three o'clock. Time to get this show on the road.

TELLUMO WAS on the treadmill, wrapping up his workout with a little cardio. Some days running was easy, and some days, not so much. After a rough start, today had become an easy day. He'd logged two and a half miles already and felt like he could run forever.

The scenery helped. Last week, when everyone had been snowed in and he'd about had the gym to himself, he'd struggled to run a mile. The people coming, going, and milling around gave Tellumo something more to watch than the gym's entrance and the numbers on the treadmill console.

Heads turned as a male voice bellowed from the weight room. Tellumo sighed and shook his head. The roar had come from a tall, lean guy in his late twenties who wanted everyone to know how hard he worked out. No matter when Tellumo came to the gym, he was always there, checking himself in the mirror for any sign of fat between each noisy set. Tellumo liked a man with more meat on his bones, more life experience, and at least a little silver on top.

Like the Silver Fox. Perhaps today his vigilance would be rewarded and the ridiculously hot middle-aged man he'd admired from afar since August would return. Tellumo knew the man's routine well enough. Boot Steppin' class at three o'clock on Saturdays and seven o'clock on Thursdays; free weights sometime between four and six on Mondays, Wednesdays, and Fridays; Zumba at six o'clock on Tuesdays; and one of the Sunday afternoon stretching classes. He missed a day here and there, but never more than a few days in a row. Snowmageddon had caused the biggest break in the Silver Fox's routine since Tellumo had joined the gym.

The Silver Fox was the epitome of the polar bear/leather daddy stereotype—beefy, with enough of a paunch to make him human, but muscular and at least six foot tall, with short-cropped salt-and-pepper hair and a matching, well-trimmed beard. He looked pissed all the time and scowled at anyone who got in his way. Dress him up in leather and chains, and assuming he was reasonably well-hung, the man could make a fortune in the porn industry.

Tellumo wondered what kind of porn the Silver Fox preferred. The porn a guy picked to watch from the nearly infinite range of options said a lot about him. A casual observer of the websites Tellumo visited could easily see what floated his boat. He couldn't explain his attraction to older men but suspected his upbringing played a role. Mother Universe had a wicked sense of humor.

The issues Trish and Jules were passionate about stemmed from the actions of greedy old white men. Given their disdain for the patriarchy, Tellumo speculated they must have been horrified to give birth to a boy, rather than the daughter they surely would have preferred. Whatever their initial reaction may have been, they loved him, and had been as good or better at parenting as others he'd known with the same job title.

Like any good son, however, Tellumo followed his mothers' wishes and directives more when they were around than when they weren't. He sometimes ate red meat and was particularly fond of veal. As Trish swore she could smell meat on him, sneaking around for the occasional hamburger or scaloppini had added a little excitement to his life. Ditto his taste in men. Old white guys were the enemy. Perhaps that's why Tellumo found them so attractive.

The Corral was filling up fast for the popular three o'clock Boot Steppin' class. Tellumo was ready to start his cooldown when the Silver Fox entered the gym. Tellumo guessed he was in his late forties or early fifties and was pretty sure he was gay. Everything about him screamed uptight in a way Tellumo found endearing. Navy stripes on the tube socks pulled up almost to his knees matched his long basketball shorts and a stripe across the shoulders of the white, V-neck, short-sleeved shirt he wore. Tellumo had seen him wearing variations on the same outfit in a wide range of color combinations, many with matching shoes.

What set the dapper gentleman apart from the rest of the guys, however, was his participation in the group classes. He was comfortable enough with his masculinity to be the only guy in a room full of women. Tellumo felt certain his female classmates watched his every move. *He* would—and did whenever he had the opportunity.

The fact the Silver Fox was an older white guy pushed all Tellumo's buttons. His mothers would no doubt rather he lived on veal for the rest of his life.

Chapter Three: Boot Steppin'

PEGGY'S SNEAKERS squished as she dragged her feet across the carpeted walkway to dry the soles. A mirrored wall brought her up short. *Good Lord!* She pulled the bottom of her jacket out of the sleeve and shifted her pants around so the seams were in the right place. She fingered the sweat-soaked curls plastered to her skull. Nothing she'd done since joining the gym had caused her to sweat so much. She could reapply the makeup perspiration had washed from her face, but fixing her hair would require the skills of a professional.

At the gym, sweaty hair was the norm. Not for her, but today had been an exception. Anyplace else, she'd look like one of those poor women who couldn't afford a good hairdresser. Shopping for a hat was out of the question. Unless Giorgio could squeeze her in for a wash and set this afternoon, she'd miss Sunday church services for the second week in a row.

Missing Christmas services had been bad enough, but Peggy didn't think God would punish her. The blizzard they'd received in response to fervent prayers for a white Christmas was, after all, an act of God. Last Sunday, services had been held for anyone able to get there, but she'd stayed home. The Lord might understand her concern about getting killed in a bad wreck on an icy road, but missing church because of bad hair was definitely a sin.

Holy Snips closed at six on Saturdays. She thought about calling ahead, but knew she'd never get an appointment. If she showed up with her hair in this shape, Giorgio would work her in. He had to. She hadn't tipped him 10 percent every two weeks all this time for nothing. *This was an emergency!*

Peggy hurried out of the locker room into the gym, wiping sweat from her forehead with the back of her hand. She made straight for the Corral, determined to cover the distance to the double doors as quickly as possible. The sooner she got to the salon, the more time Giorgio would have to work her in.

A bright yellow shape materialized in front of her, blocking her way. "Peggy Tucker!" Gladys Honeycutt looked Peggy up and down. "Ain't you a sight for sore eyes? I haven't seen you since the Sunday before Christmas!" She smiled. "You've lost weight! Run out of food during the big storm?"

Almost. Anyone else would have starved, but Peggy knew her way around the kitchen. She shook her head and forced a smile. "Good to see you, Gladys." Lying was the polite thing to do and therefore not a sin. "You and Bernie make it through okay?" Obviously, she had. The weight Gladys had gained in the few weeks since Peggy had last seen her suggested blizzards agreed with her.

"We survived." She clucked a few times and shook her head. "I swan, I've never seen so much snow in all my life!" She shook her finger at Peggy. "Bill Pinkley says we had the snowiest December since they been keeping records. Can you believe it?"

"If Bill Pinkley said so, you know it's true." Seeing an opportunity to make her escape, Peggy smiled. "Well, Gladys, I really need—"

"Yeah, we're fine," Gladys said. Her smile faded and she sighed. "Wish I could say the same for my car."

Christ! Peggy had no time for a long-winded explanation—the only kind Gladys knew how to give. She had to ask. The last thing she needed was Gladys Honeycutt telling everyone at church she'd been rude to her. "What happened?"

"Well," Gladys said, climbing back onto the thigh machine and getting comfortable. "Thursday evening, two days after the big storm, me and Bernie were watching *Tender Hearts* on television. It's our favorite show. You ever watch it?" She squeezed her thighs together with a grimace.

Jesus. Peggy shook her head. As obscene as Gladys looked clenching her thighs together, opening them was worse. Peggy glanced around to see if anyone was watching.

"Oh, Peggy! You really should. It's the best show I've ever seen. Everybody's talking about it." She grunted with effort and squeezed again.

Peggy tried to look interested as she contemplated her escape. She thought about saying she had to run to class, but leaving before Gladys explained what had happened to her car would be rude. Besides, she'd see Peggy leave class early. "I'll have to check it out. So what about your car?"

"Oh, yeah." She cleared her throat. "Well, me and Bernie was watching our show and eating supper—one of them frozen dinners. Enchiladas with refried beans and the most delicious pudding. You ever tried one?" She relaxed her thighs. "I swear, they're just as good as what you get at the old Pizza Hut where those Mexicans opened that restaurant. You know the one I'm talking about?"

Peggy nodded, and wondered if Gladys was ever going to get to what happened to her car.

"You've tried those frozen dinners or you know the place?" She clasped her thighs together again.

"Both!" Peggy resisted an overwhelming urge to shake the woman's shoulders. She had no time to waste. "What happened to your damn car?"

Gladys's head jerked back like she'd been slapped. Her thighs flopped open, her hand went to her mouth, and she stared at Peggy with wide eyes.

"I'm sorry," Peggy said, feeling like she'd struck a small child. Using a curse word was a sin. She'd do what she could to repair the damage and slip an extra five dollars into the collection basket tomorrow with her tithe. She glanced at the clock. "I'm a little pressed for time."

"I didn't mean to keep you," Gladys said, with a wounded look. "Wouldn't want you to be late for your date."

Of all the things for her to say! Peggy hadn't gone on a date since Earl passed away—like it was any of her business. She gave Gladys what she hoped passed for a knowing smile. "Well, it is Saturday night." Let her think what she would. "So… your car?"

Gladys squeezed her thighs together. "Well, you know that big sycamore tree in the side yard?"

Peggy nodded and resisted the urge to scream. "The one you've been telling Bernie to cut down?"

"The very same," Gladys said, nodding. "I'm tired of cleaning up all the seedpods." She relaxed her thighs. "Won't have to clean 'em up anymore." She shook her head. "Blasted thing fell down. Must have been all the snow. Smashed that old Buick flatter than a pancake."

"Thank God nobody was hurt," Peggy said. "I really need—"

"You coming to church tomorrow?"

Good question. "I'm planning to," she replied.

"Could I sweet-talk you into bringing a batch of your delicious cinnamon buns? Best I've ever tasted." She grinned and patted her belly. "Since we had to cancel Christmas and hardly anyone could get out last week, Pastor Brown wants to welcome everybody back with coffee and pastries before services in the morning."

"What a good idea!" Peggy's mind reeled. Pastor Brown was full of ideas requiring a lot of work from everybody but him. Still, she couldn't say no. "Be happy to." She caught Tellumo's eye and gave him a pleading look. Then she plastered a smile on her face, hoping she'd held it long enough to be convincing.

"I knew I could count on you. Thanks so much!" Gladys beamed. "I'll let you get on about your business. Have fun on your date."

"See you tomorrow morning!" Peggy said, waving as she set off at a brisk pace for the Corral. Her tennis shoes squeaked and squished with each step. Missing church was no longer an option, whether Giorgio worked her in or not. She didn't have time for a date—even if she'd had one.

Music came through the double doors where Boot Steppin' class had already started. She glanced at the clock. Three ten. Nobody should see her like this—especially Mr. Crumbly. Nobody would think she'd lost track of time lifting weights or running on the treadmill. Leaving before class ended would fan the flames. They'd wonder what she was up to and fill in the blanks with Lord only knew what. But without the keys she'd left in the Corral, she wasn't going anywhere.

TELLUMO DROPPED the speed on the treadmill to a slow walk to finish his cooldown. Mirrors and windows had fogged up around the gym. Apparently, nobody had switched the thermostat from heat to cool. He was beat. Running for another hour—long enough to bump into the Silver Fox when he got out of class—wasn't an option.

The idea of accidentally running into the older man or timing his departure so they walked out at the same time wasn't new. He'd thought about it lots of times, but doubts about how the Silver Fox would react had prevented him from acting. Tellumo had never seen him talking to anyone and had noticed he seemed to resent any intrusion. The handsome man was all business. He came, did what he needed to do, and left.

From his vantage point on the treadmill, Tellumo caught glimpses of him getting his step on. The beefy man moved with surprising grace, like maybe he'd had some dance training—ballet or contemporary. That would explain his amazing ass and the way he moved at Zumba. Tellumo shook his head and averted his gaze. His sweatpants were in the locker room, and he didn't want to have to conceal a hard-on in sweat-soaked running shorts.

He gasped when Mrs. Tucker emerged from the women's locker room. *What on earth happened in there?* Her hair was a mess, her face was flushed, and she looked like maybe she'd showered in her clothes without bothering to dry off. Upon closer inspection, her garments appeared only soaked in places—like sweat stains from a hard workout. She glanced around the gym, wiped her brow with the back of her hand, and headed toward the Corral.

The blue-haired lady in the yellow jumpsuit sprang from the thigh machine and planted herself directly in Mrs. Tucker's path with agility and speed he wouldn't have believed possible had he not seen it with his own eyes. After a moment, Mrs. Tucker gave him a pleading look, but before he could come to her rescue, she escaped her nimble captor and was on her way to the Corral. When she reached the double doors, she tapped on the window a few times, pointing and waving at someone inside, but nobody paid her any attention. She stomped her foot, put her hands on her hips, and then turned around, beckoning him over when she saw him watching her.

Curious about what she was up to, Tellumo stepped off the treadmill. He stood still for a moment to adjust to the unmoving floor, gave each leg a few shakes, and then loped toward the Corral. He had always felt an odd connection with the matronly woman—like maybe they'd known each other in another life. Her frantic waves slowed, stopping all together when he was a few feet away.

"Hi, Mrs. Tucker. What's up?" he asked.

She glanced at her tennis shoes and then met his gaze. "Could you do me a teeny, tiny little favor?"

"Sure, happy to help," he replied. "What can I do for you?"

"Well." She paused for a moment. "Something has come up and I need to miss class." She fingered the wet hair at the nape of her neck. "Could I sweet-talk you into slipping in and getting my things?" She turned and pointed to the glass. "Right over there—on the back row."

He saw the unused platform on the opposite side of the crowded room. No wonder she didn't want to go inside. Getting there and back without tripping over anyone would be difficult, even for him. "No problem. What am I getting?"

Relief flooded her face. "My towel and keys." She waved her hand. "Never mind the towel, I've got dozens of them—just the keys. They're under the step."

Tellumo took advantage of the lull between songs to slip into the room, stepping with care around the women and platforms, moving as fast as he could. Another song started. He glanced to the front of the room and saw the Silver Fox slip an elastic terrycloth band around his head—the kind women wore to aerobics classes back in the eighties. *Adorable!* Tellumo made it to the far side of the room and reached beneath the unused platform for the keys.

"Hey! What do you think you're doing?"

Tellumo turned around. "Just helping a friend." He'd seen the woman who spoke hanging with the mixed martial arts crowd. She glared at him with her hands on her hips. "Honest." He tilted his head and flashed his most irresistible smile.

"Sure you are," she said, unfazed by his charm. She folded her arms across her chest and scowled. "Lady asked me to watch her stuff."

He pointed to Mrs. Tucker. "Her?"

She looked toward the door and then at Tellumo. "Nope. This lady had curly hair—one of those hairdos older women get at the beauty shop once a week."

"Oh. It's her, I swear." Tellumo smiled, receiving nothing but a menacing glower in return. The nearby steppers stared daggers at him too. Time to make his escape before things got out of control. He turned his back on the blonde woman, reached under the towel-covered platform, and grabbed the keys.

OLIVER HAD never seen the Corral so crowded—a fact that pleased him not one little bit. He didn't have room to move around with the platforms so close together. He'd be lucky to avoid kicking anyone or stepping on someone's foot.

The instructor donned a headset and blew into the microphone a few times. "Howdy, y'all!" She winced and adjusted the volume. "I'm Angie, and this is the three o'clock Boot Steppin' class! Anyone here for the first time?" She glanced around with the same dazzling smile everyone under thirty had these days as hands went up across the crowded room. "Welcome, ladies. You're in for a treat!"

Oliver bounced on his toes and shook his arms to stay loose as Angie gave her spiel about Boot Steppin' being country line dancing with a riser thrown in. Though an improvement over the Christian pop tunes it had replaced, the twangy music had grated on Oliver's nerves at first. Now, most of his favorite songs he'd heard for the first time in Boot Steppin' class.

"We're here to have fun, okay?" Angie placed her hands on her hips and tilted her pretty head. "Alrighty, then. Let's get started!"

Since retiring, Oliver had thought about getting certified to teach a few exercise classes, but relentless cheerfulness wasn't really his thing. Never mind talking through all the huffing and puffing. The more he thought about the challenges, the more the instructors for his classes had impressed him. Angie was one of the best. She barely perspired, and the perky smile never left her face.

By the middle of the third song, Oliver and the women behind him panted and dripped sweat. The mirrors had fogged up, and even Angie glistened with perspiration. "Golly, y'all are really working hard today. It's getting hot in here!"

The song ended. Oliver pulled a terry-cloth headband from his pocket and slipped it over his head to keep the sweat out of his eyes. The ladies had shifted to avoid bumping him, giving him a little more room than he'd had when class had started, but not as much as he really needed for a good workout.

Commotion behind him drew his attention. A tattoo-covered blonde wearing one of those sports bra thingies and spandex shorts stood with her arms folded, glaring at….

Oliver gasped and almost tripped over his step. *Him!* The long-haired whippersnapper with his tattoos, piercings, gym bod, and ever-present smartphone represented everything Oliver hated about vain, disconnected, and self-absorbed twentysomethings. Sure, he was stunning, but weren't they all beautiful anymore? Perfect teeth, flawless complexions, luxurious heads of hair, and the physiques—nobody in the world had possessed such perfectly sculpted bodies when Oliver had been that age. He had little faith the most self-absorbed, narcissistic, and shallow generation in history would make the world a better place. They were too busy tapping their phones.

"Stop!" The blonde unfolded her arms and dropped into a fighting pose—karate, maybe, or tae kwon do—one of those Far Eastern styles of hand-to-hand combat. The intimidating young woman appeared to know what she was doing. The music continued, but many in the Corral had stopped to watch the drama unfolding on the back row.

Oliver kept moving, watching the scene behind him in the mirror. The young man held his hands up, palms open. A set of keys dangled from his right thumb.

Distracted by the ensuing drama, Oliver missed a change in the choreography and bumped the woman beside him hard enough to knock her off balance. He reached out to steady her, but she shook him off with a cold glare. No sweat off his back. He'd come to work, not to socialize.

He tried to focus on Angie and the complicated choreography, but couldn't look away from the back row. He couldn't hear what they were saying over the music until the song ended and the room went silent.

"I'll give you to the count of three to put those keys back where you got them," the belligerent blonde said, holding her threatening pose. "One...."

"The woman these keys belong to asked me to get them for her." The young man kept his hands up and held his position. "Go ahead. Ask her."

"Two...." She sunk lower and clenched her fists.

Oliver watched, certain the arrogant, narcissistic whippersnapper was about to get the comeuppance he deserved. The young man didn't move and looked like Tarzan from the sixties television series in a standoff with a savage beast—in sweat-soaked running shorts and a T-shirt instead of a loincloth.

"Don't hurt him!" A bedraggled stocky woman in a floral-print jacket and matching slacks stepped into the Corral and stopped inside the door. She waved, clearly embarrassed. "Sorry to interrupt." She pointed to Whippersnapper. "Tellumo was just getting my keys for me."

Tellumo? Perfect! Nobody had normal names anymore. Perhaps because everyone *looked* so much alike, unique names were all the rage. The combative blonde looked the sweat-soaked woman up and down and relaxed her stance.

"It's me." The woman fluffed the hair flattened to her head with her fingers. "I was warming up on the treadmill and lost all track of time." She smiled weakly. "Thank you for watching my things."

The music resumed. Angie's cheerful voice came through the speakers. "Come on, y'all! We're halfway there. Don't quit now!"

The tattooed woman grunted, and with a glance to the front of the room, rejoined Angie's step routine. Tellumo returned the step platform to the shelves, picked a towel up from the floor, and followed the lady in the floral print out of the Corral.

Oliver threw himself into the last thirty minutes of his step class, but couldn't stop thinking about the whippersnapper in a loincloth. Rather than the pectoral-revealing cutout T-shirts Kevin had called workout ponchos—worn by most of the more muscular men at the gym—Tellumo wore modest, loose-fitting T-shirts and sweatpants when he worked out. Oliver tried to push the image of the cocky, self-absorbed young man in clingy running shorts from his mind.

Why should he worry, anyway? Without children or grandchildren, Oliver had no stake in the distant future. The world was going to hell in a handbasket. Given the lack of ambition of the younger generation, he'd be dead long before they drove the country over a cliff—probably while texting.

Chapter Four: Home, Sweet Home

TELLUMO HURRIED out of the Corral behind Mrs. Tucker, unable to remember when he'd last been so embarrassed. Although her reaction had been over the top, the combative, overly protective woman's confusion was understandable. Between Mrs. Tucker's sweat-soaked hair and makeup-free face, she looked like a different woman.

"I never dreamed she'd guard my things so fiercely," Mrs. Tucker said, shaking her head. "Like the Bible says, you can't judge a book by its cover."

Tellumo was pretty sure books hadn't been invented when the Bible texts had been written but didn't say anything. He handed her the towel and her keys. "Are you okay?"

She nodded. "Thanks for asking, and for coming to my rescue yet again." She patted his arm and smiled. "You're a good boy."

"Happy to help," Tellumo said. He heard a commotion outside the locker rooms and turned to look.

She followed his gaze. "I've got to run," she said. "If you don't have anything else to do, stop by Trinity Baptist Church before eleven o'clock services tomorrow." She looked back over her shoulder as she hurried to the exit. "We're serving coffee and my homemade cinnamon buns. You should come."

Before he could say anything, she'd dashed out the door into the parking lot. Despite a weakness for home-baked sweets, he'd pass on her invitation. Church hadn't been part of his upbringing. His mothers believed organized religion perpetuated the patriarchy and had explored alternative paths to enlightenment, including a mishmash of traditions and rituals inspired by paganism, mysticism, self-help books, and feminist encounter groups. He'd seen more naked and bare-breasted women howling at the moon than he could count.

Tellumo watched the sexy older man through the double doors. Red-faced and glistening with sweat, the Silver Fox had slowed a bit and appeared to be conserving energy. His steps were smaller, his knee lifts a little lower, and his lunges not quite so deep as before. After a moment,

Tellumo realized he'd been staring, tore himself away, and headed for the locker room.

The custodian wheeled a Shop-Vac past him into the women's locker room. An orange construction cone with Caution Wet Floor lettered on the sides sat in the doorway. A hand-scrawled sign had been taped to the wall. "Temporarily Out of Order. Sorry!" Tellumo wondered what had happened and suspected Mrs. Tucker's apparent drenching was somehow related. She'd sure been in a hurry to leave.

Tellumo opened his locker, slipped his sweatpants over his damp running shorts, and slid into a black hoodie with a white *C* beneath four white bear claws centered on the chest. Football wasn't really his thing, but he'd enjoyed going to Nippert Stadium every fall for a game or two when he'd been a student at the University of Cincinnati. Buying the sweatshirt emblazoned with the alma mater's bear-paw logo had less to do with school pride than his preference for silver bears.

Boot Steppin' class would be over in fifteen minutes. Given the disruption he'd caused, hanging around for a chance to bump into the Silver Fox was a bad idea. The grumpy man was liable to bite Tellumo's head off for wrecking his workout.

The gray sky had lightened a bit, and the wind had died down. He shook his head in the chill air, combed his hair back over his ears with his fingers, and then raised the hood of his sweatshirt. Things were returning to normal after Snowmageddon, at least on this end of Fallisville. Business was booming throughout the little shopping center. The grocery store, nail salon, pet store, and pharmacy he passed looked to be as busy as the gym had been.

Tellumo was glad he didn't have to deal with the traffic and could walk home. In the fall, he'd often cut through the wooded buffer zone between the shopping center and his apartment complex, stopping on occasion to meditate or to watch the sun set. Staying on the sidewalk took a little longer but, until the saturated ground dried out, was the better option.

Living alone agreed with him. He thought he'd feel homesick after moving out, but he hadn't. Not one little bit. Teaching responsibilities kept him too busy to think about home. Lacking room for his mothers to spend the night, or a car so he could go home, bothered him less than he'd expected—a lot less.

Though not luxurious by any stretch of the imagination, his apartment was twice the size of the bedroom he'd grown up in, and he no longer shared a bathroom with his mothers. Opposite his bed was a dressing area with a sink and mirror between two doors. The left opened into a walk-in closet, the right into a room just big enough for a toilet and bathtub. He turned on the faucet, stepped out of his clothes, and when the water had warmed up enough, switched the flow to the handheld showerhead he'd bought to replace the original fixture.

Tellumo faced the steaming water and closed his eyes for a moment, shaking his head to wet his hair. He switched to the massage setting, turning slowly as hot bursts pelted his shoulders, back, and chest. Facing the rear of the tub, he leaned forward and back again, sending staccato pulses of hot water up and down his spine. His thoughts returned to the Silver Fox, red-faced, covered with sweat, and in his mind's eye, naked. Imagination filled the void of his knowledge with details catering to his exacting specifications.

Beneath the short-sleeved shirts the older man always wore, Tellumo envisioned nipples like pencil erasers rising from hairy pecs, with a narrow happy trail extending invitingly from his muscular chest and across his belly, drawing Tellumo's eyes downward to the shaft jutting arrogantly from his groin. He imagined the man's hairless alabaster ass gleaming in stark contrast to his tanned skin and furry thighs. Tellumo wanted to taste it, to rim his hole until he begged for something bigger and harder in its place.

Tellumo's rock-hard cock demanded attention. Had it been his offspring instead of his dick, child protective services would have been all over Tellumo, investigating claims of neglect, abuse, and cruelty. Since leaving Cincinnati, he'd embraced abstinence as a way of life—like he really had a choice. He wasn't into hookups, and nightlife in Fallisville left a lot to be desired. Masturbating was always an option, but he was seeing how long he could go without getting off for the ultimate experiment in delayed gratification.

He turned off the movie in his mind along with the water, grabbed a towel, and stepped out of the tub. Preparing lesson plans for four classes a day and grading papers had kept him too busy for extracurricular activities. If he didn't do a better job keeping up, Tellumo feared he'd be fired. The extended winter break had given him a chance to plan further ahead. Surely not having to play catch-up all the time would relieve some of the pressure. He hoped to make still more progress this evening before reviewing lesson plans for the classes he'd teach on Monday.

Struggling to keep his neck above water had interfered with more than visits home and his sex life. He knew little more about most of his students than their names. The exceptions were outliers—top performers, class clowns, brownnosers, troublemakers, and kids who maybe should have been held back a grade or two earlier in their school careers. He hoped the extra preparation would enable him to give them the attention they needed and give him time to get to know the rest of his students.

Had he been motivated by money and material possessions, Tellumo would have chosen a different profession. Changing the world was beyond his reach, but teaching was an opportunity to make a difference. Male teachers had been a rarity in his life before college, but the few who had taught Tellumo made a lasting impression. He intended to do the same for his students, and not just the attention grabbers.

OLIVER DROVE home to Thoroughbred Acres, a planned community on the south side of Fallisville with sidewalks, streetlights, and a lakeside playground surrounded by picnic benches and fire pits. Throughout the neighborhood, signs encouraged residents to Have a Nice Day, Enjoy Your Walk, and Pick Up After Your Pet. He had no way of knowing about the impact of the first two messages, but evidence suggested the third—despite his complaints to the neighborhood association, the Humane Society, and the city council—was often ignored.

He maneuvered the Taurus into his box-filled two-car garage, pushing the button on the automatic opener to close the door behind him. Although the roads had cleared, no truck had come to haul Kevin's crap away. He'd called Goodwill several times to no avail. The tight fit prevented him from opening the door very far, forcing him to slide through the narrow space and sidle between the car and the wall until he reached the door to the kitchen.

The aroma of well-seasoned pinto beans greeted him. He'd soaked the dry beans in water overnight, drained them this morning, and dumped them into the Crock-Pot with a ham hock, diced onion, and seasoning. His cooking often left much to be desired, but his beans and cornbread—except for the time he'd added a tablespoon of cloves—were crowd-pleasers.

Oliver flipped on the hallway light and headed for his bedroom. After laying out a clean pair of boxers, a well-worn flannel shirt, the pajama bottoms he called his house pants, and a pair of white socks, Oliver stripped, dropping his soiled clothing in the hamper before grabbing a fresh towel from the linen closet. He placed the towel where he could reach it and stepped into the tub.

When the water temperature was right, he switched on the shower. As he did at least once every day, Oliver cursed the low-flow showerhead Kevin had insisted on installing. Surely any savings from the reduced flow were offset by the extra time required to get wet and rinse off in little more than a heavy mist.

He lathered his hair with medicated shampoo, soaped up a washcloth, and proceeded to scrub every square inch of his body. Sandalwood filled the air—one of his favorite fragrances and a gift from Janice Downey, a frequent weekend lunch date who still taught English at Salt Lick County High. He'd given her several bars of lavender and chamomile soap—her favorites—in return. They'd given each other the same gifts for twenty years, guaranteeing at least one present they wouldn't need to exchange.

Patting his skin and hair dry—never rubbing—Oliver then draped the damp towel over the shower curtain rod to dry enough to keep from mildewing in the hamper. The thick and luxurious poker-straight hair he'd taken for granted most of his life had given way to thinning patches, a rapidly receding hairline, and an ever-expanding hair desert on top of his head he fortunately couldn't see in his reflection without the help of a hand mirror. He'd resisted the increasing salinization of his salt-and-pepper hair, starting with Grecian Formula and progressing to frequent trips to the salon for Giorgio to touch up his roots. The gray had a wiry texture he disliked and dyes couldn't conceal, forcing Oliver to keep his hair too short for expensive color treatments.

He ran a comb through the hair he had left, more out of habit than need, swiped deodorant across his pits, and slathered his face with the same moisturizer he'd used since he was a teenager, slapping on a generous amount of body lotion everywhere else. Next to liver spots—of which he had none so far—nothing aged a person like dry, wrinkled skin.

Growing older wasn't so bad, Oliver thought as he dressed. Aging, however, sucked. His mind sometimes forgot he no longer had the body of a thirty-year-old. Although a ridiculous amount of sagging had occurred slowly enough he'd barely noticed, he still didn't look his age. Some work around the eyes would knock off ten more years, but Botox and plastic surgery were on the other side of a line he refused to cross. Cosmetic procedures were like tattoos, potato chips, and an alcoholic's first drink. One was never enough. The more work aging celebrities had done, the more alike they looked—regardless of gender. The fat-lipped, wide-eyed, expressionless faces held no appeal for Oliver.

Besides, he hated having to go to the doctor. If it took a village to raise a child, keeping the little darlings alive into old age required an army of medical experts. Every time he looked up, he had an appointment with one specialist or another, none of whom ever talked with each other—at least, not about him.

A cluster of health issues around his fortieth birthday had scared the hell out of him. Exercise, good nutrition, and a daily glass of red wine kept his cholesterol, blood pressure, and sugar in check. Aside from the occasional over-the-counter painkiller, his daily fiber supplement, and a multivitamin, Oliver no longer needed medications. His only prescriptions were for various creams and ointments, prescribed by the dermatologist to control a scalp condition, a persistent itch in his ears, and a high susceptibility to foot fungus.

Oliver pulled paper towels and window cleaner from under the sink and spruced up the bathroom. Living alone agreed with him. Everything he owned was where it was supposed to be. Instead of spending half a day every week cleaning and putting the house in order, he tidied up a little at a time and put things back where they belonged when he finished using them. The house was spotless—perfect in every way. Oliver had no desire to change a thing.

PEGGY THOUGHT she'd never get home. Giorgio hadn't been able to work her in, but had stayed late to wash and style her hair. He'd urged her to forego the teased and sprayed look she'd worn for the last ten years for a sportier, easier to care for style more in fitting with her active lifestyle. Although flattered, she'd told him she'd think about his suggestion for her after photo. One didn't make a change like that willy-nilly.

For at least the thirtieth year in a row, losing weight topped her annual list of New Year's resolutions. Maybe this year would be different. Joining the gym last fall had given her a head start. She was quite proud of herself. Until Snowmageddon struck, she'd hit the gym for a class or to work out at least twice every week. The effort hadn't transformed her like she'd expected, but she felt better and could see a difference in the way her clothes fit.

The grocery stores had been packed. The store on the way home from Giorgio's shop was out of raisins, forcing her to detour halfway across town to stop at another. Running out of milk, eggs, and bread she could understand, but raisins?

Her stomach rumbled, reminding her she hadn't eaten since lunch. She'd planned to bake a chicken breast, steam some broccoli, and make brown rice for dinner, but had run out of time. Besides, the little kitchen at the duplex was too small to fix dinner and make buns at the same time. Never mind the lack of oven space. Certain she'd be up all night as it was, Peggy went through the drive-through window at the chicken place for a three-piece, all-white, extra crispy meal with mashed potatoes and baked beans, an extra biscuit, and a large diet cola.

She hadn't realized how dehydrated she was until her first sip of cola. The icy cold beverage tasted great and felt good going down. When she'd slaked her thirst, she reached into the bag and pulled out a small cardboard carton. As she'd hoped, the extra biscuit was inside. Crumbs scattered across her lap, and she moaned. The biscuit was delicious even without butter and honey, jelly, or rich and creamy gravy.

By the time she got home, Peggy had polished off two wings, the other biscuit, and her soft drink. After three trips to get the groceries inside, she nibbled on beans, mashed potatoes, and the chicken breast as she put everything away and assembled the ingredients and equipment she'd need for what promised to be a long night of baking.

Her recipe made six dozen buns. Fearing there wouldn't be enough, and knowing none would go to waste no matter how many she made, Peggy had decided to double the recipe. Given the size of her mixing bowls and oven, she'd have to make the buns in two batches. Making the buns would take at least three hours. Since she could only fit two pans of a dozen buns in her oven, baking would take another three hours.

She poured warm water into a large mixing bowl and checked with a thermometer to make sure the temperature was in the desired range before adding the yeast. After a few minutes, she added sugar, a hefty sprinkle of salt, ginger, flour, and an egg; beat the mixture with her electric mixer for a couple of minutes; and then covered the bowl with plastic wrap. While the yeasty mix proofed, she hurried to her bedroom, where she had a much easier time shedding her active wear and spandex attire than had been the case at the gym. The long flannel gown and fluffy slippers she put on were a lot more comfortable too.

Back in the kitchen, she uncovered the dough and added raisins, shortening, and more flour, kneading the soft dough on a floured board until it looked the way she wanted. After setting the dough to rise in a greased bowl, Peggy filled her Big Gulp travel cup with ice and diet cola, opened the bag of potato chips she'd picked up at the store, and plopped on the living room sofa to watch a little television.

The VCR blinked twelve o'clock, as usual. The fake grandfather clock her last husband had given her, God rest his soul, said a few minutes after eight o'clock. She hit the guide button on the remote and scrolled through the channels for something watchable before settling on a movie she hadn't seen on the Lifetime Movie Network—her favorite channel next to the Oprah Winfrey Network.

An hour later, Peggy returned to the kitchen to see her dough had doubled. She punched it down, divided it into quarters, and left it to rest while she mixed brown sugar with cinnamon for the filling. With a rolling pin, she flattened each dough ball into a rectangle. After slathering the dough with melted butter and the filling mix, she rolled it up like a jellyroll and sliced each roll into eighteen one-inch pieces she then placed in three pans to rise.

She was enjoying her second movie when the time came for the step that set her cinnamon buns apart from everyone else's. She blended some brown sugar with a splash of vanilla, a pinch of cinnamon, and a cup of heavy cream, spread the mix over the top, and then placed two of the three pans into a 375-degree oven to bake. When they were done, she'd make the glaze.

Four hours later, Peggy slid the last two pans into the oven. Her arms were numb from all the kneading she'd done, her back ached, and thanks to her earlier workout in the tiny little stall at the gym, her left elbow was bruised. Muscle soreness tormented her midsection with every move she made. She longed for a hot bath and the comfort of her bed.

While the last pans baked, she moved the most recent batch to come out of the oven from the pans to a wire rack and glazed them. For quality control, she'd eaten a bun from each batch, and while they'd all passed muster, she could taste the ginger more in the last batch—a slip with the measuring spoon she'd noted on the recipe card to repeat next time.

By the time she'd finished packing the buns, with sheets of wax paper between the layers, into one of three plastic storage bins that, until a few hours ago, had held her summer clothes, Peggy was exhausted. The kitchen looked like the window had been left open during Snowmageddon. A dusting of flour and confectioner's sugar covered every surface, including the mountain of dirty dishes rising from the sink and extending across the surrounding countertop.

The mess could wait until morning. Too tired for even a quick shower, Peggy fell into bed. Her last thought before she fell asleep was she maybe should have rinsed her feet. If washing them would make a difference, she'd have gotten up. After all this time, she didn't see the point.

Chapter Five: Best Friends

OLIVER SCOWLED at the steaming trash can and then examined the contents of his refrigerator. How the beans had turned out too salty to eat remained a mystery. Cooking had never been his forte. He could clean like nobody's business, organize clutter like the professionals on an episode of *Hoarders*, and iron like a fifties housewife. His skill in the culinary arts, however, left much to be desired.

Problems varied with the food he prepared. Over- or undercooking was common—especially on the grill where Oliver took blackening to new heights. He often omitted essential ingredients because he overlooked them in the recipe, forgot to add them, didn't like them, or had none on hand. On occasion, he added ingredients twice—the likely problem with his salty beans. Bad substitutions ruined many a good dish, like the hamburgers he'd made with vanilla yogurt when he'd been out of the sour cream called for in the recipe. Or he'd use the wrong ingredient accidentally, like three tablespoons of cayenne pepper instead of cayenne seasoning in red beans and rice nobody could eat. How was he supposed to know they weren't the same thing?

His worst offenses were the personal touches added to make a dish his own, like the pinto beans he'd ruined with cloves. Dill pickle juice hadn't kicked up the flavor of his chili the way he'd expected either. Same with the half cup of sugar he'd added to his spaghetti sauce or the mint leaves he'd stirred into scalloped potatoes for a Kentucky Derby party.

A combination of delivered food, takeout, and frozen entrees had sustained him after Kevin left. The days, however, hadn't been long enough to burn enough calories to offset what he consumed. He hadn't really tried to change his ways until the scales, shrinking clothes, and the threat of new prescriptions had forced his hand.

There was plenty of food in the fridge—just nothing he wanted to eat. The full freezer offered different choices to reject. Free of the sugary cereals, cookies, snack cakes, and the like he'd banished from his kitchen, nothing in the cupboard appealed to him either. His mother would have said he must not be hungry. Were she or anyone else here to cook for him and clean up the mess, he'd have no trouble making a selection.

The shrill ringing of the telephone startled him. Since his mother had passed away, only telemarketers, pollsters, politicians, and scammers ever called him. He scowled as he lifted the handset from the receiver. "Hello."

"Hello to you too, you crotchety old man. Have I called at a bad time? Who peed in your Wheaties?"

Oliver laughed. "Fiddledeedee, if it isn't Scarlett O'Mara. I thought you were a telemarketer."

"As God is my witness, if you ever call me that again...."

"Sorry, Letty." Her siblings—Gerald, Suellen, and Carreen O'Mara—hadn't been teased the way she had about the Tara-inspired names. By high school, even her mother had stopped calling her Scarlett.

"Don't you have caller ID?"

"I keep forgetting to pick up the little box that shows the number," Oliver said. He wasn't sure it would work with his wall-mounted, rotary-dial telephone. "I need to get a new phone first—maybe one of those cordless models so I can walk around the house when I'm on a call."

"Geez, Ollie. We're almost two decades into the twenty-first century and you're stuck in the seventies. What are you up to?"

Oliver ignored her dig. "Just trying to figure out what to cook for dinner."

"You're cooking?" She clucked several times. "Eating your cooking has to be the worst part of being single. Your chocolate mashed potatoes stand out as the most disgusting dish I've ever seen."

For Christmas dinner one year, he'd whipped grated baker's chocolate into mashed potatoes for a truly unfortunate dish even he'd agreed looked like steaming poop on the plate. "Ha! You know me so well. Despite the appearance, they didn't taste all that bad." Oliver sat down at the kitchen table and crossed his ankles. "Believe it or not, I'm doing better."

"Yeah." Letty snorted. "Like worse is possible. Funny what you can do with nobody around to do for you."

"Like you'd know. Sid has waited on you hand and foot since the day you met him." Letty hadn't been the first to blame functional incompetence for Oliver's lack of skill in the kitchen. True, his more memorable failures had been epic. But he hadn't messed up on purpose and had been embarrassed more than once—especially when guests had been his victims. "Everyone gone from your place?"

"Finally." Letty sighed. "I'm delighted to see my grandkids come, and just as glad to see them go—especially this time. Thanks to Snowmageddon, the three-day visit—already a good two days more than I can really handle—turned into ten days."

"I can't even imagine." Oliver whistled. Spending Christmas Day in Dayton with his best friend, her husband, and their progeny—four handsome sons, their respective wives, six grandsons, and one overindulged granddaughter—was hard enough to stomach. "Sorry I couldn't make it."

Letty laughed. "Yeah, I bet. Fifteen minutes with any two of my grandkids is ten more than you can stand."

Oliver nodded and stood. "I can't disagree. In my defense, other than your little darlings, high school students are the youngest kids I've been around since I was a kid." He paced from one side of the kitchen to the other as he talked. "How'd your long-suffering husband hold up?"

"Fine, until two days after Christmas when the wine ran out." She snorted. "Boys had to physically restrain Sid to keep him from hiking four miles through two feet of snow to the Liquor Barn."

"Poor guy." From the moment they'd met forty years earlier, Oliver had liked affable Sid. The handsome, good-natured bear of a man adored Letty and had never objected to or resented her close relationship with Oliver.

"I love them dearly," Letty continued. "But a week with a house full of people makes for a lot of work. Hell, I'm ready to retire from the kitchen and housework, but my daughters-in-law show no sign of taking over and are worse cooks than you are."

"If one of your boys had married Julia Child, you'd say the same thing," Oliver said.

"What is it with you and Julia Child? If any of my boys married her, I'd have a whole lot to say before I ever got around to her cooking. She's older than we are, Ollie."

"You wouldn't approve of a May-September relationship?"

"Julia Child and my *oldest* son would be more like early January and late December. I guess if she had a foot in the grave and a shit ton of money…."

"She's already dead." He bit back a remark about the second or possibly third wives some fraction of her sons was likely to have in another twenty years. Teasing remarks about her kids didn't always go over as intended. "When do you want to get together to catch up?"

"I don't know—after ten days with the clan, I might not come up for air until March."

"You know you're always welcome. Give me enough notice to spruce things up and lay in the requisite supplies."

"Fine—but no more substitutions. If what I eat is going to kill me, give me the real thing, not some low-fat, artificially sweetened, gluten-free processed crap."

"Yes'm, Miss Scarlett."

"One more time and I'll order my hot new overseer to take you to the barn."

"Can you go ahead and set that up? I haven't been laid since Kevin left."

"That has to be some kind of record."

"If you must know, it's not." She didn't need to know the record, aside from his recent dry spell, had been the years from birth to age nineteen.

"Childhood doesn't count."

Oliver laughed. "I can't wait to see you. We'll hang out like old times, when we shared that crummy little apartment on the corner of High and Rose. Remember?"

"Vaguely." She laughed. "And I'd prefer to keep it that way. Thank God we didn't have smartphones. Imagine some of the pictures we could have taken."

"I don't know what you're talking about." Oliver smiled. "I'm the same wholesome, law-abiding citizen I've always been."

Letty guffawed. "You can sing that song down there in Fallisville all you want, but me, Sid, and a few folks back in Lexington know better."

"Dementia, I'm sure." He sniffed. "There's not a scintilla of proof."

"There has to be a Polaroid out there somewhere."

"Impossible." Although unlikely one would ever turn up, the risk terrified him, prompting him years ago to burn a shoebox full of snapshots he'd received in response to an ad he'd placed in the back of a gay magazine, along with his collection of 16mm porn. Nightmares about the handful of incriminating photos he'd sent to other men finding their way to Fallisville had ceased on his retirement, but the thought still gave him a sick feeling in the pit of his stomach.

"Hold on to that fantasy, Ollie. Whatever gets you through the night."

"Sometimes, it's a second glass of wine. Something about a barn, a studly overseer, and a few bales of hay will do the trick tonight." He was only half joking.

She sighed. "I didn't ask about your love life—"

"Because you know I'll call you when and if I ever get laid again."

"My kids didn't wake me in the middle of the night as much as you did and, unlike you, were never shitfaced when they did." She paused. "Well, except for a few calls when they were in college."

"Sorry." He shook his head. "In those days my long-distance bill was more than my rent."

"Mine too. I'm close to Suellen and Carreen—Gerald too—but you know stuff I could never tell them, some even Sid doesn't know about."

"We've got enough dirt on each other to sink a good-sized ship."

Letty laughed. "I'll never tell."

"Because you know what would happen if you did." He laughed in turn. Like anyone cared about the embarrassing incidents, secret crushes, and opinions too honest for anyone else's ears they'd shared with each other over the years.

"Well, darling, I won't keep you. Sid is standing at the door rubbing his crotch. Looks like Momma's gonna get laid."

"Go ahead, rub it in. Do y'all still make all that noise? If I had a dollar for every night you two kept me awake…."

"We tried to be quiet. You should hear us when we have the house to ourselves. Want me to leave the phone off the hook so you can listen?"

"No," Oliver said, shaking his head. "That's quite all right. Tell Sid I said hello."

"Will do, darling. I'll be in touch about our tryst. Love you!"

"Love you too."

The line went dead. Oliver hung up the phone and smiled. He envied Sid and Letty Dawson. They'd had their share of ups and downs—he'd heard at least one side of every major fight they'd ever had. But after all these years, they'd never stopped loving each other like the teenagers they'd been when they'd first fallen in love.

He'd often wondered how different his life might have been had his first love been other than a no-good, two-timing, sorry-ass, lying son of a bitch—not that he was bitter or anything. What shouldn't even have been a one-night stand had lasted six long, miserable years. Faith that early struggles would strengthen the relationship had kept him from giving up. Now he knew better. Things never got better—only worse.

In hindsight, Oliver saw he'd fallen for different versions of the same guy five times. Trouble was, none of them had actually been the man he'd believed them to be. He'd been conned, and with each failed relationship, the walls went up a little higher. His biggest fear was that the fortress protecting his heart had become impenetrable.

TELLUMO PUTTERED around the apartment after his pulsating post-workout shower, working on lesson plans, playing video games, and reading. Having his very own bathroom was the best part of living alone. Long, soaking baths had become a new nighttime obsession. To enhance the experience, he'd splurged on patchouli-scented candles, incense, and soaps, and an assortment of shampoos, conditioners, oils, and lotions.

Soft music played from the smartphone sitting atop the towel-covered toilet seat, along with a razor, scissors, comb, nail clippers, and a stemless wine glass filled with ice, Lambrusco, and slices of orange, lime, and lemon. His mothers called the citrusy concoction grown-up Kool-Aid, but instant sangria was the name he preferred.

The instrumental arrangements on the playlist another subscriber on his music service had shared provided the perfect background. The eclectic assortment spanned the centuries and included everything from the classics to electronic dance music. The result was an interesting and upbeat mix of songs he never tired of hearing and, after he'd e-mailed the creator of the list a thank-you message, a new virtual friendship.

The music faded and his phone vibrated. A picture of his best friend filled the screen—an over-the-top parody of the duck-lipped, arched-eyebrow, look-how-clever-I-am selfies used so often as profile pics on social networking apps. He swiped the screen, and Melody Abshire's smiling face replaced the still image.

"Hey, Moe! You in the tub again?" She screwed up her face and peered back at him. "Point that thing lower. I want to see how much of a man you really are."

Tellumo laughed and was tempted to flash her. "You know it's bath time, and for the umpteenth time, I'm not showing you my junk."

"Good, because I'd never show you mine either."

"Never say never." He winked at her. "You're looking good. Love the new haircut."

"Really? Mom hates it—says I look like a cancer survivor."

"I disagree. It's short, but flattering. Let me see the back." Her face fell away as she raised the smartphone above her head. "Don't go so fast! The image is blurring."

"Oh, sorry."

"You look like a different person. Without all that hair, your eyes pop, and who knew you had such cute ears?"

"Thanks!" Her face grew serious. "I felt naked at first, and then like a huge weight had been lifted from my shoulders—literally and figuratively."

"You've been hiding beneath that gorgeous red mop for as long as I can remember. Did you save the hair?"

"Gave it to a charity that makes wigs for kids with cancer." She furrowed her brow. "Who'd save it?" She shuddered and shook her head. "Then would I leave it to somebody when I die? Granny Mel left me a big ole hank of her hair. Woo-hoo!"

"I'd treasure it." Tellumo's family tree dead-ended with Jules and Trish. Before his birth and the legalization of gay marriage anywhere, they'd legally changed their last names to Magnamater. On medical forms and other records, they claimed to be sisters, and looked enough alike to disarm contrary suspicions.

"Oh yeah, sorry." Mel furrowed her brow and frowned. "I wasn't thinking."

"It's okay." He wondered if growing up with a grandfather or two and a few uncles might have averted his attraction to older men.

"You have to wonder what they're trying to forget."

"Or don't want me to know." Tellumo shrugged. "I'll never know. They don't talk about the past, but I get the impression neither had a very happy childhood." He raked his wet hair off his forehead with his fingers. "Maybe I should cut my hair short—pick a trendy style from a poster for one of the boy bands topping the pop charts."

She brought the phone up close to her face until the bridge of her nose and her eyes were all he could see. "Don't you dare!"

He stood and reached for the bath sheet hanging from the towel bar. "I'm going to set you down for a minute." After securing the towel around his waist, he picked up the phone again. "Why not?"

"Your hair is your best feature. Not that there's anything wrong with the rest of you." She smiled. "Not so far as I know, anyway. Have you met anyone? Made any new friends?"

Tellumo shook his head. "Honestly, Mel, I know it's been almost six months, but I'm still basking in the solitude."

"The gang asks about you all the time. Nobody has seen you on Twitter or Instagram for months."

"Really? I've been too busy for much social networking." He studied his reflection in the mirror, stroked his cheek, and then decided to wait until morning to shave. "Pretty sure everyone has my number and e-mail address."

Mel shrugged. "Yeah, you know how it is. Cincinnati is the center of the universe, and if you're not here, you don't exist."

He leaned his phone against the liquid soap dispenser beside the sink. "I haven't tried to contact them either." The astringent he applied cooled his face and neck. "Haven't had time."

"Trish calls about once a week." She looked at him and screwed up her face. "Lean down here."

He complied with her request. "Close enough?"

She nodded. "Trim those brows, bro!"

"Yes, ma'am." Tellumo retrieved the comb and scissors from the towel-covered toilet seat, combed his brows upward, and snipped. "What do you and Trish talk about?"

"She says she's checking to see how I'm doing and then grills me about what you've been up to like the good cop in a crime drama."

"Subtlety has never been her strong suit."

"She asks if I've spent the night at your place every time she calls."

"There's no room for overnight guests. Jules says I should sleep on the couch and let her and Trish sleep in my bed."

Melody wrinkled up her face. "Ew!"

"I could never fool around with anyone in my bed if the two of them slept in it. Does that make me weird?"

She shook her head. "No, you'd be weird if you could. So I can't come for a visit? Not seeing you for Christmas was a huge disappointment." She batted her eyes. "I wouldn't mind sleeping on the couch."

"Of course you can visit—whenever you want. You wouldn't have to sleep on the couch either."

"I couldn't take your bed away from you."

"You wouldn't have to. Sleeping with you would be fun."

"I sleep commando."

"Me too."

"Unfair. You're gay, so sleeping naked with me would be more likely to gross you out than turn you on. But I'm straight, and you're a man. A mighty fine specimen I might add."

"Titties turn me on."

"Yeah, old man boobs. A perky set like mine would freak you out."

"Old man boobs?" Tellumo laughed. "You're a riot."

"It's funny because it's true."

"When do you want to come down? I'm too busy with school to entertain during the week, but weekends are good."

"Let me get through the next few weeks and we'll see what our calendars look like around Valentine's Day."

"Sounds good to me. Love you." He kissed his fingertips and pressed them to the phone.

Melody smiled and repeated the gesture. "Love you too, Moe."

The image on the screen shrank and then disappeared, leaving the familiar grid of icons. He raked his fingers through his hair and smiled. A visit from Mel would be nice. He made a mental note to pick up some pajamas.

PEGGY OPENED her eyes, wincing as she raised her head to check the time. Every muscle in her body ached. She wanted to get out of bed, but moving hurt too much. When she attempted to rear up on her elbow, pain shot through her shoulders and down both arms.

No bones appeared to be broken. She didn't feel sick or have a headache, and other than the angry purple splotch on her left elbow, she could detect no swelling or bruising. She didn't think a stroke or a heart attack was the problem. She could move whatever she wanted, but any movement caused something to hurt. Pressing her forearms, biceps, and abs hurt too, but she couldn't stop herself. Instinct told her kneading and massaging the sore muscles would help.

What she really needed was a hot bath—and the sooner the better. It was already half past seven o'clock. A huge mess to clean up waited in the kitchen, and she needed to get to church early enough to unload and arrange the cinnamon buns on serving trays. She rolled onto her side and willed her feet to the floor, groaning as she rose to a standing position.

She started to make the bed, but stopped. Bending over hurt too much. Nobody but her and God would know the difference. She moved toward the bathroom with a gait somewhere between limping and staggering. Pain shot through her thighs with each shuffling step. Twisting even the slightest bit left or right brought pain to her sides.

Pushing through her agony, she twisted the stopper for the tub to fill up, turned on the water as hot as it would go, and removed her clothes. Raising her flannel gown over her head nearly brought tears to her eyes. After slipping the inflatable horseshoe collar around her neck to keep her hair from getting wet, she eased down in the tub, adjusted the temperature of the water pouring from the spout, and waited for the tub to fill and the heat to work its magic.

The neighbors on the other side of the duplex were fighting again—noise she wouldn't hear had she turned on the radio. Oh well. Too late now. In her tender state, the thought of walking across the room to turn it on and climbing back into the tub held no appeal. The shouting would turn to lovemaking soon enough, hopefully somewhere on the other side of the duplex so she wouldn't have to listen to the obscenities they hurled at each other as they fornicated. She sometimes got up and pounded on the wall. Never stopped their rutting, but at least they quieted down some.

In the distance she heard her phone ringing. Crap. Who on earth would be calling at this hour? Probably a wrong number. By the time she could dig her phone out of her purse, the caller would have hung up. If she got out of the tub, she'd need a fresh towel too. Whoever it was would have to wait until she finished her bath.

She sank down onto her inflatable collar. Wisps of steam rose from the surface, and the mirror above the sink fogged up. Every move she made hurt, but soaking seemed to help. She didn't feel quite as stiff as before, and the pain had either lessened or she'd simply gotten used to it.

Pushing against the tub with her feet, she eased into a sitting position and squirted Dove body wash into a wet facecloth. After slipping the collar from her neck, she massaged her shoulders with the soapy washcloth, groaning now and then as she worked her way slowly down her body to her feet. The pressure felt good against her sore muscles.

The third time the phone rang, curiosity got the best of her. She pulled the stopper, sluiced tepid water from the spigot over her body to rinse off the soap as the tub drained, and then grabbed the towel hanging from the shower-curtain rod to dry off. Calling anyone before nine in the morning or after nine in the evening was rude unless it was an emergency. She pulled her robe on and headed to the kitchen where she'd left her purse. After some digging, she pulled out her phone and flipped it open to see who had called.

Lurleen Owen's number appeared on the little screen. She hadn't left a message. Ignoring the dirty dishes and the rest of the mess, Peggy pushed the button to call her back.

"Oh, Peggy! Thank God it's you. I've been worried sick! Are you okay? I was about to call the sheriff to see if he'd drive over to check on you."

"Hello, Lurleen," Peggy said, taken aback by the concern of the woman who'd been her best friend since shortly after she'd moved to Fallisville. "I'm a little sore, but otherwise I'm fine. What makes you ask?"

"All that snow was bad, but this ice storm is worse. Do you have electric? Trees are down all over town. Half of Fallisville is without power."

Bill Pinkley hadn't said anything about freezing rain. Peggy pushed a button on the remote control and, after the television came on, switched from Lifetime to Channel 13. "I've got power. What ice storm?" She pushed the curtains back from her living room window and looked out. Icicles dangled from the eaves, tree branches were sheathed in a layer of ice, and the evergreens along the fence were bent nearly double. The porch, sidewalk, and the street in front of her house glistened with a half-inch sheet of frozen precipitation.

"The roads are a solid sheet of ice. Bill Pinkley says to stay home unless it's an emergency."

The woman across the street let her boxer out. The dog stepped off the porch, lost his footing, and slid down the sidewalk on his belly with splayed legs. He struggled to get back on his feet for a moment before giving up.

"So I see," Peggy said. Her neighbor covered the icy porch and sidewalk with a rug, and went back inside, coming out a moment later with another rug.

"You have plenty of food to eat? Bill Pinkley says the temperature's not supposed to get above freezing until Wednesday or Thursday."

Peggy eyeballed the plastic cinnamon-bun-filled containers stacked by the door. "Reckon I'll get by."

Chapter Six: Back to Normal

"SEE YOU this afternoon, Jack!" Tellumo called to the driver as he hopped off the bus, excited to face another day. The two weeks since the holiday break had gone much better than had the start of the fall term. An ice storm had pushed the return to classes back two more days, giving him time to complete tentative lesson plans for the rest of the school year.

He let himself into his classroom, slid his backpack under the desk, and hung his coat on the hook behind the door. Being well prepared made him feel better about his teaching ability. His students seemed more relaxed too. Discussions were livelier, he had fewer discipline problems, and through writing assignments, he'd learned at least a little about every young man and woman in his four classes.

He pulled a stack of papers from his backpack before shoving it back under his desk and sat in the well-worn captain's chair he'd inherited from the teacher who'd had the room before him. Like Salt Lick County, the students in his classes weren't particularly diverse. Tellumo had been surprised grocery stores offered choices other than white for bread and vanilla for ice cream. Asians, Hispanics, and African Americans lived in the area, but he saw few minority students in school and had none in his classes.

Southern Baptist was the prevailing faith, with Church of Christ a distant second, just ahead of the Mennonites whose farms dotted the countryside on the western side of the county. A smattering of Methodists, Episcopalians, Presbyterians, and Catholics brought up the rear. Agnostics, Buddhists, atheists, and others who weren't Christian kept a low profile.

Nobody was very poor or, aside from a few horse farm owners on the south side of the county, particularly wealthy. The unemployment rate stayed below state and national averages. A manufacturing plant for a foreign automaker, a light bulb factory, and a nearby hub for a national delivery service were the largest employers, followed by the hospital and then the county government, including teachers, firefighters, and peace officers. County residents, even teenagers who wanted to work, had little trouble finding jobs.

Tellumo heard a knock, but before he could answer, the door opened. Janice Downey, the head of the English department, poked her head into his classroom. "You sure you don't mind giving up your planning period?"

Tellumo smiled and shook his head. "Don't mind a bit."

"Good. See you in the lounge after second period." She disappeared, and the door closed behind her.

Tellumo wasn't sure what he'd gotten himself into. Taking on extra responsibilities hadn't crossed his mind last year, but the steep learning curve had flattened out a bit and the extra preparation had freed up some time. When Ms. Downey had asked at yesterday's faculty meeting for a volunteer to be the advisor for the *Salt Lick County Review*, after a long uncomfortable silence, Tellumo had raised his hand.

Although he hadn't seen any literary works from his students, several showed promise. Involving them in the selection and editing of the pieces for the magazine would be a great learning experience, and a mentoring opportunity for him.

First hour he taught a mythology elective for juniors and seniors. As early arrivals trickled in, Tellumo didn't look up from the papers he was grading. He was a busy man. His time was important and not to be wasted. Tardiness wasn't tolerated. Hopefully, future employers of his charges would thank him.

When the bell rang, every seat was full. Sticking to his guns had worked. He wasn't here to befriend his students or to win any popularity contests. Given the scant age difference between him and the seniors, boundaries had to be maintained.

Salt Lick County High students self-selected into the usual crowds found in high schools across the country. Some of the tribes played well with others, and some didn't. Tellumo often divided his classes into small groups for discussion, separating friends and circulating around the room to make sure everyone participated. The cliques were still intact, but with each passing day, more open to interacting with outsiders. Or at least that's what he told himself.

By the time his second-hour freshman composition class ended, Tellumo was ready for a break. The good teachers he remembered from his school days had made thinking on their feet look easy. Keeping freewheeling discussions about the timelessness of a good myth and the keyhole structure for organizing an essay from veering too far off subject had required his full attention.

The sound of slamming lockers and the low roar of conversation filled the crowded corridor. The sea of students with backpacks slung over their shoulders moved at a snail's pace, but teachers had an advantage. A conga line three students deep going the wrong way parted, allowing him to join the slow-moving queue on the other side of the hallway. Sensing his presence behind them, students shifted to either side and a path opened before him.

The lounge, for lack of a better word, was almost as noisy and crowded as the hall had been. Lounge implied something much nicer than the ragtag collection of chairs, wobbly tables, and other furnishings crammed into the small room. Refuge was a better descriptor, or maybe shelter. An ancient refrigerator hummed in the corner. Vending machines, one for soft drinks and another for snacks, did a brisk business. A vintage toaster oven and the oldest microwave Tellumo had ever seen sat on the counter next to a deep sink that, judging from all the paint stains, once belonged to the art department.

Ms. Downey pulled a mug from the microwave, tossed the steaming teabag into a trash bin beside the sink, and with a wave, beckoned for Tellumo to join her at a nearby table. "Care for tea? This is chamomile. If you've got a mug, there are half a dozen different kinds in the drawer beneath the microwave. Help yourself."

"I'm good, thanks." Tellumo smiled and took a seat across from her.

By the time the bell rang for third hour, the lounge had cleared of everyone but the two of them. She looked over her mug at him, sipped her tea, and smiled. "I'm glad you're here."

He looked at her, unsure what she meant. "Thank you."

She met his gaze and smiled again. "Now that we're halfway through the school year, how do you feel about teaching here at Salt Lick County High?"

The question surprised him. Was this the meeting he'd dreaded, when she'd tell him things weren't working out and they were going to have to let him go? "Well…." Tellumo paused to collect his thoughts. "I'm still sorting things out. Last year was rough, but I'm feeling more on top of things and a lot better now."

She nodded. "Teaching right out of school is a tall order. The learning curve for a first-year teacher is pretty steep."

"I'll say." He relaxed. Her words didn't sound like the preface to a firing.

"I'm very impressed with your performance. Most new teachers need two or three years in the classroom to get to where you are."

Tellumo was shocked. "Seriously?"

"You're surprised?"

"Frankly, yes." He shrugged. "Believe it or not, I was afraid you were going to let me go."

She laughed and patted his arm. "Mr. Magnamater, I've taught for twenty-eight years and been department head for ten." She paused and took a sip of her tea. "I've seen a lot of teachers come and go. Most were pretty good educators. Many were extremely talented. But only a handful have the kind of gift for teaching I see in you."

"I… er… I don't know what to say."

"Teaching isn't something you do—it's who you are." She watched him over her mug for a moment. "Between the low pay and long hours, disinterested students and overengaged parents, and interference from local, state, and federal officials, anyone who isn't born to teach leaves in the first two or three years." She shook her head and then held his gaze. "It's who you are, from the moment you wake in the morning until you fall exhausted into bed two or three hours later than you planned because you still had work to do."

He nodded. "I want to make a difference."

She looked at him for another long moment. "You already have. That mean you're done?"

He furrowed his brow. "No, of course not. I'm just getting started."

"Trying to make a difference will break your heart, if it doesn't drive you crazy first. Forget about it." She shook her head and looked off into the distance for a moment before looking back at him. "You'll change lives." She cupped her hands around her mug and leaned forward. "But never in ways you planned, would expect, or could ever predict."

"Thanks for the advice." Tellumo thought he understood what she was telling him. The destination mattered less than the journey to get there. "I'll try to stay in the moment."

She nodded. "It's all you've got." She took another sip of tea. "By the way, I'm not the only one to have noticed your gift for teaching. Mr. Wyrick cites you as an example for using technology in the classroom."

"The principal?"

"Do you know another Mr. Wyrick?" She smiled. "He agreed with my suggestion to have you take charge of the *Salt Lick County Review*. You have the skills to move our little literary magazine into the twenty-first century. Switching from print to an online version will save money, and give more exposure to the kids whose work gets published too."

His head reeled. "But, I volunteered."

"True." She shrugged, and her face grew serious. "If you hadn't volunteered…." She smiled and stood. "But you did, so win-win, right?"

She had a point. Though he'd been a reluctant volunteer, nobody had held a gun to his head. The tech wrinkle was a new twist that made the job even more attractive to him. "Right." Tellumo smiled. "So what do I need to do?"

"Everything except write the submissions." She leaned over and pulled a thick folder from her bag. "Here's the file the previous advisor kept."

Tellumo picked up the folder and thumbed through it.

"We're a little behind schedule. The submission guidelines should have gone out last fall." She shrugged. "Submissions rarely come in before March anyway. I think you'll be fine." She rinsed out her mug in the paint-spattered sink and placed it on a paper towel to dry. "Any more questions?"

"Not at the moment." He stood and pushed his chair back under the table. "I'll look the file over and get back with you."

"Nobody is going to micromanage you," she said as they moved toward the door. "The old notes are FYI only. You're free to go about this however you see fit."

"Thanks, Ms. Downey." Tellumo held the door open for her. "I'm honored, and I really appreciate your faith in me."

"Like I said, I'm glad you're here. Keep up the good work." She turned and walked down the corridor to her classroom.

After she rounded the corner, Tellumo did a happy dance in the hall. The custodian came out of the boys' bathroom and caught him midleap. His face grew hot, but after the custodian gave him a wink and a thumbs-up, Tellumo smiled and resisted the urge to skip back to his classroom.

OLIVER SAT up and stretched. Two o'clock, according to the digital alarm clock on his bedside table. Some days, he could get through the early afternoon hours without a little shut-eye, but more often than not, heavy lids and frequent yawns forced his hand.

Aside from the naps he'd only been able to enjoy on weekends and days off before, retiring had not changed his sleep habits. Whether he wanted to or not, Oliver jumped out of bed by five thirty every morning and had done so for as long as he could remember. Snoozing until six thirty was a rare treat that threw him off schedule and made him feel like he was playing catch-up for the rest of the day.

Not that he would have minded sleeping in now and then. A high-fiber diet was the problem. Come five thirty, four thirty daylight saving time, he had to go to the bathroom—no ifs, ands, or buts about it. His mother, God rest her soul, had said he should be grateful to be so regular.

He sauntered into the kitchen to make coffee. After he filled the tank with water and added the desired quantity of beans, the built-in grinder roared to life for a moment and then came to an abrupt stop. As the coffee brewed, he checked his curbside mailbox to see if the postman had made his rounds yet. He had, leaving two magazines, a couple of credit card offers, a flyer from the local cable provider, and another membership solicitation from AARP.

Oliver subscribed to two weeklies, one for news and the other for the reviews and clever cartoons. Staying on top of current events and popular culture had been mandatory when he'd taught history. These days, he stayed hopelessly far behind and, on occasion, tossed half a dozen or more unread issues in the recycling bin. The mystery was how he'd ever found the time to read them in addition to working all day and either grading papers or updating lesson plans at night.

The beeping coffeemaker greeted him when he returned to the kitchen. Perfect timing. He filled his favorite mug to the rim. He'd abandoned a preference for a hefty measure of cream and sugar early in his teaching career. Coworkers had used the condiments he'd provided, but never replaced them. He'd grown tired of subsidizing his colleagues and had learned to like his coffee black.

He placed the coffee on a coaster and fell into his recliner. The motor whirred as his head dropped back and the footrest came up. He pulled a legal pad and pen from beneath the end table beside him and grabbed his coffee. Since retiring, Oliver had split his free time between gardening and the book he'd always wanted to write: a gay history of the United States.

He hadn't known he was gay until Letty had taken him to a gay bar his sophomore year in college. Things were different in the 1970s. Homosexuality was considered a mental illness and, in all but twenty states, a crime.

Awareness of his sexual preference had launched a lifelong curiosity about the subject. He'd read everything he could get his hands on. The more he read, the more frustrated he became. Entries in dictionaries and encyclopedias, newspaper articles he found on microfiche at the public library, and the books he read—fiction and nonfiction—shed little light on the history of same-sex attraction in the United States.

To satisfy his curiosity, Oliver had obtained a post-office box his junior year and placed classified ads in several gay magazines. Hundreds wrote him to share personal histories, recollections, and details about gay life where they lived. He had boxes full of their letters, dating back almost forty years. Each one was different, but in the end told the same story.

His ongoing curiosity had motivated him to pursue a degree in history. His thirst for knowledge, however, had remained unquenched. Oliver knew far more about the subject than had any of his professors. Most hadn't heard of the Compton or Stonewall riots that had taken place in the previous decade.

Fear he'd never find a job with a degree in history motivated a change in majors. Absent a passion for any particular career, history education looked like the best option. Jobs were easy to find, the benefits were great, and the history courses he'd completed counted toward graduation requirements. Time off for summers, holidays, and weekends sealed the deal.

Teaching had been easier then. Students paid more attention in class, did their homework, and read assignments. When parents met to talk about poor grades, their wrath had been directed at the child rather than the teacher.

In his third year, he'd settled into the job and commuted back and forth from Fallisville to Lexington for graduate school. The letters he'd saved and continued to receive in response to his ads provided a wealth of information for his master's thesis, "The Simultaneous, Independent Development of Homosexual Communities Across the United States in the Early Twentieth Century." He'd hoped to follow up with his book, but teaching turned out to be a lot more time-consuming than he'd expected. Until he retired, he hadn't had the time.

In retrospect, he was glad. The book he'd have written then lacked the scope of what he now had in mind. The pace of change blew him away. Only a lunatic fringe still considered homosexuality a mental illness. Conversion therapy had been exposed as a scam and had been outlawed in places. Rather than raiding gay bars or setting up entrapment schemes, law enforcement agencies had liaisons to maintain good relations with the gay community.

How many hours had he spent over the years discussing the current state of affairs with gay men his age and older? They'd come much further than anyone had predicted. The possibility homosexuals would ever legally marry or be elected to office had never come up until ten or fifteen years ago.

A few of his pen pals and old friends still corresponded with him, by letter primarily—now and then by telephone. Most were gone now, many before their time. Alcohol, drugs, suicide, murder, and disease had each taken a toll on his Rolodex. Oliver wondered why he'd survived when so many he'd known, fucked, or partied with had not.

So many lives cut short. Oliver shook his head. They'd lived in the shadows, hidden from view, keeping secrets and telling lies because they had no other choice. Sharing their stories was his duty—an obligation not just to his friends, but to generations of gay men who'd lived and died before him.

He wished they could be here to see how things had changed. The mothers who'd once demanded their children be protected from homosexual predators were PFLAG members who marched in pride parades. HIV was no longer a death sentence. Trans people were everywhere, and nobody much cared. Bisexuality was the fashion for high school and college students. Lines were blurring. Nothing was black or white anymore.

Oliver didn't miss teaching, but couldn't complain. He'd put in his time, done everything his bosses had ever asked him to do, and though always underpaid for his time and effort, had earned enough for a comfortable lifestyle. He'd paid his dues and early retirement was his reward. His history of gay America would be his legacy.

PEGGY WORKED at the Fallisville branch of the state Division of Driver Licensing and had for seventeen years now. The way she issued and renewed licenses had changed with new technology, but her duties remain largely unchanged. She hated her job and couldn't wait until she'd put in enough time to retire.

Meeting new people every day had been fun for the first six or eight years, and tolerable for maybe another five. Somewhere along the way, she'd stopped caring who anyone was, how long they'd waited in line, why they lacked appropriate identification, or what important person they knew and planned to complain to in Frankfort. She knew the relevant laws and regulations as well as she knew her Bible, and followed them with equal rigor.

"I'm sorry, ma'am. I can't accept this as proof of your Social Security number," Peggy said, handing the card back.

"Why the hell not? It's my Social Security card!"

"Ma'am, please watch your language, and you don't need to yell. I'm standing right here." Peggy pointed to a sign listing acceptable documents. "Says right there we can't accept laminated cards."

"That's bullshit!"

"I'm sorry, ma'am. I don't make the rules. Next!"

"You can't just dismiss me like that! I need my driver's license. Let me talk to your supervisor."

Peggy pointed to another sign. "There's his contact information. Please step aside so I can help the next person in line."

The young woman folded her arms across her chest and glared at her. "I've been here for four hours! Not until you either let me talk to a supervisor or give me my driver's license."

"Ma'am, step aside, or the state police officer over there waiting to give driving tests will escort you out." Silly girl. Like she was the first to challenge Peggy's authority. Resistance was futile.

The young woman stepped away from the counter. "Fucking bitch," she mumbled, loud enough for everyone to hear. "She'll be sorry she messed with me. My father plays golf with the governor."

Peggy bit back a sarcastic response. She'd won the battle. The impertinent young woman could have the last word.

Her next four customers had everything they needed. Peggy liked people who read and followed directions, but the problem customers made the work memorable and kept the days from running together. She helped when she could, especially if she liked the person. A lot of the time, however, there was nothing she could do.

Working for the state suited her. As long as she did her job, nobody paid much attention. She was a tiny little cog on the giant wheel of an enormous bureaucracy. Even with the extra income from her fancywork, she had to watch her pennies, but she made enough money to cover her expenses. The benefits were great: holidays off, a generous vacation allowance, and paid sick days, plus health insurance and a pension plan.

Peggy glanced at the clock. Twenty more minutes and she could close the door. After she'd taken care of anyone still in line, she could leave. Her tolerance for complications decreased significantly during the critical period between the door closing and her departure. The state didn't pay extra for staying after hours, and she resented the imposition on her time—especially when she had plans. Lurleen was meeting her for dinner at the Dinner Barn up by the interstate, and she didn't want to be late.

"Next!"

Only two customers remained when she closed the door. Peggy didn't get her hopes up. Appearances could be deceiving. One problem child could take fifteen or twenty minutes.

Exactly eleven minutes later, she left, locking the door behind her. Aside from the first one being a little talkative, her last two customers had followed directions and been easy to assist. Good thing. She was more than a little hungry. Since the big cinnamon roll binge during the days she'd been home for the ice storm, she'd redoubled her efforts to lose weight and had been bringing salads with her to work every day.

The Dinner Barn stayed busy for breakfast, lunch, and dinner. Although she'd gotten away from work fairly early and made good time, Lurleen had arrived before her. Peggy was surprised to find a place to park next to Lurleen's Camry.

Despite the chilly air, Lurleen sat outside in one of several rocking chairs. "Want to play checkers?"

"No, thanks," Peggy said. "I'm starving. Ready to eat?"

"Yes, ma'am." She got up from the chair and followed Peggy inside. "I was gonna put my name in, but there wasn't a line so I figured I'd wait 'til you got here."

A polite young man led them to a table for four. Peggy dropped her purse in the far chair, added the coat she slid out of, and sat down across from Lurleen. "Sorry you had to wait."

"No trouble. I didn't have nothing else to do anyway." She smiled. "Kinda like it that way." She reached across the table and squeezed Peggy's hand. "You're looking good! How much have you lost?"

Peggy returned the squeeze. Her new diet was unlike any she'd tried before and seemed to be working. "Twenty-three and a half pounds all together. Best diet I've ever tried. I've lost nine and a quarter pounds since I started and have no trouble sticking to the program." She opened her menu to study the selections. "What's going on with you?"

Lurleen shook her head and opened her menu. "Not a thing. Since Henry died, I just lay in the recliner drinking beer and watching television." She smiled. "It's what he'd want me to do."

Peggy laughed. "I wish Earl had taken care of me the way Henry took care of you." She shook her head. "Man didn't have a dime. I had to pay for his funeral."

"Yeah," Lurleen said, nodding her head. "Me and Henry, we did okay. Sure, we had our ups and downs. Who doesn't?"

"Amen to that." Peggy's marriages had involved a lot more downs than ups. "Did I tell you what I did with all Earl's dirty magazines?"

"No." Lurleen snickered. "If Henry had any, he either gave 'em to somebody before he died or hid them where I'll never find them."

"Earl's went with him to the great beyond." Peggy smiled. "I packed them all up in a brown paper bag the funeral director put in his coffin."

A waitress stopped by the table. "Hey, y'all. I'm Kelly, your server. What can I get you to drink?"

"Coffee for me," Lurleen answered.

"I'll have a large diet cola," Peggy said. "And could we have an order of potato skins?"

"Yes, ma'am." She smiled. "I'll be right back with those drinks."

Lurleen closed the menu and placed it on the table before her. "Don't get me wrong. I loved Henry. He was a fine man, and we had a good marriage."

"But?" Peggy said, raising her eyebrows.

"Well, aside from having the place to myself, nothing much has changed since he died. For the last fifteen years, he did his thing and I did mine." She smiled. "I miss him, but sometimes I feel guilty for enjoying my life so much without him."

"Do you think you'll marry again?"

Lurleen shook her head. "Never say never, but I don't think so. Marriage is a raw deal for women. Money isn't an issue, thank God." She met Peggy's gaze. "What about you?"

"I'd like to marry again, but not just any man." She leaned forward. "I want to live in a nice house again, with a man who'd like to go to church with me." A man like Mr. Crumbly.

The waitress plunked a diet soft drink down in front of her. "Those potato skins will be right out. Y'all ready to order?"

"Two potato skins about fills me up." Lurleen said. "Bring me a salad, with Thousand Island dressing." She handed her menu to the waitress.

"Did you want the Caesar salad, the Cobb salad, the steak and shrimp salad, the fried or grilled chicken salad, or a plain house salad?"

"I reckon the plain one is fancy enough for me."

"Alrighty, then." She turned to Peggy. "And for you, ma'am?"

"I'll have the four-piece fried chicken dinner with mashed potatoes, macaroni and cheese, fried okra, and fried apples."

"The deluxe dinner only comes with three sides. Did you want to pay extra for the fourth?"

Peggy nodded. "Oh, and I'd like a side of gravy too, and extra biscuits. For dessert, I'd like the deep-dish apple cobbler with ice cream and extra whipped cream."

"Yes, ma'am!" The cheerful waitress wrote on her pad for a moment. "Those potato skins should be up now."

Lurleen sipped her coffee. "Tell me about this diet you're on."

"Well," Peggy said, "I eat a light breakfast and lunch, and snack on celery, carrots, and fruit in between meals."

The waitress dropped a plate of potato skins heaping with cheese, bacon, chives, and sour cream between them with two small plates. "Need any catsup or anything?"

"No, thanks," Peggy said. She removed her watch and set it in front of her on the table so she could keep an eye on the time. She grabbed a plate and stabbed two skins with her fork. "Then for one hour every day, I can eat whatever I want."

Chapter Seven: Technical Difficulties

OLIVER PACED the kitchen as far as the telephone cord would allow. Talking to computers pissed him off. He couldn't press anything with his rotary dial phone, and none of the numbers the saccharine voice ordered him to press or say were the option he wanted.

"Again?" He held the handset at arm's length and yelled, "Please let me talk to a live person!" He held the handset against his ear.

"I'm sorry, I didn't understand you. Could you please repeat your selection?"

Oliver palmed his forehead. "Operator! Operator! I need to talk to a real person!"

"I apologize. We seem to be having trouble communicating. Hold for one moment while I transfer you to an operator for assistance."

He heard a click, and then an enthusiastic voice. "…only on Starz, one of 245 channels available for one low price when you select the Hollywood Package from Worldwide Communications. Ask your customer service representative—"

"Thank you for calling Worldwide Communications. I'm Eric. In order to better assist you, could I please have your address?"

"I live at 182 Calumet Circle, Fallisville, Kentucky."

"With a *Ph*?"

Oliver thought for a moment. "No… that's an *F*."

"Thank you. Can you hold for just a second while I wait for this to come up?"

"I've invested far too much time to hang up now."

"I apologize for the delay. I'm sure we'll be able to resolve your issue in no time. What's the weather like there today?"

"Cold."

"Can you give me the last four digits of your Social Security number?"

"Yes. Seven, seven, six, three."

"Graham O. Crumbly?"

"Yes, Oliver Crumbly."

"All right, Mr. Crumbly. Thanks for bearing with me. How can I help you today?"

"I want to know why my bill went up this month."

"Have you recently changed your plan? Looks like you're eligible for an upgrade to silver. Would you like to hear about the advantages the silver package has to offer?"

"No, I haven't made any changes, and no thank you."

"I see you only have cable service with Worldwide. We're offering a great deal on a telephone/Internet/cable package. The six-month introductory rate is the same as you're paying now."

"No, thank you. Your cable service is bad enough. Can we talk about my bill?"

"Absolutely! Let me pull up your last statement and we'll figure this out."

Oliver wanted to ask if he had a mouse in his pocket but kept quiet.

"Okay, Mr. Crumbly. I've got it. What seems to be the problem?"

"I want to know why my bill went up."

"Can you hold a second while I take a look?"

"Sure." What else was he going to do?

"Yes, sir, looks like your bill is two dollars and eighty-three cents higher this month. Nothing to worry about."

"Oh, I'm not worried. I'm pissed. I didn't do anything different. Why doesn't my bill stay the same?"

"The number of days in the billing cycle varies, which affects local, state, and federal taxes, access charges, and usage fees. Your monthly bill can vary by as much as five dollars a month."

"But December and January both have thirty-one days."

"I'm sorry, sir, those charges aren't up to Worldwide Communications. You'll need to contact the originators. How about a free introductory month of HBO for your trouble?"

"The originators?"

"Yes, sir. If you go to our website and click on billing, you'll see a map of the United States. Just click on your state to find contact information."

"I don't have a computer."

"I'd be happy to connect you to a recorded message with contact information for originators in all fifty states."

"No, thank you."

"Is there anything else I can help you with, Mr. Crumbly?"

"Anything else? You haven't helped one little bit."

"How about that free introductory month of HBO?"

Oliver hung up the phone. He longed for the days when customer service meant something other than trying to sell him crap he didn't want or need. Carefully screened, highly trained automatons like Eric offered absolutely no help with nauseously cheerful optimism. Yelling at the happy campers served no purpose beyond making him feel bad about losing his temper. He felt sorry for Eric's significant other. Life with a professional anger diffuser had to be frustrating.

Not that Oliver would know. Starting with his father, the men in his life had thrived on fanning tiny embers of anger into giant flames of rage. Keeping the peace and dodging the minefield of actions likely to ignite his father's ire were survival skills he'd developed as a child that hadn't served him so well later in life.

His failed relationships followed the same pattern. For years, Oliver would roll with the punches, collecting resentments like postage stamps or old coins. Then—seemingly out of the blue—a tiny, insignificant infraction would unlock the door to his unvoiced resentments. When the explosion came, the relationship was over. Apologies and pleas for forgiveness fell on deaf ears.

As far as Oliver was concerned, his exes had vanished from the face of the earth. Staying friends hadn't been an option. Truth be told, none of his exes possessed traits he valued in his friends. Why he couldn't have figured this out before getting seriously involved with them was a mystery.

Not really. Oliver knew exactly why he'd fallen for all five men. Great sex. Meeting them in the moments before last call while three sheets to the wind hadn't helped. Proclaiming everlasting love for each other over breakfast the next morning never ended well. In truth, the proclamations had come later with both Tim and Kevin, but still no more than a few weeks after meeting, with the same disastrous result.

He had no one to blame but himself. Nobody had forced him into a relationship. He'd invited each of them to move in because he was lonely and desperate to be loved. He shook his head. Some things never changed.

His drinking days had ended long ago, and he hadn't stayed up past eleven o'clock for about as long. Unless a handsome, horny, and drunk delivery driver with a thing for older men rang his doorbell, getting laid was unlikely. Winning the lottery would be easier than falling in love again.

He needed to hit the gym. Working out burned energy and relieved stress. Being the only place besides the grocery store and the post office he ever went, Fit as a Fiddle also offered his best chance for meeting someone. Even if it didn't, he'd still want to work out, but the possibility Mr. Right could be waiting for him was sometimes the extra push he needed to get out the door.

TELLUMO COULDN'T figure out what was wrong with the new web page for the literary magazine. Everything looked right, but an extra space would be all it took to keep the page from loading correctly on the school's website. He'd studied the HTML coding until his eyes crossed before giving up and closing his laptop. Finding the problem would be easier after a good night's sleep.

He retrieved his backpack from under his desk and a red envelope fell to the floor. "To Mr. Magnamater" was inked on the front in block letters. The card inside appeared to be homemade. A photo of a gymnast caught midflip, upside down, and high in the air, was printed on the front. Inside, a handwritten message in the same block letters read "I'm head over heels in love with you." Beneath a heart drawn around the words, the card was signed "Your Secret Valentine."

Tellumo smiled. His best friend, Melody Abshire, had sent similar Valentine's greetings to every male teacher she ever had from middle school until she'd graduated from high school. The first few had been more or less legitimate schoolgirl crushes. The rest had been sent as a joke. The more gullible victims received additional cards now and then for the rest of the year—some for several years.

The fun part came after the recipient found the card. When Melody had let him in on her little game, the two of them had engaged in a relentless campaign to make the victim believe one of them had been the sender. Tellumo had blown Melody's moon-eyed stares, batted eyelashes, and coquettish grins out of the water their senior year. Staring at Mr. McCord from across the cafeteria while savoring every delicious bite of an especially long banana had caused the poor man to drop his tray and scurry, red-faced, from the room.

When Jack dropped him off at his bus stop, Tellumo was still smiling and more than a little curious about the identity of his alleged secret admirer. The envelope and card yielded few clues. The female gymnast on the outside and use of the first person inside proved nothing, but he suspected the card had come from a member of the opposite sex.

Aside from the occasional schoolboy crush, Tellumo had avoided Cupid's arrow. He wasn't attracted to guys his own age and had no interest in the older gay men who frequented Cincinnati's bars and partied like they were still twenty-two. What other people did was their business, but drugs held no allure for him. Never had. He might have tried pot once upon a time, but smoking, no matter the substance, couldn't possibly be healthy. Until street dealers were regulated for quality control, using illegal drugs was playing Russian roulette—with several bullets in the chamber. Old age appealed to him far too much to cut his life short doing anything reckless.

The mailman left Valentines from his mothers, Mel, and Eduardo Clemente, the older man who'd given him Trish's Christmas gift. They'd met online and gone to dinner a couple of times in his freshman year at the University of Cincinnati. Eduardo had proclaimed his undying love for Tellumo on their third and final date and had since followed up with at least a card and sometimes a gift on his birthday, Valentine's Day, and randomly throughout the year when he'd seen or heard something to remind him of Tellumo. The friendly but distant e-mails he sent to acknowledge Eduardo's generosity fanned the flames, but ignoring him would be wrong. The lonely man meant no harm.

Tellumo let himself into his apartment, dropped his backpack and mail on the counter, and slid out of his jacket. If he wanted a faithful and devoted companion, he'd get a dog. The man he desired would challenge him physically, mentally, and spiritually. He'd yet to meet anyone under forty who'd come close to fitting the bill—over forty either, for that matter.

A casual observer might say his desire for a man like the Silver Fox was pure Freud, given that Tellumo grew up with two mothers. Father issues may have played a small role, but he didn't think so. Jules had filled any paternal void with alacrity and a robust masculinity, teaching him to play football, baseball, and basketball and, after a run-in with a bully in the fourth grade, how to fight. The mere thought of Trish saying "wait until Jules gets home" still tied his stomach in knots. Jules had never spanked him, but every time he got in trouble, she'd led him to believe his luck had finally run out. Dreading the beating he never got had been punishment enough.

No, his attraction to older men didn't stem from any deficits in his upbringing. Rebellion may have played a small role, but he had no interest in rubbing his mothers' faces in anything and knew they'd ultimately come to accept anyone with whom he chose to spend his life.

Tellumo changed into workout clothes and headed to the gym. Valentine's Day was to blame today, but the gym was a little less crowded with each passing week. In another month or two, the New Year's resolution crowd would quit coming, returning in January with ten or fifteen pounds they got for Christmas. Tellumo scrolled through the playlists on his smartphone on his way to the weight room until he found the one he wanted. He dropped his towel on an empty bench and then picked up a couple of ten-pound dumbbells for a quick warm-up.

He gasped when the Silver Fox came out of the locker room. He turned toward Tellumo, their eyes met, and his heart leaped into his throat. His face grew hot, and he forced himself to look away as the Silver Fox neared, then stopped at the bench beside his. Tellumo thought maybe his crush was making a friendly gesture, but the towel and water bottle he spotted on the floor between them suggested he, not the handsome older man, had been the interloper.

Tellumo swapped his ten-pounders for a pair of twenty-fives and did some alternating curls. He stared at himself in the mirrored wall, willing his eyes not to stray to the bench beside him. The man of his dreams reclined beneath a barbell with his legs apart and his hands gripping the bar. Tellumo resisted an overwhelming urge to fall to his knees to nibble the tender inside of the gorgeous man's thighs. His shirt shifted upward, providing Tellumo with a glimpse of a furry belly, untouched by the gray sprinkled throughout his beard and the remaining hair on his head.

After three sets, Tellumo reclined on the bench for some dumbbell flyes. He couldn't see the Silver Fox without turning his head but heard him grunting as he worked through a second set of bench presses. Tellumo had reached the end of his first set of flyes when he heard a gasp, followed by a yelp and a garbled cry for help. He jumped to his feet when he saw the Silver Fox was pinned beneath the barbell.

"Let me help you," Tellumo said. He moved behind the bench and stopped, his crotch inches above the handsome face. Their eyes met—the Silver Fox's irises were the darkest brown Tellumo had ever seen. The fear written on his face surprised Tellumo. Unlike the vulnerable man before him, the Silver Fox had seemed invincible. Tellumo leaned over and hefted the heavy bar off the guy's chest and back onto the supports.

He sat up, nodded at Tellumo, and then stared at the floor. "I'm so embarrassed."

Tellumo wanted to sit beside him, to drape his arm across his shoulder to give him an encouraging hug. "Don't be. Happens to everyone sooner or later." He extended his hand. "Tellumo Magnamater." His heart rate increased by a good 25 percent when the Silver Fox shook his hand. The firm grip made his knees weak.

"Oliver Crumbly." He released his grip and gave Tellumo a weak smile. "Thanks for coming to my rescue."

"Don't mention it. Glad I was here." Truer words had never passed his lips. Meeting Oliver Crumbly was, so far, the high point of his year. "Ready to try another set? I'll spot you this time."

"I don't know…." His shoulders sagged and his chin fell to his chest.

Tellumo folded his arms across his chest and studied Oliver's face. Their eyes met again. The submission in Oliver's dark brown eyes surprised and excited him. Tellumo got the distinct feeling Oliver's thoughts were running in more or less the same direction. "What are you waiting for?"

The harshness of his tone surprised him and seemed to please Oliver. He lay back down on the bench, gripped the barbell with both hands, lifted the bar from the support, and then lowered it to his chest.

"Push."

Oliver grunted with effort as he straightened his arms.

"Give me another one."

After a quick nod, Oliver again lowered the bar to his chest, straining with effort as the bar slowly rose back to the starting position.

Tellumo held his palms open beneath the bar. "Come on, big boy. One more."

"I can't," Oliver said, shaking his head.

"Do it." He looked past his hard-on into Oliver's eyes.

Oliver licked his lips before raising the bar off the support. Tellumo kept his upturned hands under the bar as Oliver lowered the heavy weight to his chest. "I can't," Oliver grunted.

"Yes, you can. Do it. I'll help."

The right side of the bar came up a bit, followed a half second later by the left. Oliver grunted, trembling with effort as he dug his heels into the floor to push the bar off his chest.

"Come on, you're almost there. Push!"

With one final grunt, Oliver straightened his arms and heaved the bar onto the support. He wiped the sweat from his forehead with the back of his hand and sat up, pushing his elbows back as far as they would go to stretch the overworked muscles in his chest.

The air between them crackled with sexual tension. Tellumo thought about inviting him home for a massage, but held his tongue. Despite his submissive demeanor, Oliver Crumbly struck him as the kind of man who liked to be in control.

No need to rush. The door between them had opened—on Valentine's Day, no less. Where it would lead remained to be seen. In the meantime, Tellumo could wait. He had all the time in the world.

PEGGY SPENT Valentine's Day evening cross-stitching the Ten Commandments, snacking on the heart-shaped box of chocolates she'd bought on the way home from work as she switched between *The Newlywed Game* and a *Love, American Style* marathon. A few of the vignettes made her cry. But then, so did many of the commercials and a few questions on the game show.

She wanted to marry again so badly she could taste it. "Get a dog," Lurleen had suggested, but a dog was an additional expense, a liability Peggy couldn't afford. What she needed was an asset: a man of means with a nice car, a grand house in need of a woman's touch, and maybe some grandchildren to spoil.

Money certainly wasn't the only factor, though. Married people lived longer than single people. Finding another husband was a matter of life or death.

Available men were scarce. At Trinity Baptist, they were as rare as a short sermon from Pastor Brown. Frankly, she'd expected more for her tithe. Granted, 10 percent of her meager salary was a paltry sum, but she also donated freely of her time and gently worn clothing, and had baked enough cakes, cookies, pies, and pastries for fundraisers and church socials to feed everyone in China. She'd reaped no rewards from all her doing unto others and felt a little shortchanged.

Until somebody died, the church offered little hope. She could understand their desperation, but the way some women went after new widowers was shameful. Peggy hoped to find a man before she reached that point. (Of course, if Walter Addison were to suddenly become available, all bets were off.)

The few eligible bachelors she encountered through her job looked right through her—until a problem they thought they could screw themselves out of arose. Peggy Tucker was not, nor had she ever been, that kind of girl. She'd had relations outside of marriage one time, when Rodney Brubaker had taken advantage of her in the backseat of his Monte Carlo at the drive-in movie her sophomore year in high school. Like the Bible says, fool me once, shame on you; fool me twice, shame on me.

The gym was full of men, but the vast majority were half her age or younger. She lacked the body, the libido, or the money to be one of those cougar ladies. The older men were married or more interested in hanging out with each other than in talking with her. Although she'd made little progress toward making his acquaintance, Mr. Crumbly wasn't simply her best hope. He was the only man in Fallisville who fit the bill.

Of course, the beard would have to go, and he'd have to become a member of Trinity Baptist Church. She was too old and had invested too much time and energy generating goodwill in the congregation to start over with another church. No siree Bob. She'd look like a traitor if she were to change churches.

Setting her fancywork aside, she got up from her rocking chair and sat at the dining room table in front of her computer. The desktop she'd broken down and purchased to sell her wares online would go back to the spare bedroom should she ever have dinner guests. Stepping over the cords wasn't especially convenient, but she had a clear view of her television and the street in front of her duplex.

She flipped the switch and waited for the screen to fill with bright yellow tulip blossoms. Spring flowers were her favorites. She'd stopped by the Hugo Fallis House a few days earlier for a quick stroll through the still-dormant garden. The crocus were up, but hadn't yet bloomed. Real tulips wouldn't flower for another two months.

Golden tulips filled the screen, and the machine whirred and hummed for a while until the icons popped up. She double-clicked on the one she wanted, typed PeggySews into the space for her username, and entered her password, I<3Jesus. The dial tone came through the speakers, followed by the whine of the modem, and then a male voice said, "Welcome! You've got mail!" Getting Internet access from her cable television company cost too much. Besides, technology baffled her. She couldn't even set the clock on her VCR.

Clicking on the little mailbox revealed eight messages. Three offered products for masculine enhancement, two promoted pills for maintaining an erection, and the rest had been forwarded from Christian Bazaar, the website where she sold her handiwork. A woman in Topeka wanted a set of her Praise the Lord potholders, someone in Bishop, Georgia, wanted to know if the Jesus Saves towels came in red with black embroidery, and the last was an order for twelve Hand of God oven mitts from a church in Hattiesburg, Mississippi.

The potholders—her most popular product—weren't a problem. She tried to keep six or eight of her best-selling items in stock, but was out of oven mitts. Lurleen didn't mind helping when Peggy got behind, but Snowmageddon and the cinnamon bun ice storm had given her time to catch up on back orders. The towels weren't currently available in red and black, but she'd be happy to make a set in six to eight weeks for the extra 25 percent she tacked on for custom orders, plus shipping and handling.

She was about to sign off when a chime sounded and a box popped up in the lower right corner of her screen. A similar box had surprised her a few weeks ago with a lewd comment from someone called HornyDevil, followed by an obscene photograph she wished she'd never seen. Rather than arresting the man for indecent exposure, the police had suggested she block him, which she'd finally figured out how to do on her own, no thanks to the 911 operator.

Hi, Peggy. The message was from LonelyNFallisville. Peggy stared at the screen with butterflies in her stomach. How did he or she know her name? Should she answer? What if the person on the other end was a rapist, or worse? She thought about how to respond.

More words appeared. *What does Peggy sew?*

She palmed her forehead and giggled. Whoever was talking to her had run across her username. They didn't know her from Adam. She typed in her response. *Mostly linens and kitchen accessories.*

The chime sounded. *You make sheets and towels? <scratches head>*

A second earlier, and she'd have spewed diet cola all over her monitor and keyboard. Instead, her midswallow laughter caused the bubbly beverage to go down wrong. She coughed, pounded her chest a few times, and then sipped from her Big Gulp as she contemplated her response. *No, I embellish them.*

BeDazzler? Ronco Stud Setter?

Peggy threw back her head and laughed. *Embroidery, cross-stitch, a little beading.*

Fancywork! Why didn't you say so? An emoticon with a toothy grin followed.

Nobody knows what I'm talking about when I do! At least, nobody under forty years old ever had. Before she hit enter, curiosity motivated her to add a question of her own. *What do you do for fun?*

Idiots!

She thought he'd ignored her question, but then the chime sounded again. *Read some, watch a little television, hit a class or work out at the gym.*

Peggy furrowed her brow, squinted one eye, and stroked her chin. Fit as a Fiddle, and Body by God before it, offered a wide variety of classes. She'd watched the free ones long enough to decide which warranted the old college try. Not that she'd ever actually gone to college. Vocational school had taught her more than she needed to know for her state job.

Very few men participated in the group classes, at least not the free ones. In her time at the gym, Peggy had seen two. Tellumo sometimes caught the yoga class. Mr. Crumbly, however, rarely missed either offering of Boot Steppin' class, and from what she'd seen, knew the Zumba choreography well enough to teach the class.

It had to be him. She couldn't ask him outright—what if she were wrong? If she asked what he looked like or requested a picture, he'd expect the same in return. She typed two words. *What gym?* She'd add a smiley face if she knew how. Before hitting Enter to send the message, she paused. Was she being too forward? Too direct?

No, she wasn't. The good Lord filled the oceans with fish, but somebody still had to reel them in. She'd gone a long time with nary a nibble. Maybe her luck had changed.

She hit Enter, the voice said, "Good-bye," and she was back at the log-on screen. Attempts to sign back on were greeted with requests to try again later. The automated helpline she called offered a decidedly unhelpful array of choices, each leading to more options, none of which involved talking to a real person.

Two hours later, she finally heard "Welcome! You've got mail!" Along with messages about her account being compromised at a bank she'd never heard of and pills guaranteed to make her lose weight without dieting or exercising was a message from LonelyNFallisville.

Her heart jumped into her throat. She clicked on the message and stared. *Was it something I said?* The words were followed by the teary-eyed sad-faced emoticon.

Although somewhat relieved, she didn't know what to do. If she didn't reply, he'd think she wasn't interested. Not that she was, but she might be—especially if the sender was Mr. Crumbly. Replying would lead him to conclude she was either desperate, easy, or both. She certainly wasn't easy. No siree Bob.

Lurleen would tell her to ignore him. Easy to say from atop the mountain of money Henry had left her. From below sea level where Peggy lived, things looked a little different.

Dear Lonely,

Okay. Now what?

I got knocked offline. Enjoyed our conversation. Hope to chat with you again.

There. Honest, straightforward, and to the point. Still, one never knew what else he might read into her message.

God be with you. Peggy.

That should do it. She sent the message, logged off, and returned to her cross-stitch. Perhaps her prayers had been answered. Like the Bible says, the Lord works in mysterious ways.

Chapter Eight: Twitterpated Consternation

As OLIVER waited for the traffic light to change to green, his thoughts returned—again—to the moments following his embarrassing failure in the weight room. Fear he'd get pinned beneath the bar had always kept him from pushing too hard. If Tellumo hadn't invaded Oliver's personal space, he wouldn't have gone too far today either.

But he had.

When he'd come out of the locker room and found Tellumo set up beside him, Oliver should have switched to another bench. If he hadn't nearly finished his workout, he would have moved, and the entire incident never would have happened.

But he hadn't.

Tellumo's proximity had prevented Oliver from focusing. A whiff of the young man's patchouli had distracted him. He should have heeded his trembling arms and stopped. Had he been paying attention, he would never have attempted that fateful lift.

A horn sounded. Oliver realized the light had turned green and hit the accelerator. The entire weight-room incident had been Tellumo's fault. Had he any manners, he'd have moved to an open bench when Oliver returned from the locker room.

But he didn't, so he hadn't, and that was that. Tellumo was guilty as charged. Case closed.

Except the case wasn't closed—not even close. Loose ends trailed like strands from a cheap feather boa. Getting pinned beneath the barbell had upset Oliver, but the rescue had rocked his world. The lean thighs inches from his head; a tantalizing glimpse up the leg of Tellumo's running shorts; the narrow waist widening to a broad chest; muscular arms reaching for the barbell; his handsome face framed by chestnut tresses; and those piercing green eyes....

Oliver's cock stirred in his pants. "Quit that!" Oliver swatted his crotch and then dialed the radio to a station that featured oldies from the 60s, 70s, and 80s. The good old days, when a selfie was rubbing one out in the shower, and nobody had cell phones, computers, or the World Wide Web standing between them and the real world.

The familiar music failed to distract Oliver from the events at the gym. Tellumo coming to his rescue was really the smallest part. Had things stopped there, his heart wouldn't be racing and his palms would be dry.

But things hadn't stopped there. Oliver should have sat up, thanked Tellumo for saving him, and then packed up and gone home. Instead, he'd done what Tellumo had asked him to do. Not asked so much as ordered.

And he'd liked it. Not just a little either. Submitting to the young man's will had turned him on. Oliver was used to taking charge and being the one in control. He called the shots, and his exes had gone along. Their input hadn't mattered. It was his way or the highway. Trusting someone else to take control was a new experience.

Obviously that's all it was—a novelty. As usual he'd blown things out of proportion. Submitting to Tellumo's requests made sense, really—like getting back on the horse after a fall. Losing control had frightened him. Despite the extra reps Tellumo had gotten out of him, Oliver wasn't sure he was ready to try bench presses again without a spotter.

Not that he had to worry about that. The young man's proposal to lift weights together also made sense. As he'd pointed out, they already worked out at the same time, and having a workout partner would make them more accountable. No harm in that.

The way Tellumo had taken control, and the resulting pair of boners, hadn't factored into his decision to accept the offer. Oliver's thinning Rolodex held fewer and fewer cards. More of his friends had died than were living, and he couldn't remember the last time he'd added a card.

Oliver had little interest in befriending the poster boy for the modern generation. He and Tellumo were as different as night from day and, other than weight lifting, had nothing in common. Their simultaneous erections didn't mean anything. His overwhelming desire to please Tellumo was an expression of gratitude for having been rescued. That's all. His recollection of time stopping when Tellumo had looked into his eyes in the seconds before lifting the barbell off Oliver's chest was a glitch in his memory. No electrical current had passed between them. Absolutely not! The very idea of him and someone like Tellumo was preposterous.

He turned into his driveway, punched the door opener, and pulled into the empty garage. A combination of bad weather and the annual "out with the old" upsurge in donations had delayed the arrival of the Goodwill truck until two days before Valentine's Day. He hadn't made up his mind for sure, but was thinking about setting up a seed-starting operation in the now empty side of the garage to grow some vegetables for a summer garden and colorful flowers to perk up the landscaping around his house.

Oliver heard the telephone ringing and hurried into the kitchen. "Hello?"

"Hey, Ollie. It's me."

"Hi, Letty," Oliver said. She didn't sound at all like herself. "What's up?"

"Would this weekend be okay for the visit we talked about?"

"Is everything okay?" In response he heard silence, then ice clinking against glass. "Letty?"

"If it's not a good time to come, just say so. I know it's short notice."

She'd slurred the words. Something was up, but he knew better than to ask again. Whatever was bothering her, she'd tell him, sooner or later. "This weekend is perfect. Will you drive down Friday or Saturday?"

"Friday. I'll be in Fallisville by two—three at the latest." More clinking. "Probably drive back to Dayton after the rush hour traffic clears on Monday morning. Is that okay?"

"Fine with me," Oliver replied. "I can't wait to see you." Her breath caught, and Oliver thought he heard her sob. "Are you okay, Letty?"

"I've gotta run, Ollie. We'll talk Friday."

"Whatever you say." Instead of a reply, he heard the dial tone. He returned the handset to the cradle of the wall-mounted telephone, his hand lingering for a minute like letting go would be deserting his friend. Letty had something to tell him, and her secret—whatever it was—wasn't good news.

PEGGY LOOKED back and forth from the monitor on her dining room table to the pillowcase in her lap she was embroidering with Pray the Lord my Soul to Keep. Calling in sick to work had cured the bad attitude greeting her when she'd awakened. The bonus day off enabled her to finish her custom orders and make a dent in replenishing her backup stock.

The desktop computer wasn't usually on when she worked, but she couldn't turn it off. Good thing she didn't pay by the minute for Internet access. She wasn't exactly waiting for a message from LonelyNFallisville, but her heart skipped a beat, nonetheless, when the chime sounded and the box with his handle popped up on her screen.

Hello gorgeous! How was your day?

She giggled, felt her face grow hot, and typed *You don't even know what I look like*. But then she deleted the words she knew would incite yet another request for pictures she didn't have and wouldn't send if she did. *Same old same old. At least tomorrow is Friday*. She added a smiling emoticon. *Have a good day?*

I did. A thumbs-up filled the chat box. *Spent all day wondering what meeting you would be like*.

Peggy wasn't about to admit she'd spent a significant fraction of her time wondering the same thing. She still couldn't prove Lonely and Mr. Crumbly were one and the same, but without a picture or concrete evidence, she couldn't disprove it either. He was available, interested in her, and from the sound of things, everything she'd ever wanted in a man. If she asked for his picture, he'd expect one in return. No point messing things up. She finally typed *Oh you didn't!*

Busted. A red-faced emoticon popped up.

I knew it! She couldn't remember when she'd had so much fun.

Thought about what to order for lunch for five minutes. Otherwise, all you.

LOL. Silly man.

It's true! I swear!

You say that to all the girls.

All the girls? In Fallisville? At my age? ROFL!

Laugh all you want, Peggy thought. She knew better. There were ten or fifteen lonely women for every eligible bachelor over the age of forty in Salt Lick County. Even losers like Marvin Shankley could pick from half a dozen or more wanton hussies desperate for a man's affection. Not her. No siree Bob. She had standards.

Meet me for coffee somewhere? Before she could reply, another message popped into view. *Name the time and the place. Anywhere you want*.

Until she lost twenty more pounds, she'd rather not meet him at all, but she couldn't hold him off forever. He could meet her at church, but Gladys Honeycutt would have a field day. She'd never been in one of those pricey coffee shops, but suspected diet cola wasn't on the menu. Hot tea tasted like it was missing something—like a stew without meat. Ice cream could be made with the sugar and cream she'd need to make coffee palatable.

Meeting in public offered safety, but also meant being seen with him. What if it wasn't Mr. Crumbly and he was black, or Jewish, or God forbid— one of those liberals? What would people say?

He could be a serial killer. The other day, she'd watched a movie on Lifetime about a murderer preying upon lonely women who responded to his personal ad. She hadn't met Lonely through an ad, but still… better safe than sorry.

But then, what if it was Mr. Crumbly, and he was everything she thought? The man looked like a movie star. She snorted. The moment he saw her, he'd vanish into thin air, never to be seen or heard from again.

My treat. A winking emoticon followed.

The longer she dragged this out, the more his rejection would hurt. Like the Bible says, nothing ventured, nothing gained. Her hands shook so much she had to switch to two-finger typing. *Seven o'clock tomorrow evening at the Dinner Barn?* She read the message over twice to make sure there were no typos and then hit Enter.

"Good-bye!"

"Dammit!" She slammed her hands on the table. The little Indian man she finally reached after calling the toll-free number for help said anything could have knocked her offline. Nothing could be done to make her dial-up connection any better. Adding a bill for Internet access was the only solution, he'd explained, before she'd finally hung up.

When she was able to reconnect, as expected, she found a message from him in her in-box. *Let me know if you change your mind. I really want to meet you.*

She clicked on Reply, but couldn't think of what to say. Sending an e-mail message was different from chatting—more deliberate and a lot less spontaneous. Using the exact same words in an e-mail message that she'd last typed in the chat box struck her as too forward. She stared at his words until she lost her nerve, then discarded her blank reply and signed off.

The grandfather clock in the living room gonged four times. Her father had spanked her good at age seven for opening the cabinet of her grandpa's grandfather clock and playing with the weights. After Grandpa died, her cousin Glenda Carpenter—who'd continued to sit on Grandpa's lap long after she had children of her own—had inherited the beautiful family heirloom. The weights never moved on the battery-operated replica Earl had given Peggy the following Christmas.

She ought to go to the gym. If she started cooking now, she could eat dinner from five to six and then drive over to Fit as a Fiddle for Boot Steppin' class at seven. The exercise would do her good.

Since the end of January, her weight had plateaued. In fact, despite sticking to her diet and exercise program for longer than ever before, she'd somehow gained five and two-thirds pounds. The mystery of the extra weight confounded her. Perhaps she'd added muscle, or was retaining fluids. Whatever the cause, she'd stay the course. Like the Bible says, persistence is its own reward.

TELLUMO DROPPED his backpack beside the door and fell onto the couch, exhausted from what had to have been the longest day in history. Lying awake half the night wondering who'd sent him the card hadn't helped. Not only was the identity of his secret admirer still a mystery, after today, the pool of likely suspects had expanded to include four teachers, two cafeteria workers, a security guard, and about 80 percent of the students at Salt Lick County High. Since they couldn't all be in on the gag, his runaway imagination was most likely to blame.

And karma. In the past twenty-four hours, Tellumo had developed a much greater appreciation for karmic justice. He'd be a silver bear himself before he atoned for the years he and Melody had engaged in a prank he now found far less amusing.

Melody's long-awaited visit was a day away. Tomorrow their as yet unplanned adventure would begin. Spontaneity worked for them. Were Jules and Trish coming instead, he'd have planned every minute. Sitting around shooting the breeze with his mothers invited an inquisition. Stopping the questions was impossible, but staying busy slowed them down and gave him time to recover between grillings.

Melody's impending visit had slipped his mind when he'd asked Oliver to work out with him. He had a feeling canceling the first time would not be well received. Tellumo didn't want to mess things up right out of the gate. Begging off to run to the gym so soon after Melody arrived wouldn't be very hospitable, but unlike the intractable Oliver Crumbly, she'd understand.

The sour-cream pound cake he planned to bake after his workout would soften the blow. Tellumo pulled eggs, sour cream, and butter from the refrigerator and set them on the counter so they'd be at room temperature when he returned. Melody, a self-proclaimed connoisseur of the buttery cakes, considered his recipe the best she'd ever tasted.

The themes in his backpack could wait to be graded. He changed from work clothes to gym attire, scarfed down a peanut butter and blackberry jam sandwich, and chugged a glass of milk. Considering his longer-than-usual to-do list for the evening, he'd skip his customary postworkout cardio.

Otherwise, he'd have to cut his bath short, which he'd rather not do. Another long, leisurely soak was unlikely until Melody returned to Cincinnati.

The sun had set and the temperature had dropped a good ten degrees since Jack had let him off and he'd walked home from the bus stop. Were he going any farther than the gym, he'd have gone back for another layer. His coat barely fit in the locker as it was. He pulled his hands from his pockets and picked up his pace from a brisk walk to a jog.

When he reached the entrance to the gym, Mrs. Tucker was right behind him. He held the door open for her.

"Good grief, Tellumo. Why didn't you call me? I'd have been happy to pick you up. You're going to catch yourself the death of a cold."

"That's mighty nice of you, Mrs. Tucker. I don't have to walk far. My apartment is right behind the shopping center."

"Are you here for Boot Steppin' class?"

"No," Tellumo said, shaking his head. He hadn't thought about it being Thursday. "But I'm tempted." He smiled. "Leg day." He walked along beside her toward the Corral.

"Oh, I see." She furrowed her brows for a moment and then smiled. "Do you know anything about computers?"

Tellumo stopped. "Having problems?"

"I keep getting knocked offline." She blushed. "I have a dial-up connection."

"What's dial-up?"

Her face fell. "Oh, never mind. If you don't know, you won't be able to help."

"You never know," Tellumo said. "I'd be happy to come by to take a look."

"Tonight?" Her face lit up.

"No, sorry." He shook his head. "I'm tied up until Monday." The sad, defeated look on her face broke his heart. "I've got company coming from out of town. If you wouldn't mind her coming along...."

"Mind?" She beamed. "I'd love to meet her!"

Tellumo could see she had the wrong idea but wasn't about to correct her.

"Tell you what." She stopped outside the Corral. "How about six on Saturday? I'll cook dinner for you."

"Oh, no... I couldn't—"

"I insist! Feeding you is the least I can do."

He pulled his smartphone from his pocket. "Okay, but really—don't go to a lot of trouble."

"No trouble at all. I get tired of cooking for just me. Any requests?"

Telling her he didn't normally eat meat would be rude and, he suspected, a huge mistake. Home-cooked meat was a delicacy—a rare treat he never had at home. He shook his head. "No. Surprise me."

"The nearest bus stop is at least a mile away. I'll pick you up."

"No," Tellumo said. "That's okay. My friend has a car. What's your address?"

"I live out near Thoroughbred Acres, 716B Hummingbird Lane. Want me to write out directions for you?"

"My phone will show us how to get there." He held the door open for her. "Looking forward to it!"

"Me too!" She waved. "See you Saturday."

Tellumo waved back and turned toward the weight room. A familiar voice called his name.

"Hey," Oliver said. "Got a minute?"

"Sure, what's up?" The top of Tellumo's head reached Oliver's chin. He fought the force drawing his eyes downward and focused on Oliver's face.

"I'm glad I ran into you. Something has come up and I'm not going to be able to work out with you tomorrow."

"I'm sorry. Monday, then?" He hoped his relief didn't show.

Oliver nodded. "That works. Thanks for understanding."

"No problem. See you Monday."

Tellumo watched Oliver walk to the front of the room and set up his step through the window before heading toward the weight room. His Friday afternoon dilemma had been resolved, and Saturday evening with Mel and Mrs. Tucker would be fun. The dinner she'd prepare would no doubt beat his cooking or anything served anywhere he'd have taken Melody. In the meantime, he'd see what he could find out about this dial-up thing she'd mentioned.

Chapter Nine: Roll Out the Red Carpet

WHEN THE doorbell rang, Oliver turned on the coffeemaker, slid a pan of apple turnovers into the oven, and hurried to greet Letty. His hand trembled as he reached for the knob. The knot in his stomach tightened when he opened the door.

"Letty!" The smile he tried putting on to welcome her, made difficult by concern for his lifelong friend, never reached his lips. One glimpse of her jaundiced and tear-streaked face told him the news was every bit as bad as he'd feared.

She fell into his open arms and burst into tears. He held her for a moment as she sobbed into his chest and then steered her inside, kicking the door closed behind him to keep from letting go of her. Words escaped him, but for now, none were needed.

He stood in the entryway holding her as she cried for a long time, ignoring the beeps indicating the coffee had brewed and, a few minutes later, the kitchen timer he'd set for the turnovers. Dread kept him from letting her go or asking what was wrong. He'd find out soon enough.

She raised her head, sniffed, and pushed him away. "Is something burning?"

Before he could reply, the smoke detector went off. He ran into the kitchen, yanked the charred triangles from the oven, and tossed them—pan and all—out the back door. Then he turned on the fan over the stove and the ceiling fan, opened a window, and fanned the air around the smoke detector until the screeching stopped.

"You baked for me?" Letty snickered and wiped the back of her hand across her cheek. "You shouldn't have."

Oliver laughed. "It's some kind of curse."

"Karma." She laughed so hard she could barely get out the words. "For that awful... Julia Child getup... you wore... for Halloween."

Oliver's face grew hot, and he laughed so much he had to hold his sides. "Oh my, I'd forgotten all about that."

She snorted. "You and your selective memory. I suppose you don't remember the dildo rolling pin either."

"I plead the Fifth," Oliver gasped, wiping tears from his eyes.

Letty guffawed, dropped her purse on the kitchen table, and plopped into a chair. "Oh shit, Ollie. It feels good to laugh."

"Coffee?" Oliver got his first good look at her since she'd come through the door. She'd lost weight and looked more tired than he'd ever seen her. The knot in his stomach returned.

She nodded. "Love some. Black is fine."

He filled two mugs, set them on the table, and sat across from her. She met his gaze, and they watched each other sipping coffee for a long moment.

"Aren't you going to ask what's wrong?"

Oliver shook his head. "You'll tell me when you're ready." He started to add he didn't want to know but was afraid she'd misunderstand. Burying his head in the sand wouldn't change the facts.

"I couldn't tell you over the phone." She smiled. "Never know who's listening these days."

"Yeah," Oliver said. "The CIA keeps a close eye on us retired history teachers."

"I've got cancer."

Oliver's heart sank. He reached across the table and took her hands in his. "Oh, Letty. I'm so sorry."

"Lost my appetite right after Christmas. When my lovely yellow tan arrived a week or so later, Sid made me see the doctor."

Cancer wasn't the death sentence it had been in the past. There were treatments now. Lots of people recovered. "How bad is it?"

"Stage three. I'm eaten up with the stuff."

Oliver felt like he'd been kicked in the stomach. Still, modern medicine worked miracles every day. "When do you start treatment?"

She looked at him for a long moment. "I'm refusing the treatment. Unless it's caught early, people don't get over pancreatic cancer. They die." She sobbed and then took a deep breath. "If I thought chemotherapy and radiation would save my life, I'd go for it. But that cure is worse than the disease, and I'm going to die anyway...."

He squeezed her hands. "I completely understand." He did, but part of him—most of him—wanted her to fight the dread disease. They might only talk a few times a year, but Letty was always there when he needed her. The thought of living without the comfort of her presence scared him.

"Well, I'm glad you do because Sid doesn't have a clue." She pulled her hands away and wiped a tear from her cheek. "I get it. He's not ready to give up." She looked at Oliver. "If he had cancer, I'd be the same way."

She shook her head. "Staying sick and losing my hair through months of treatments isn't worth a few extra weeks."

Oliver wanted to cry, but he had to be strong. He'd leaned on Letty so many times over the years. Now she needed to lean on him. "Have you told the boys?"

She slurped her coffee and shook her head. "Not until Sid and I are on the same page. I can't handle them ganging up on me."

Oliver nodded. He couldn't imagine how hard that conversation would be. "Is he coming around?"

"Sid's a real trouper." She smiled. "I tell him what I think, he says what's on his mind, and ninety-nine times out of a hundred, we agree."

"And that one time?"

"He eventually figures out he's wrong and comes around."

Oliver laughed. "If he knows what's good for him." Letty was feisty and more than a little headstrong. Early in their marriage, Sid had sometimes called in the middle of the night, wondering what he'd done to warrant banishment from the bedroom. Oliver sympathized but had been no help in identifying a cause—even when he thought he knew.

"He's really having a hard time with this." She clenched both hands around her mug. "We always figured he'd go first."

Oliver didn't know what to say. He was having a hard time with the news too. Like Sid, he'd never thought about outliving his best friend. Unlike Sid, Oliver had no sons, daughters-in-law, or grandkids to help fill the void. He couldn't think about that now. This wasn't about him. He took her hands in his. "I'm here for you, Letty, anytime."

"I know." She squeezed his hands. "That's why I'm here."

Oliver got up and closed the window. "Getting chilly."

"A little bit," Letty said, rubbing her shoulders. "But you couldn't ask for a prettier day."

"Anything in particular you want to do while you're here in beautiful Fallisville?"

"Even after all the years you've lived here, I still snicker when I hear the name of this town. Great place for a dildo factory."

"Hugo Fallis settled here in the late eighteenth century—"

"Hugo?" She snorted. "Are you kidding me?"

"What's so funny?"

"What a name! For a minute, I thought you said huge old phallus." Her titters turned to belly laughs. "Wonder if the name fit."

"I'm not touching that," Oliver said. He wondered if her apparent penis obsession had anything to do with Sid. "So what shall we do?"

"We're *not* going to sit around here moping and crying all weekend." She shook her head. "I'm cried out."

Oliver placed their empty mugs in the dishwasher and turned off the coffee pot. "You up for a walk?"

"Shit. You're doing it too."

He looked across the kitchen at her. "Doing what?"

She met his gaze. "Treating me like a fucking invalid. My appetite comes and goes, cancer cells have taken up residence in my lymph nodes, my skin is jaundiced—yellow has never been my color—but at least for now, I'm not sick."

Oliver nodded and the light came on. Sid, her most ardent admirer, had always spoiled her rotten. She'd never complained about him waiting on her hand and foot before. The cancer diagnosis must have changed his behavior in the bedroom.

"I'm sorry. Let me try again." He cleared his throat. "I'm going for a walk." He smiled. "You going to sit there on your lazy ass or come with me?"

TELLUMO COULDN'T tell whether he or the kids in study hall—his last class of the day—were more anxious for the bell to ring. After weeks of cold, dreary weather, the unseasonably mild temperatures and a dazzling, cloud-free sky made everyone want to be outside. Sticking to lesson plans and maintaining order after lunch, always a challenge on Friday, had become more difficult with each passing hour.

He looked up from the tablet where he'd been entering grades and glanced around the room. Every student sat on the edge of his or her seat. Books and other possessions had been stowed in the backpacks slung over their shoulders. When the bell rang, they leapt from their seats like racehorses breaking from the starting gate and rushed for the door.

A moment later, the echoes of their footsteps faded and silence fell over the school. During the week, the building remained open until eight or nine o'clock for club meetings, rehearsals for musical performances or theatrical productions, and other after-school activities. But on Fridays, unless a football game or a dance was scheduled, the doors were generally locked by four thirty—five at the latest.

The weather was so nice, had he not been expecting Melody at his apartment, he'd have walked home. The first bus after school let out was always standing room only, so Tellumo usually waited at his desk another thirty minutes for the next bus, using the time to grade a few papers, catch up on his recordkeeping, or prepare for the next day.

He heard a knock and looked up to find Melody standing in the doorway, grinning from ear to ear as she took in Tellumo and his classroom. "Stand up, Mr. Magnamater. Let me look at you."

Tellumo stood, pulled the gray jacket Trish and Jules had given him for Christmas from his chair, and slipped it on. "What do you think? Teacherly enough?"

She folded her arms, studied him for a moment as he neared, and then nodded. "Casual, yet professional, stylish without being too trendy, and very flattering."

"Thanks!" He wrapped his arms around her. "I'm so glad to see you." He squeezed her tight, kissed her forehead, and then released her. "And a little surprised." He glanced at his watch. "I wasn't expecting you for another hour."

"Sorry." She shrugged. "I was so excited to see you, I hit the road a little early."

"Spared me from watching for you. Let's get out of here."

She stepped back. "I'm ready when you are."

He pulled his backpack out from under the desk, locked the door behind them, and headed toward the entrance, holding hands with his best friend.

When they passed the principal's office, Melody stopped and rapped on the glass door. Mr. Wyrick looked up and waved. "Thanks so much," she said, loud enough for anyone still in school to hear. "I should have stayed in my car and waited for you, but I wanted to see your classroom," she whispered as she waved at Tellumo's boss. "He gave me directions."

By the time they got to the parking lot, the last of the busses was pulling out of the semicircular driveway. Melody's yellow VW Beetle, with eyelashes mounted above the headlights and daisy decals scattered from the hood to the rear and down both sides, stood out from the pickup trucks, minivans, and SUVs surrounding it.

"Vanessa is looking good."

Melody unlocked the doors. "The daisies have done more for her than a good tune-up. She runs like a charm now."

Tellumo slid into the seat, closed the door, and fastened his seatbelt. "Want me to put my address in the GPS?"

"Nope." She shook her head. "I put it in as soon as I got here." She hit the gas, sending gravel flying across the parking lot.

"I picked up stuff to make pizzas for dinner. Is that okay?"

"You couldn't have made a better choice." Mel nodded. "Ready-made crust?"

"Are you kidding?" Tellumo shook his head and smiled. "Kneading and tossing the dough is the fun part of making pizza."

"What kind of toppings did you get?"

"Just vegetables."

"Seriously?"

He nodded. "I'm pretty sure you'll thank me tomorrow."

Mel laughed. "Are you trying to tell me something?"

"Yeah, but nothing about you."

"That's a relief. I've put on a few pounds since you last saw me."

"You've always been on the skinny side." He grinned. "Matchstick."

"I can laugh since nobody calls me that anymore. So what are you trying to tell me?"

"Oh, yeah." Tellumo chuckled. "We're having dinner with a friend of mine."

"The Silver Fox?"

"No, Peggy Tucker. We met at the gym. I have a feeling she'll serve a feast."

"Oh, okay. I hope so. Think she'll make dessert?"

"I bet she does—we'll see. By the way, I did meet the Silver Fox."

"Oh?" She glanced at him and returned her gaze to the road. "How did that go?"

"Nothing like I expected." Tellumo told her about rescuing him at the gym. "I don't know what came over me." He shook his head. "Something in his eyes…."

"Will you see him again?"

Tellumo nodded. "We're going to work out together."

"You're his trainer?" She threw him a quick glance. "I didn't know you were taking clients again."

"He's not a client." Tellumo thought about the kind of training session he'd like to have with Oliver and his face grew hot. "We're just workout buds."

Mel smirked. "Isn't that a category for gay porn?" She shot him another glance.

"What do you know about gay porn?"

"Have you been hiding under a rock?" She shook her head. "The Internet has leveled the playing field. Women can enjoy watching two guys getting it on the way straight men enjoy lesbian scenes."

"What's your favorite category?" Part of him didn't want to know, but curiosity got the better of him.

"I haven't really watched enough to have a favorite. Is kissing a category?"

"Probably so. If people can do it, they have a category for it somewhere."

The trip home went by fast enough for Tellumo to reconsider his decision to pass on buying a car. Not stopping at every corner between the school and his apartment made a big difference.

"Maybe I will buy a car," Tellumo said as they pulled into his apartment complex. "Thirty extra minutes on either end of my day doesn't sound like much, but five extra hours a week is a lot of time."

"Your mothers would expect you to visit every weekend."

"Not if I don't tell them." Tellumo laughed.

SINCE EARL had gone to meet his maker, Peggy Tucker hadn't cooked for anyone but herself. Lurleen joined her for dinner now and then but hardly counted as she ate like a bird. Throw her a couple of soda crackers and a piece of cheese and she was happy.

Flush with cash from a flood of orders for Valentine's Day gifts, Peggy had gone all out, paying as much for one meal as she normally spent on a week's worth of groceries. She'd splurged, selecting name brands over store brands, fresh over frozen or canned, and regular over fat-free, lite, or sugar-free. She'd probably overestimated what she needed, but like the good book says, better too much than not enough.

Peggy couldn't wait to meet Tellumo's girlfriend. What a lucky young woman. Such a nice boy, and handsome too. Now that she'd gotten to know him, she didn't mind the pierced ears or tattoos so much. As Lurleen had pointed out, all these young people had at least one or two of each—some you could see, some you couldn't. At least he wasn't covered with them.

She moved the computer back to the dresser in the spare bedroom, tossed a tablecloth over the dining room table, and hauled her fancy silver and china out from under the bed. Her everyday dishes would have been fine, but the occasion called for her best, and she intended to deliver. Lurleen said she'd gone overboard. The boy was coming to look at her computer. His friend was coming along because they already had plans. There was no occasion.

Peggy loved her like a sister, but sometimes Lurleen's negative attitude got on her nerves. Rather than half-full or half-empty, Peggy's glass bubbled over. Every cloud had a silver lining. Life was too short to waste time pining for things she'd never have. She focused on possibilities. Like finding a husband.

Charles Manson found a wife. God willing, surely she could find a husband. The odds were against her, but as long as she could walk up the aisle—or roll, if necessary—another marriage was still possible. She knew God stayed busy answering prayers from around the world, many from people far worse off than she. Sending a good man her way was such a tiny little thing.

A yellow VW Beetle covered with daisies pulled into the driveway. Peggy glanced at the clock—six o'clock on the nose. She checked everything in the kitchen one last time, adjusting the temperature on all four burners and both Crock-Pots before hanging up her apron and hurrying to answer the door.

"Come in!" She smiled and held the screen door open for them.

Tellumo gestured toward Melody. "Mrs. Tucker, this is Melody Abshire, my friend from Cincinnati."

"Nice to meet you, Mrs. Tucker," Melody said, offering a long, narrow gift bag. "This is for you."

"You shouldn't have!" Peggy tried not to stare at the ring in her lip or the daisy tattoo on her neck. "Thank you so much!" She took the bag and ushered them into the dining nook. "No need to be so formal. We're among friends! Call me Peggy."

"The table is beautiful," Melody said. "I love your china! Is it Butterfly Meadow?"

"It is, thank you." Peggy beamed. These days, young girls didn't know a thing about china unless they were looking to register a pattern. "With so many choices, I like to have never made up my mind, but I have no regrets. It's durable, dishwasher safe, and still available just about anywhere."

"Smells great in here," Tellumo said. "I hope you didn't go to a lot of trouble."

"Oh, no trouble at all," Peggy said. "Take a look at my computer, and then we'll eat."

"Oh," Tellumo said. "About that...."

"We spent the morning researching dial-up," Melody interjected.

"What did you find out?" Peggy hoped they'd be able to solve the problem. Getting knocked offline every time she chatted with Lonely was frustrating. "My computer is in the spare bedroom."

"Well." Tellumo scratched his head. "There's really no need to look. The problem isn't your computer; it's your connection. Dial-up is the worst."

Melody nodded. Peggy had to admit, even with her tattoo, piercing, and mannishly short hair, she was a pretty girl.

"Oh, dear," Peggy said. She didn't have the money for anything else. "I guess I'll just have to live with it."

"Maybe not," Tellumo said. He pulled one of those smartphones out of his pocket and tapped on it several times. "I didn't realize you lived so close to Salt Lick County High."

"Does that make a difference?"

He looked up from his phone and grinned. "Sure does. You're close enough to use the school's Wi-Fi." He grabbed Melody's hand. "Which one is the spare bedroom?"

"First door on your right."

"We'll have you fixed up in no time," Tellumo said.

He and Melody disappeared into the spare bedroom. She thought about standing in the door—to prevent any hanky-panky—but Tellumo didn't strike her as the type for such shenanigans, given the circumstances, so she returned to the kitchen. The gift bag contained a bottle of wine—something pink—with a screw cap, thank God, rather than a cork. Beer and hard liquor were from the devil, but even Jesus drank wine. She didn't have any wine glasses but believed the stemmed goblets she'd picked up at a garage sale would work.

Melody poked her head out of the spare bedroom. "We're done! Got a minute so we can show you how it works?"

With the patience of saints, she and Tellumo explained about the wireless Internet connection and showed her how to access her e-mail and Christian Bazaar accounts.

"I can't believe the difference," Peggy said. Everything looked the same, but pages loaded in the blink of an eye and the long pauses and the screeching of the modem were gone.

"If you have any trouble, call me." Tellumo wrote his number down on a pad next to the keyboard.

A timer sounded. "The rolls are done," Peggy said as she hurried toward the kitchen. "Y'all ready to eat?"

Melody fell in behind her. "Anything I can do to help?"

"No." Peggy shook her head as she grabbed a potholder and pulled the rolls from the oven. "I've got everything under control. Grab a plate off the table and help yourself."

"Smells great," Tellumo said.

"Yeah, sure does." Melody licked her lips. "Those yeast rolls look delicious! Are they homemade?"

Peggy nodded. "Thank you." She pointed to a platter of sliced roast beef on the counter. "Here's the main course. On the stove are mashed potatoes, corn on the cob, green beans, and mushroom gravy." She gestured to the Crock-Pots sitting on the counter on the other side of the oven. "There's macaroni and cheese on the left, and broccoli casserole on the right."

"Wow," Tellumo said. "This is amazing."

"For real," Melody added. "I don't know where to start."

The more she was around Melody, the more Peggy liked her. "Anywhere you want. Be sure to save room for dessert."

"Oh, thanks for the warning," Tellumo said as he slid several slices of roast to his plate with a serving fork. "What's for dessert?"

"You have your choice. There's blackberry jam cake with caramel icing, chocolate meringue pie, or pineapple upside-down cake."

"All homemade?" Melody looked at her with eyes wide.

Peggy nodded. "That ready-made stuff isn't any good."

"Wow," Melody said. "Sure wish I knew how to cook like this."

Tellumo laughed. "Yeah, me too."

Peggy liked this girl. She and Tellumo made a nice couple. Like the good book says, the way to a man's heart is through his stomach. "I'd be happy to share my recipes with you."

Melody's face fell. "Not sure that would do much good."

Bless her heart. Kids today couldn't boil water, much less prepare a home-cooked meal. "Next time you come to town, we'll fix dinner for Tellumo, and I'll show you a few tricks." Passing her cooking skills to Melody appealed to her and was the least she could do.

Chapter Ten: Secret Pacts

OLIVER AWOKE Sunday morning with a splitting headache. The aspirin he'd chased with two glasses of water before falling into bed hadn't prevented the hangover he'd known was coming. Every heartbeat exploded in his temples. The incessant throbbing reminded him why he'd long ago sworn off drinking more than a glass or two of wine.

The pounding intensified when he stood to make his way through the dark room, faded into the background when he stubbed his toe on the bathroom doorjamb, and after he flipped the switch, returned with a vengeance in response to the blinding light. "Dammit!" He hopped on one foot, massaging his aching toe with one hand and his temple with the other. After a moment, he downed more aspirin, splashed his face with cold water, and proceeded with his morning ritual.

Despite the dark cloud hanging over them, the first full day alone with Letty in more than twenty years had passed quickly. Not talking about cancer was like trying not to scratch an itch. No matter how hard they'd tried to avoid the subject, every conversation ended with her illness. Somehow, they'd still laughed more than they'd cried.

The enticing aroma of fresh-brewed coffee hastened his progress. Whether from the aspirin or the hot shower, his headache and the pain in his toe had eased a bit. He folded his pajamas, slipped into his house pants and a well-worn flannel shirt, and then made the bed. Although the sun wouldn't rise for another hour or so, he pulled back the curtains and opened the blinds. Unlike Kevin, who'd preferred keeping the windows covered, Oliver had nothing to hide.

"Good morning, Ollie." Letty, wearing a long flannel nightgown, sat at the table with the newspaper spread before her, sipping coffee. "I messed up your paper." She smiled. "Sorry. I know it chaps your ass."

"Retirement has mellowed me out." He pulled a mug from the cabinet, filled it with coffee, and sat across from her. "You're also sitting in my spot, and I didn't make you move."

"Like I would…."

Oliver laughed. "Good point. Sleep well?"

"Passed out is more like it." She massaged her temple. "Between the two of us, we put away three bottles of wine last night."

"Four, counting the chardonnay we had with lunch."

She shook her head. "Doesn't count. Our little afternoon nap wiped the slate clean."

Pointing out she'd downed three glasses for every one he'd consumed served no purpose. Besides, as far as he was concerned, her terminal diagnosis was a free pass to do whatever she wanted.

"Sid said hello."

"You talked with him again?"

She nodded. "I called him when I woke up this morning. Payback for cutting our nap short."

Oliver laughed. "I'm glad he came around."

"Me too. I knew he would, sooner or later." She wrapped her hands around her mug. "He's calling the boys today about getting together for dinner next weekend."

"Need my help?"

"Your help…? In the kitchen?" She shook her head and laughed. "Thanks, but no thanks. My sweet husband is hiring a caterer."

"Sid is one in a million," Oliver said.

"Yeah." She stared at the table for a moment. "He's going to be lost without me." She looked over her coffee at him. "Too bad he's not bi. You'd take good care of him."

"Don't get me wrong. I love Sid like a brother." Oliver smiled. "But going after my best friend's husband, even if he were interested in me—and Sid, most definitely, is not—would be disloyal."

"Oh, Ollie." She sighed. "Sometimes you're so naïve. Dying women leave husbands to friends all the time."

"Well, in that case, tell Sid if he ever wants to take a walk on the wild side, I'd be happy to show him around."

Letty laughed. "He's known that since before we got married. Did I tell you Kevin hit on him?" She shook her head. "I swear, what you saw in that sorry excuse for a man is beyond me."

Oliver's face grew hot. "You did tell me, and in hindsight, I'd have to agree."

She reached across the table and patted his arm. "You're a good guy, Ollie—better than Kevin, Tim, Angelo, what's-his-face, or Steve deserved. I hope one day you find a guy like Sid."

"Well, that ship has sailed. The pool here in Fallisville is pretty shallow. If I haven't met him by now, it's not going to happen."

She shrugged. "Who says you haven't already met him?"

"Unlikely." Oliver shook his head. "Aside from a few codgers I've kept up with over the years, the only gay man I've met since Kevin left is a self-absorbed twentysomething gym rat with perfect teeth, glorious hair, piercing green eyes, and a physique Michelangelo would admire."

"Oh yeah. The one you can't stand but can't seem to stop talking about. He sounds hot." Letty smiled. "So you like him?"

"Good grief! He's younger than your boys."

She shrugged. "Age is just a number."

"What happened to Julia Child and the January-December thing?"

"Only applies to my boys." She smiled. "Double standard. Go ahead, sue me. Is he a good kid?"

"I really don't know him well enough to say. Maybe?" He told her about Tellumo coming to his rescue. "An older woman—one who joined the gym during those dreadful Body By God days—seems to have taken him under her wing."

"Oh yeah, I'd forgotten about the biblically based gym. What a hoot." She watched Oliver for a moment. "Sounds like you've judged this kid without knowing much about him."

"I know enough."

"Like what?" She snorted. "Other than he's gorgeous and thirty years younger than you."

"So what if he is a good kid? What could we possibly have in common?"

"You both go to the gym. That's one thing more than you had in common with any of your exes."

"Oh come on, Letty. You're being ridiculous."

"Am I?"

"Even if I was interested—and I'm not—who says he's interested in me?"

"He wants to work out with you. That might not sound like a big deal, but having raised four boys who were big into sports, I can tell you a workout buddy is special."

She had a point. After a few sessions with Kevin ordering him around, Oliver had insisted on going to the gym alone to work out, a habit Kevin later took advantage of for his liaisons.

"Think about it." She smiled. "You couldn't do much worse than Kevin."

"That's what you said about Tim." He smiled. "Anything you want to do today?"

"Would it hurt your feelings if I went back to Dayton?"

"A little bit, but I'll get over it." He winked. "I can never get enough of you."

"I'll come back for another visit." She nodded in confirmation. "I promise. Being here with you has been great. Just what the doctor ordered."

"Come any time." He shrugged. "You and Sid are about the only people in the world who never get on my nerves."

"We feel the same about you." She took another sip of coffee. "Probably something to do with living together in our formative years."

"That place was also our first apartment." He shook his head and chuckled. "We didn't have a stick of furniture."

Letty laughed. "Furnished that dump with cinder blocks, plywood, and whatever we could salvage and thought we lived in splendor." She sighed. "Good times."

"How could thirty years have passed…?" The naïve, callow young man he'd been hadn't survived the ravages of time. "We've changed so much."

Letty met his gaze. "We haven't changed—we've grown." She reached across the table and took his hand in hers. "When you come out from behind that curmudgeonly shield, you're still the Ollie I've always loved."

"I love you too, Letty." He pulled a hand away to wipe a tear from his cheek with the sleeve of his flannel shirt.

"My dearest friend." She squeezed his hand and regarded him with an earnest expression. "Every time you get hurt, you add another layer to your shield." A tear slid down her cheek. "The weight of it is crushing you."

Oliver had no words. A lump formed in his throat. Swallowing didn't make it go away.

"That you've been hurt so much breaks my heart." She released his grip and wiped her eyes with a paper napkin. "You always try so hard to do the right thing." She shook her head and wiped another tear away. "Those guys were lucky to have you, and not one of them even met you halfway."

Oliver shrugged. "Yeah, I really know how to pick 'em."

"True." She finished off her coffee. "You're impatient, trust too much, and let the wrong head call the shots."

"I plead the Fifth."

"You're wiser now. More independent too." She took his hands in hers again. "The next man in your life, whether it's this kid you keep trashing or someone else, deserves a fair shot. Don't hold the sins of the motley crew from your past against him. Come out from behind that monstrous shield and let him see who you really are."

"What's the point?" Oliver's chin fell to his chest. "Even if I could get past my thing with his generation, he's way too young."

"See? You've known the guy less than a week and have already written him off." She squeezed his hands hard. "It's not like you've got cancer...."

He looked up. "I'm sorry." He felt like a heel. What could be more insensitive than pissing and moaning about his lack of a love life when his best friend was dying of cancer?

"Change your perspective a bit?"

He nodded.

"Keep an open mind—that's all I'm asking."

He came around the table and kissed her on the cheek. "I promise I'll try."

"Good." She stroked his cheek with the back of her hand. "Guess I need to hit the shower and get moving."

"How about some breakfast first?"

"Sure." She smiled. "I even have a request."

"Really?" Oliver's chest puffed with pride. Requests for his custom dishes were rarer than snow in summer.

"I see you've got blueberries in the fridge."

He nodded. "I eat them with yogurt for breakfast."

"I'd love your green eggs and ham omelet."

Oliver laughed. Rather than the striking color contrast he'd envisioned, blueberries had turned the eggs a lovely shade of green. "I don't have ham, but bacon works just as well."

TELLUMO AWOKE with a lightly snoring Melody curled up against him. Her cheek rested on his right arm; his left arm was draped across her waist. A raging hard-on he hoped she wouldn't notice and an overwhelming need to pee competed for his attention.

Relief for his overfull bladder waited in the bathroom. The boner would go away by itself. Eventually. Abstinence made the dick grow harder, he'd learned. Still, the longer he went without, the less jacking off appealed to him and the more determined he became to wait for the right occasion.

Melody stirred against him and sighed. "Good morning, sunshine."

He kissed the top of her head. "Good morning."

"This is so nice." She snuggled back into him. "Do we really have to wait until we're forty?"

Tellumo hugged her and shifted his position to put a little more distance between her ass and his morning wood. "That's the deal. Some lucky man will fall head over heels for you long before then."

"Yeah, right." She kissed his arm. "I still think thirty-five makes more sense—in case we want children."

"We can always adopt." He slid his arm from under her neck and sat up. "You hungry?"

"I don't know how, but I am." She rolled onto her back and groaned. "After yesterday, I need to fast for like a week."

"I ate enough pot roast for Trish to smell meat on me for the next week. The vegetables would have been enough." He patted his belly. "I could eat my weight in that Crock-Pot broccoli casserole."

"Yeah, and that macaroni and cheese was to die for." She fisted the sleep from her eyes. "I can't believe the three of us ate two-dozen yeast rolls."

He smiled. "I wasn't keeping count, but I'm pretty sure Peggy ate half of them."

"I don't know," Melody said. "I got distracted and lost count after four. Soaking up mushroom gravy with homemade yeast rolls is the most sensual food experience I've ever had."

"Isn't she sweet?"

Melody nodded. "A real peach." She snickered. "Sounded like her neighbors were practicing for some kind of verbal sex competition."

Tellumo chuckled. "More like a marathon. Dude had some serious staying power." His cock bounced in defiance of his desire for the erection to go away.

"The longer they went at it, the harder pretending I didn't hear anything became." She looked at him. "Watching Peggy squirm didn't help, and I didn't dare look at you."

"I almost lost it the second time she turned up the volume."

"Me too!" She giggled. "But you have to admit, the religious music worked there toward the end."

"Oh, Jesus! Fuck me!" Tellumo said in a falsetto voice. "The crucifix bouncing on the wall and 'Just a Closer Walk with Jesus' blaring in the background did me in."

"Me too." She shook her head. "Pretending I didn't hear anything would have been easier if Peggy hadn't been so mortified. She turned red as a beet!" She furrowed her brow. "Something about her reminds me of Jules."

"My mother?" Tellumo groaned. "I've got to pee so bad it hurts to laugh. Hold on to that thought." He got up, walked into the bathroom, and closed the door.

"Yeah," she continued after he came out. "They're as different as night and day. Peggy is straight, religious—I've never seen so much Christian kitsch in all my life—and about as femme as they come."

"That's for sure." Tellumo walked into the kitchen and opened the refrigerator. "And also, unlike Jules, a great cook. Do you want jam cake, upside-down cake, or pie for breakfast?"

"Oh, please—no more carbs. I need something healthy." Melody sat on the edge of the bed and stretched. "I can't put my finger on it…. Something about her…." She shook her head and then shrugged.

"I love her determination." Tellumo opened the produce drawer. "Nothing ever gets her down. How does an omelet with egg whites, onions, and green peppers sound?"

"Delish!" She got up and headed toward the bathroom. "Do I have time to freshen up?"

"Take your time." He smiled. "Unlike yesterday, we're not on any schedule today."

"Well, I do need to head back sometime this afternoon." She extended her lower lip. "Seems like I just got here."

"Yeah I know." Tellumo nodded as he gathered up the desired items. "Having you here has been easier than I expected."

"Thanks a lot."

"You know that's not what I meant. I didn't think my apartment was big enough for company."

"It's not." She smiled. "Unless they share your bed. That couch sleeps for shit."

"I knew we'd have a good time, but worried we might get on each other's nerves."

She smiled. "I wasn't worried. I mean, heck, we're farting buds."

Tellumo laughed. "I'd forgotten about that."

"Because I won." She slipped into the bathroom and closed the door behind her.

He pulled a knife from the drawer and retrieved his cutting board from the cabinet. The weekend had passed in the blink of an eye. He hadn't realized how much he'd missed her. Video chats were nice, but no replacement for hanging out.

Melody's visit forced him to do something besides playing video games, catching up on chores, grading papers, and going to the gym. He didn't regret putting her visit off for as long as he had, though. His first few months on the job, weekends had been the only time he'd had to catch up from the previous week and to plan for the week to come.

But he could afford to take a break now and then, couldn't he? High praise from Janice Downey and being so much more on top of things gave him some breathing room he hadn't had before. The weekend with Melody had been the perfect antidote to his work-obsessed weeks.

By the time a freshly showered Melody emerged from the bathroom, Tellumo had made the bed, straightened the apartment, and changed from his pajamas into jeans and a T-shirt.

"I could live in your bathroom." She put her suitcase on the bed. "It's what makes this your place."

"What do you mean?"

"From your custom paint job and fabric choices to the fancy showerhead, every detail screams Tellumo Magnamater." She smiled. "In a good way."

"Ready for an omelet?"

She nodded and took a seat. "I'm starved." She eyeballed the plate he placed before her and grabbed a fork. "Looks delicious."

"Nothing to it." Tellumo dumped his omelet from the skillet onto his plate and sat beside her. "I've been thinking, maybe you ought to take Peggy up on those cooking lessons." He looked at the floor and dug his toe into the carpet. "I mean, if you want to...."

Melody swallowed a mouthful of eggs and then set her fork down on her plate. "You know, Moe, now that you're out of school and settled into a job you're going to have for the foreseeable future, it wouldn't hurt for you to lighten up a bit and maybe make some new friends."

Tellumo's face fell. He pushed bits of green pepper around on his plate. She was right. More balance in his life would make him a better person and a better teacher too. "Yeah, I know." He met her gaze. "I can't expect you to run down here to keep me company every weekend."

She shrugged. "I don't know. The drive here wasn't nearly as bad as I expected. The worst part was getting out of Cincinnati."

"I'd love for you to come back." He looked up. "Not every weekend. I'd fall behind on my grading and never get anything done."

"Every weekend?" She folded her arms and looked at him. "Believe it or not, I have a life too." She smiled. "Once or twice a month is doable. Laid-back little Fallisville is a nice change of pace from the big city."

"Good." He grinned. "Everyone in town will think we're sleeping together."

"Uh, Moe. I hate to be the one to break it to you, but we did sleep together."

"You know what I mean."

"Sure I do. But they don't, and showing up now and then with me on your arm will keep them guessing."

"I don't have anything to hide." He pointed to the pink triangle tattooed on his right shoulder. "Besides, anyone who sees this knows I'm gay."

"Has Peggy seen it?"

Tellumo thought for a moment. "Yeah. I wear sleeveless shirts or tank tops at the gym sometimes. She'd be blind to miss it."

Melody scoffed. "She thinks I'm your girlfriend. Her whole demeanor changed after I recognized her pattern." She shrugged. "She doesn't know I worked in the china department at Macy's for almost five years."

"I noticed the change too." He folded his arms across his chest and stroked his chin. "Leading Peggy to believe something that isn't true is wrong."

"You haven't lied or hidden anything from her. She put two and two together and came up with six or seven." Melody raised her palms. "I suspect she's not a fan of the gays…."

The words stabbed him like a knife. Technically, six months of abstinence meant Tellumo wasn't any kind of sexual—homo, hetero, or anything else. The idea that Peggy might treat him differently if she knew upset him. He'd done nothing to mislead her, nor would he. If she asked him outright, he'd tell her the truth. But until then, he'd let her think what she wanted to think.

PEGGY WAS a changed woman. In fewer than twenty-four hours, she'd fallen head over heels in love. Although they'd only just met, already the minutes passed like hours when they were apart.

The magic Internet connection Tellumo had hooked up had won her over in record-breaking time. Not since she'd become enamored with her first cordless telephone had a device so profoundly impacted her life. He'd also rearranged the wires, eliminating the need for all but one cord to step across when she was set up at the dining room table.

She flipped open her ringing cell phone. "Good morning, Lurleen. I was about to call you."

"You sound mighty chipper this morning. I take it things went well last night."

"We had a lovely time. They stayed until almost nine o'clock!" She didn't mention how embarrassed she'd been about her neighbors fornicating through dinner.

"Have enough to eat?"

"Barely." Peggy had hoped there'd be enough leftovers for two dinners, but wasn't sure she even had enough for a full hour. "They raved about your broccoli casserole." Lurleen didn't need to know Peggy had doctored up the recipe to keep it from tasting so bland.

"I'm glad they liked it. Is she a big girl?"

"No." Peggy shook her head. "Tiny little thing. Cute as a button, with short red hair, pretty blue eyes, and a few freckles."

"You fix 'em a plate to take home?"

"Just dessert." With all the cooking she'd done yesterday, damned if she was going to cook again today. "I'm telling you, Lurleen, those kids must have hollow legs. There wasn't much left."

"Was that boy able to fix your computer?"

"Did he ever! Turns out I'm close enough to use the high school's wireless Internet. It's a hundred times faster than the dial-up connection, and free!"

"Free? I'm sure somebody pays for it. Probably the taxpayers."

"Well, I'm a taxpayer too." Mostly. The Lord got his 10 percent, but she didn't declare the income from her fancywork on her tax return. "Besides, with all the noise I have to put up with for band practice, football games, and everything else that goes on at that place, free Internet access is the least they can do."

"Of course you're right, as always. Think they're in love?"

"Beyond any doubt," Peggy said. "They're darling together. You should see the way they look at each other."

"What does she do?"

"Teaches second grade at a private school in Cincinnati. I bet her students love her. She looks like she'd be good with kids." Peggy clucked several times. "Poor girl doesn't know how to cook, though. I offered to give her some lessons."

"How nice of you! Did she take you up on it?"

Peggy shook her head. "Not yet. She took my phone number. Tellumo said he wants to learn how to cook too. Isn't that sweet?"

"Very. Didn't you say he had a pink triangle tattoo?"

"Yes, on his shoulder. Does it mean something?"

"You'd have to ask him."

"I will. You've made me curious."

"Listen, I'm not going to be able to sew with you Tuesday."

"Oh, Lurleen! I was counting on you. Melody took pictures of everything we make with her camera. I've been uploading them to Christian Bazaar and sales have taken off."

"I'm glad your little business is doing so well. You really ought to look into one of those fancy new sewing machines I was telling you about."

"I'd never figure out how to use one. Are you sure you can't help?" Peggy didn't know how on earth she'd get all those orders completed without her. "I'll buy your dinner again."

"Already got plans. Marvin Shankley is taking me to Fallis House for dinner."

"Are you serious?"

"He's a nice man. We have a lot in common."

Like what? She didn't ask. Truth be told, Lurleen's husband had been more than a little odd too. Henry had preferred documentaries to reality shows and read books like he was still in school. "Fallis House makes the best bread pudding I've ever tasted."

"I hear it's good, but I'm always too full for dessert. Well, Peggy, I'll let you get back to whatever you were doing. Just wanted to let you know I'm not coming Tuesday."

"Thanks for calling. Y'all have a good time." She hung up and found Gladys Honeycutt's number. The quality of her work fell short of Peggy's standards, and she tired of listening to the woman talk about everyone in town, but like the good book says, desperate times call for desperate measures. She was about to place the call when a message from LonelyNFallisville popped up.

Hey, beautiful! An animated emoticon winked at her. *Having a good day?*

Her heart jumped into her throat. She closed her phone, placed her fingers on the keyboard, and thought about how to respond. *Best day ever!*

A giant smiley face filled the box. *What makes today so special?*

Switched from dial-up to wireless. She added a winking smiley face with wings and a halo.

Welcome to the 21st century!

Before she could respond, another message appeared.

We have so much to talk about. What can I do to convince you to meet me?

What do you want to talk about?

Anything. Everything. You. Me. Us.

Her heart skipped a beat. *How about we start with you?*

What do you want to know?

What didn't she want to know? Peggy lost track of time as they chatted and hadn't laughed so much in years. Her willingness to answer the same question and a desire to confirm Mr. Crumbly was on the other end guided her interrogation. She didn't hold his sometimes fuzzy responses against him. After all, she hadn't been entirely forthcoming either. If she was right about his identity—and she was certain she was—she still didn't know much about the man.

Tell you what....

She stared at the screen but didn't have to wait long for his next message.

Tuesday night, from six o'clock to seven o'clock, I'll be at the Dinner Barn in one of those rocking chairs.

Peggy was 99.5 percent sure the man on the other end was Mr. Crumbly, but he didn't know that. She had to maintain the ruse. *How will I know it's you?*

I'll have a red carnation.

She stared at the screen, unsure of how to respond. Men weren't exactly beating down the door to ask her out. The red carnation added an element of romance, but she didn't want to seem overeager. Unlike those women Gladys told her the smooth-talking Vic Hunter had bedded—including a few from church—she wasn't man crazy. No siree Bob. Why buy the cow when the milk is free?

Oh, dear. The blinking cursor taunted her. She pecked out a response. *Let me think about it.*

The chime sounded and more words appeared. *If you like what you see, say hello.* A smiley face flashed pearly whites at her.

Appearance wasn't the issue—at least not for her. Lust provided no foundation for the kind of marriage she envisioned. Even with the beard, Mr. Crumbly was a fine-looking man. Any woman would be proud to stand beside him. What he'd think of her was the bigger concern.

Chapter Eleven: Close Encounters

TELLUMO CONSIDERED skipping his workout and staying home to grade papers. Saturday with Mel had been the first day he hadn't worked on school stuff since moving to Fallisville. Her Sunday afternoon departure had left ample time to prepare for the week ahead, but he couldn't shake the feeling he should make up for the time he'd missed.

Until Mel's visit, Tellumo hadn't realized how lonely he'd been. School and his personal training clients had kept him too busy for much of a social life in Cincinnati. When he wasn't asleep, at the gym, or in class, he was at the library studying. Student teaching had kept him even busier. Still, he'd hung out with classmates at Espresso Yourself once or twice a week, barhopped with Mel a few times a month, and gone on the occasional date.

He shut his laptop, stood, and stretched. The papers could wait. After an always challenging Monday at school, a trip to the gym would do him good. Nobody would die if he didn't finish grading tonight. Except for a few overachievers, his students wouldn't care.

When Tellumo stepped outside, he caught a whiff of wood smoke. Sweatpants and a lightweight jacket offered scant protection from the chill wind, but he wasn't going far. He shoved his hands deep into his pockets and quickened his pace.

The receptionist at the gym flashed him a perky smile. "Hi, Tellumo." She glanced at the clock. "You're running late tonight." She scanned the barcode on his Fit as a Fiddle key tag and handed back his keys.

"Hey, Tiffany." He smiled. "I was going to stay home but couldn't miss a chance to see you."

"You sweet-talker, you." She winked at him. "My offer still stands."

"I promise, you'll be the first to know." Conversion wasn't really in the cards, but should he—for some reason—suddenly become heterosexual, or even bi, Mel would have his head if anyone found out before she did.

Tiffany laughed. "Have a good workout."

The piped-in country music competed with the din of the mostly male crowd, divided more or less equally into two groups. Some preferred working out alone—including a significant fraction Tellumo believed were gay—and focused on getting in and out without wasting any time. The others lifted weights with one or more buds. The larger the group, the more likely they were to be straight and the less exercise actually took place as they stood around telling war stories, bragging about conquests, and exchanging exercise and nutrition tips.

Tellumo was surprised to see Oliver Crumbly curling barbells in the weight room. The icy glare he shot Tellumo surprised him too—until he remembered their six o'clock appointment. He hurried over to him. "I'm so sorry. I don't even have a good excuse. I got busy this weekend and completely forgot about meeting you." He swallowed. "I should have put our appointment on my calendar. I'm so sorry."

Oliver glowered at him for a long moment without saying anything. The scheduling snafu clearly hadn't won Tellumo any points. He was relieved when Oliver's brows knitted and his angry scowl melted into a pensive frown.

"I'll let it go this time," Oliver said. His piercing gaze said he meant it too. "I waited a few minutes, then went ahead with my regular BTC workout for Monday."

"BTC workout?" Tellumo shook his head. "Haven't heard of that one."

"It's three workouts a week with B-day, T-day, and C-day."

Tellumo screwed up his face and scratched his head. "I'm still not getting it."

"B-day is buns, belly, and biceps. T-day is traps, triceps, and thighs. C-day is chest, calves, and clavicle."

"Clavicle?"

Oliver shrugged. "Best C-word I could find for shoulders."

Their laughter broke the tension. "You should smile more often," Tellumo said. Even when he scowled, Oliver was a good-looking man. A smile kicked him into the realm of gorgeous.

Oliver studied Tellumo's face for a moment. "I would if everybody'd stop pissing me off."

For a minute, Tellumo thought Oliver was serious. The gleam in his eye, however, gave him away. Tellumo snickered. "Everybody?"

Oliver nodded.

"I can't imagine how hard that must be for you."

He nodded again. "We all have our burdens."

From the look on his face, Oliver appeared to believe Tellumo bore a much heavier load than did he. Showing up late hadn't helped. Good thing he'd decided to come to the gym instead of staying home and grading papers. "Your BTC workout sounds pretty good. How long have you been doing it?"

Oliver blushed. "Eight years, but I've only been religious about it for the last year or two." He glanced down at his shoes, then back to Tellumo. "T-day and C-day seem to be working for me, but on B-day I should maybe focus less on my buns and more on my belly."

Tellumo's face grew hot. Focusing on Oliver's buns was his job. "Changing your workouts might help, but considering how long you've been exercising, I'd say your diet is to blame."

Anger flashed in Oliver's eyes. He glared at Tellumo for a moment, and then his expression softened. "I have a thing for doughnuts."

"What kind?"

Oliver met his gaze. "Cake. Chocolate-dipped once in a while, and cinnamon-powdered now and again, but the plain cake doughnuts are my favorites."

"Me too!" Tellumo beamed. "Any idea how many calories are in a plain cake doughnut?"

Oliver shook his head. "Nope. Couldn't be worse than glazed."

Tellumo pulled his smartphone from his pocket. "You're in for a shock." He tapped the keyboard a few times and touched Go. "A plain cake doughnut has about 320 calories, but glazed are less than 200 calories."

Oliver gasped. "Are you serious?"

He held up the phone so Oliver could see the screen. "Surprised me too."

"You looked that up, just now, on your phone?"

Tellumo nodded. "It's not on the phone. I searched the Internet."

"And you got the answer that fast?"

He nodded again. "You don't have a computer?"

Oliver shook his head. "Never needed one."

Tellumo wondered if he'd heard right. "Never needed one?"

"Nope. When I need to look something up, I go to the library."

Tellumo could survive without food or water longer than without the Internet. He stared at Oliver for a long moment. "What kind of phone do you have?"

"A wall-mounted rotary dial in the kitchen and a princess on the nightstand in my bedroom. Both beige."

Rotary dial? Tellumo could hardly believe his ears. "No cell phone?"

Oliver shook his head. "Nope. Never needed one of them either."

The thought of a world without smartphones and the Internet was almost enough to make his head explode. He couldn't conceive of such a place. "What do you do?"

"I'm retired."

Tellumo nodded. Not the answer he was looking for, but he let it go. Asking how Oliver filled his days was probably a bad idea anyway.

"We on for Wednesday?" Oliver glanced at his watch. "I haven't eaten yet and need to stop at the store before I go home."

"Sure," Tellumo replied. "This time I promise not to forget." He pulled out his phone and touched the calendar icon. "Six o'clock?"

Oliver nodded as he picked up his gym bag and water bottle. "Your calendar is on that thing too?"

"My life is on here," Tellumo said, and was only half kidding. "Music, pictures, games, books, my address book…."

"What happens if you lose your phone?" He folded his arms across his chest with a smug look on his face.

"No big deal," Tellumo replied, enjoying Oliver's surprised expression maybe a little too much. "Everything is backed up in the cloud."

"I see," Oliver said. His furrowed brow and pursed lips told a different story. "I'd never figure out how to use one."

"Yeah, you would." Tellumo smiled. "The menus on the old flip phones were a lot more complicated, and not nearly as useful. You should get one."

"Maybe I will." He extended his hand. "See you Wednesday."

Tellumo gripped Oliver's hand, still warm from the workout gloves he'd removed, and pumped. "I won't forget this time, I promise."

Oliver gave him a curt nod and headed for the exit. Tellumo had been lucky. If he hadn't shown up when he did, Oliver very likely would have written him off and had nothing to do with him again. He pulled out his phone, went to the calendar, and set a reminder. He had a feeling Oliver wasn't the kind of guy to give someone more than a second chance.

FOR THE first time since the cinnamon bun weekend, Peggy Tucker went off her diet. She had no choice. Orders for her merchandise were pouring in, and nobody had the time or talent to help fill them.

On the way home from work, she stopped at the fabric shop for supplies, picked up shipping materials at the office supply store, and then hit the drive-through window at the Dairy Freeze. She downed a double cheeseburger, a large order of their delicious crinkle-cut fries, and a chocolate milkshake with whipped cream and a cherry on top in the car in less than ten minutes. With so much to do, she couldn't afford a whole hour for dinner.

The dark computer monitor mocked her as she embroidered. She thought about checking her e-mail for new orders but already had more than she could handle in the stack she'd printed out the day before. Nothing would please her more than chatting another evening away with Mr. Crumbly, but like the good book says, business before pleasure. A sizeable dent in the backlog would keep her from feeling guilty about taking a night off to meet him too.

Her little sideline was fast becoming a full-time job. Until now, keeping up with orders hadn't been a problem. Repeat customers and word of mouth accounted for some growth, but sales had really taken off since she'd uploaded Melody's photographs.

She set her embroidery aside and rifled through the stack of orders. A few could be filled from the overstock she kept on hand. The rest needed something she'd have to make. Filling those orders in a week would be a tall order—even were she to forego sleep.

Finishing pieces in minutes rather than hours would make a huge difference. Industrial embroidery machines cost a lot more than she could afford, but she had enough money in her PayPal account from recent orders to pay for a fancy sewing machine—top of the line, maybe. The challenge— and the reason she hadn't already bought one—was getting the machine to replicate her designs. The demonstration video she'd watched at the fabric store showing how the easy-to-use software worked assumed far more knowledge about computers than she possessed.

She started to ignore her ringing phone, but curiosity got the best of her. The number flashing on the screen wasn't familiar. Whoever it was, she'd get rid of them quick. She had way too much to do to waste time on polls or sales pitches. "Hello?"

"Hi, Peggy, it's Melody Abshire—Tellumo's friend."

"Melody! You didn't have to explain who you are." Who could forget such a precious little girl? "I'm so glad you called!" Elated would be more honest, but she didn't want to seem overeager. "How are you?"

"So kind of you to ask. I'm fine. Thanks again for the delicious dinner."

"You're very welcome." Peggy beamed. Praise was the best part of cooking for others. "Have you thought any more about those cooking lessons?"

"Yes, ma'am. That's why I'm calling." Melody cleared her throat. "I'm driving down to Fallisville the first weekend in March. If you're sure it's not an imposition...."

"An imposition?" She chortled. "Whatever gave you that idea? Nothing would please me more. Any requests?"

"I keep dreaming about yeast rolls and mushroom gravy. Unless they're too hard for a beginner...."

"Too hard?" Peggy stood and walked into the kitchen. "Cooking is all about practice. Nothing to it once you learn the basics."

"That would be great!" She paused for a moment. "In return, I'd be happy to take more pictures for you, maybe show you something besides emoticon shortcuts on the computer."

"Sweet of you to offer." Instead of saying Melody didn't need to do a thing, as she'd intended, an idea popped into her head. "Your pictures have made a big difference in sales. I can hardly keep up!"

"That's great! I'd offer to help, but I can't even thread a needle."

Peggy laughed. "I'm sure you'd pick it up fast enough." She glanced at the stack of orders waiting to be filled. "Know anything about embroidery software?" She explained what she'd learned about programmable sewing machines.

"I don't," Melody replied. "But I took a computer-assisted design course at the community college. It can't be very different from other design software. Let me do some research."

"Thanks, dear." Peggy glanced at the clock. "Dinner at six on Saturday?"

"If you don't mind...."

"I wouldn't have offered if I minded." Sometimes a sense of duty or obligation compelled her, but not this time. "The yeast rolls take a while." She squinted for a moment as she thought about the steps in her recipe. "Is three thirty too early?"

"Not at all. Can I bring something?"

Peggy smiled. Such good manners! "Just that handsome Tellumo."

Melody laughed. "If I ate your yeast rolls without him, he'd never forgive me. See you soon!"

The call boosted Peggy's spirits. As problems went, more orders than she could handle was a good one to have. Without pushing her prices into the stratosphere, making things by hand fast enough to replace what the state paid her was impossible. If Melody figured out how the software worked, she could show Peggy. A high-tech sewing machine could turn things around.

The request for cooking lessons tickled her pink. Lurleen didn't care diddly-squat about the recipes Peggy had tried, tinkered with, and perfected over the years. If Peggy died first, Lurleen would toss the lot of them in the garbage without so much as a second glance. Just the thought brought tears to her eyes.

Whether Melody could help with the embroidery software or not, Peggy was thrilled. Teaching her how to cook was a way to make sure her recipes lived on. The love she'd poured into cooking would live on too.

FEW THINGS annoyed Oliver as much as grocery shopping. He hated every grocery in town. For the same basket of goods, he could pay too much and get great service at one store, pay the lowest prices and get no service at another, or opt for average prices and crummy service at a third.

Bad service made his blood pressure go up. The last time he'd decided to save a few bucks, he'd feared his head would explode when he'd spent forty-five minutes in line waiting to check out at the only open register. Since then, he'd avoided the low-end option like the plague. Higher prices at the nice store forced him to cut back elsewhere, leaving him no choice, more often than not, but to settle for mediocre service and higher prices than he really wanted to pay.

Stopping at the store on his way home from the gym helped. Making a special trip to buy groceries was enough to put him in a bad mood for two or three days. He'd tried stocking up to keep from having to go so often, but ended up throwing food away that spoiled before he could eat it, and still having to shop every few days anyway for milk, berries for his morning yogurt, or something he'd forgotten or suddenly decided he needed. Going more often and buying less was a pain, but it saved money because so much less went to waste.

Tellumo's tardiness, although not unexpected, pissed Oliver off enough for him to consider driving to the high-end store, where he'd be less likely to blow up at anyone. He would have, but an astronomical heating bill had placed considerable strain on his already tight budget. If he hadn't been anxious to get home, he'd have hit the low-end store, saved some money, and blown off some steam yelling at rude customers and incompetent employees. As usual, the middle option was really his only choice.

Why they bothered putting up stop signs and painting arrows in parking lots was a mystery. Insurance purposes, he supposed. Nobody paid them any mind. He honed in on an open space as someone pulled through from the other side. Oliver glared, and would have given the stupid bitch the bird, but he was trying to break himself of the habit. He'd almost gotten his ass kicked the last time he'd flipped someone off.

Nobody heeded the signs on the doors either. He had to fight against the flow of idiots leaving through the In door, only to wait while some asshole stopped to do something with his smartphone. By the time Oliver reached the produce section, he was foaming at the mouth.

When had grocery shopping become a group activity? The shitty aisles were barely wide enough for a single file of grocery carts to move in each direction. Bringing friends and neighbors along was ridiculous. Standing around talking seriously messed with the flow.

Shopping with a passel of kids in tow was equally annoying, but understandable. Babysitters weren't cheap. Herding the screaming little monsters through the store was punishment enough, though he did wish, as he'd committed no crime, he could skip the sentence. He'd also like to have a word with the son of a bitch who invented the extralong carts for children to ride in.

Half the people in the store were talking on one of those goddamn cell phones. He imagined himself yanking the device from some asshat's hand and screaming into the phone "She's too busy to talk right now, call back later."

No matter what he needed, someone stood between him and the shelf with the item he desired. It was uncanny—like they knew. If it wasn't some old lady trying to decide which soup she wanted, it was the restocking clerk blocking the aisle. The whole fucking world conspired to drag out his trip to the goddamn fucking grocery store as long as possible.

Oliver was hangry—starving and pissed off. He took a deep breath and counted to ten. A doughnut would tide him over until he got home, except he hadn't put any in his cart. He really should pay more attention to labels. The nutrition information on the boxes he compared confirmed what Tellumo had told him. Cake doughnuts were too fattening, and glazed hit his stomach like a ton of bricks. Varieties with reduced fat or less sugar tasted like cardboard.

"Hello, Oliver."

He turned to the familiar voice. "Janice!" She hugged him, and he pecked her on the cheek. "Good to see you."

"You too." She smiled. "I've missed you."

"I've missed you too." His face grew hot. "It's almost March, and we haven't sat down together since before Christmas."

"The weather threw us off our routine. Can you believe the winter we've had?"

Oliver shook his head. "Between the snow and the ice—"

"Hey, you two wanna talk about the weather someplace else? I'm trying to do some shopping here."

Janice smiled at the man in a cement-spattered jacket and jeans who glared at them. "Fuck off, asshole."

Oliver's jaw dropped, and he quickly shifted to one side so the purple-faced man could pass. He glowered at them as he went by but remained silent.

"Pushy people piss me off," Janice said. "He should keep his bitchy comments to himself, like the rest of us do."

Oliver laughed. "We need to get together… soon."

"Doing anything tomorrow evening?"

He thought for a moment. Tuesdays he usually went to Zumba, but he wasn't especially happy with the new instructor. "Nothing I can't do some other time."

"Great!" She pulled a smartphone from her purse. "Six thirty? At the Dinner Barn?"

He nodded. "Works for me." The food at its best was mediocre, but cheap, and more often than not, he'd been satisfied enough with the service to leave the full 15 percent for a tip.

"Then it's a date." She fooled with her phone for a moment, then dropped it back in her purse. "Glad I ran into you."

"Me too." Oliver glanced over his shoulder and saw a line of carts waiting to get by. "Looking forward to catching up."

"Me too." She smiled and then gave her cart a push. "See you tomorrow!"

Hanging out with Janice Downey was the one thing Oliver missed from his teaching days at Salt Lick County High. Next to Sid and Letty Dawson, she was his closest friend. He felt bad for letting so much time go by without at least giving her a call.

Her smartphone surprised him. She and Oliver had been the last to switch from paper files and grade books to computerized recordkeeping. In truth, he'd never made the change, and as far as he knew, she hadn't either. When Frank Wyrick became principal and mandated the switch after Elmer Lebus retired, Oliver and Janice relied on student teachers to update online attendance records, enter grades, and prepare progress reports for them.

Perhaps technology wasn't all bad. Tellumo's search had turned up exactly what he wanted to know in a fraction of a second. Hours and hours poring through card catalogs had yielded few answers to a long list of questions Oliver had for the book he wanted to write. Going to the library for more research was a frustrating and futile act he'd finally given up. Writing around the gaps in his knowledge had taken the wind out of his sails and produced still more questions.

He'd ask Janice about her apparent conversion at dinner. Her easy use of the smartphone was encouraging. Maybe old dogs could learn new tricks.

Chapter Twelve: Missed Connections

PEGGY GLANCED at the clock. Twenty minutes had passed since she'd closed the door to the driver's license office. As was always the case when she had plans after work, the last customer of the day tested her patience.

"No, not your library card," she shouted as she slid the well-worn plastic back to the elderly man. "Your Social Security card."

He cupped a hand to his ear. "What?"

"Your Social Security card," she yelled.

A confused look came across his face. "Security guard?" He shook his head. "No, honey. I'm retired."

Peggy took a deep breath and counted to ten as she slowly exhaled. *What would Jesus do?* Curing the old man of his deafness wasn't an option. If working miracles had been in her bag of tricks, she'd be happily married to Mr. Crumbly by now.

A truck that had been parked in front of the office all afternoon roared to life, lurched into gear, and drove away. The late afternoon sun streamed through the unobstructed window, illuminating the sign she pointed to a hundred times every day. She came around the counter, crooked her finger at him to follow, and then pointed to the first item on the list.

He squinted for a moment. "Social Security card? Why didn't you say so?"

Between the sign and a few handwritten notes, she managed to verify the information she needed to reissue the driver's license he'd misplaced. Getting him to sit still for his picture had further tested her patience, but after four attempts—three more than she usually needed—she finally got a good shot of his face.

"Here you go, Mr. Ferguson," she hollered.

He studied the freshly laminated license for a moment and then shook his head. "This picture makes me look old. Can you take another one?"

She came around the counter again, took him by the elbow, and steered him toward the door. "Now look here, Mr. Ferguson," she whispered, smiling sweetly. "You've wasted enough of my time. Now leave... before I hurt you."

"What did you say?"

"Go home," she whispered. The smile never left her face as she held the door open for him. "Have a good evening," she yelled as she closed the door behind him.

She locked up, turned out the lights, and exited through the rear. The cold weather had taken its toll on a battery she should have replaced last fall. If the car failed to start and she had to ride the bus home, she'd never get to the Dinner Barn. She turned the key, held her breath for a moment, and then let out a huge sigh of relief when, after a few stutters and stammers, the engine started.

The drive home cost another ten minutes. Peggy shut the front door to her duplex behind her, tossed her coat over the back of the sofa, and kicked off her shoes. Getting to the Dinner Barn by seven was still possible, but left no time to waste. She hurried down the hall to the bathroom, leaving a trail of discarded clothing in her wake, and turned on the hot water for a quick bath.

Rushing to get ready for such an important occasion was unsettling. She hadn't even decided what to wear yet. Staying home from work had crossed her mind, but Patsy Curtsinger, who filled in for her when she was out, was enjoying a week in Fort Lauderdale. Calling Frankfort for a replacement would invite scrutiny she didn't want or need.

On days she missed work, fear of Channel 13's investigative reports on the work habits of county and state employees kept her inside the duplex with the blinds drawn. Had she stayed home, she'd have risked her job to visit Holy Snips for the makeover Giorgio had promised. Her transformation was far from complete, but updating her hair and makeup might keep Mr. Crumbly from recognizing the frumpy woman he'd overlooked at the gym.

Peggy drew in her breath as she slid into the tub. Her arms prickled with goose bumps. In hindsight, she maybe should have waited an extra few minutes for hot water to reach the tap before flipping the stopper. Her legs felt like poorly plucked chicken skin, but shaving would take too long. He wasn't going to feel her up at the Dinner Barn. She'd just have to wear pants.

Her ablutions complete in record time, Peggy stepped from the tub, wrapped a towel around her torso, and padded to the bathroom door to check the time. A trail of puddles marked the path she'd taken. Getting to the Dinner Barn before seven o'clock was still possible, but she really had to hurry.

She slid into her Spanx and smoothed out the wrinkles from the panties she wore underneath. Her closet was full of clothes she'd never wear again but couldn't part with. If she got rid of them, she knew from experience the weight would come back sure as shooting, and she'd have to spend money she didn't have to replace them.

The pants she tried hung like a burlap sack. Cinching up the waist bunched up the fabric too much to conceal with a sash or wide belt. Leaving her blouse untucked didn't work either.

Nothing in her closet fit. With more time, she could have altered something. She yanked a black shirtdress off the hanger and tried it on. A belt at the waist improved the fit. A bit dressy for the Dinner Barn, but she'd run out of time and would have to make it work. She'd explain she'd just come from…. Well, she'd figure that out on the way there.

Bare legs wouldn't do. With no time to back up and start over, she pulled dark pantyhose on over her Spanx, slid into a pair of low-heeled black pumps, and threw a string of fake pearls around her neck. A quick glance at the clock made her gasp. Driving fast while putting on makeup wasn't easy, but she'd done it before. She grabbed her purse from the dining room table and hurried out the door, fishing for the keys inside as she made her way down the sidewalk.

The headlights she'd left on in her haste to meet Mr. Crumbly cast a dim glow. Peggy glanced skyward as she mumbled a quick prayer and then opened the door. The dome light flickered dimly. When she stuck the key in the ignition, the buzzer letting her know the door was still open bleated a pathetic warning. She turned the key, but nothing happened.

She pumped her foot on the gas, gave the dashboard a good whack, and tried again. Her heart sank. The horrible clicking sound couldn't be good.

Giving up wasn't her style, but she'd run out of options. If she sprouted wings and flew, she still wouldn't make it on time. Peggy folded her arms across the steering wheel, lowered her head to her wrists, and cried like she hadn't cried for a long, long time.

TELLUMO PUSHED back from the counter and the submissions for the literary magazine he'd been reviewing on his laptop and stretched. Although the deadline was two weeks away, he'd been thrilled about the quantity awaiting his review. He'd since discovered the quality of a hefty percentage left much to be desired.

The reason was obvious. To encourage submissions, teachers in the English department had offered extra credit. They had not, however, specified minimum requirements. A number of students had exploited the loophole, submitting some of the shortest essays, stories, and poems he'd ever seen—a few too clever and well written to leave out.

Serious submissions ranged from pretty good to great. The variety impressed him too, with something to catch the eye of a wide range of readers. Publishing the *Salt Lick County Review* online kept him from having to worry about the page limits and budget constraints of a print edition. Good or bad, Tellumo was inclined to accept them all—to embarrass the kids who hadn't really tried, if nothing else.

For a different reason, two short stories and a poem got his attention. He'd pared down the list of suspects, but the identity of his secret valentine remained a mystery. A coworker couldn't have slipped into his classroom without Tellumo or someone else noticing, except for the custodian, and everyone knew he was sleeping with the school librarian. Tellumo's secret admirer had to be a student, most likely in one of his classes.

Two of the authors, girls in his mythology course who giggled and blushed whenever he so much as looked at them, were already suspects. The third—a shy young man in the freshman composition class he taught—had escaped Tellumo's notice previously, but now topped the list. His obviously autobiographical story about falling for his teacher who, aside from her gender, sounded an awful lot like Tellumo, hit too close to home to ignore.

His smartphone, still silenced from his day at school, vibrated on the counter. After a quick glance to see who was calling, he swiped the screen and lifted the device to his chin. "Hello, Jules. What's up?"

"Trish's fortieth birthday is coming up soon. Have you thought about what you want to do to celebrate?"

"Sorry, I haven't." The end of March didn't seem very soon to him, but Jules had a business to run and liked to have her ducks in a row. Time was money. "Have something in mind?"

"Nothing in particular…."

He smiled and waited for her to continue.

"I know you're too busy to spend the weekend in Cincinnati…."

"I'll make time."

"I thought maybe we'd come to Fallisville for the day."

Tellumo pulled up his calendar. Trish's birthday fell on the last Saturday in March. He furrowed his brow. "I'm surprised. You've been begging me to come home for months."

"We know how busy you are."

"Really, Jules. I don't mind. Trish only turns forty once."

"Um."

"Sounds like you don't want me to come home."

"No, that's not true at all. We'd love for you to come."

"But?"

"Well, um. You'd have to sleep on the living room sofa."

"Oh?" He swallowed.

"I'm sorry, honey." She paused. "The first few months, we kept your room the way you left it." She cleared her throat. "Between the television and radio ads, our listing in the *Rainbow Business Directory*, and the website you set up, business is booming. Trish stays home now to handle all the paperwork, take calls, and schedule appointments. Your old bedroom is the new headquarters for Amazon Home Repair."

Tellumo nodded. "It's okay. Not using so much of your living space makes no sense."

"I'm glad you understand. Trish was afraid you'd be upset."

The loss bothered him more than he expected. He'd left nothing important behind and had grown too accustomed to having his own space to go home again without feeling cramped. But still….

"Are you there?"

"Yeah, sorry. I was checking my calendar. I'll make reservations at the Fallis House for dinner. I've never been, but everyone says it's great."

"Perfect. We'll pin down the details a few days ahead of time. Everything okay with you?"

"Yeah, much better than last year." He told her a little about his classes and the work he and a team of students were doing for the literary magazine.

"The excitement and enthusiasm in your voice makes me very happy. Loving what you do makes life a lot easier."

"I had good role models."

"I don't know. We might have worked too much. Do something besides work all the time. A life away from the job will make you a better teacher. I'm sure of it."

After they said their good-byes, Tellumo shoved his phone into his pocket, fell back on his bed, and sighed. His unwillingness to go home had been a temporary state, induced by the pressures of his new job. He'd known he'd return to Cincinnati sooner or later. Spending a few days at home for Christmas had always been the plan, but he hadn't had time to reschedule.

Not having a bedroom in the home he'd grown up in wasn't the end of the world. Trish and Jules would still welcome him with open arms whenever he wanted to visit. He'd slept on the living room sofa many times, but falling asleep watching television was different. No more waking up in the middle of the night and going to bed.

Tellumo jumped when the smartphone in his pants pocket came to life. He yanked the device out, gave it a swipe, and stared at the screen. "Hey, Mel. What's up?"

"I was going to ask you the same thing." She pursed her lips and studied his face. "Who died?"

"Did Jules tell you to call?" Her eyebrows went up and she chewed on her lip, but she didn't say anything. "Just as I thought."

"Like I wasn't going to call later anyway." She gave him a concerned look. "You okay? She said you might need a friend."

"My old bedroom is corporate headquarters for Amazon Home Repair."

"Tired of waiting for a man to do the job? Call the Amazons!" She laughed. "Has to be one of the best slogans of all time. I'm surprised they worked out of Jules's van for so long. I see their logo on trucks and vans all over Cincinnati. How many employees do they have now?"

"None. They're subcontractors."

"All lesbians?"

"No." Tellumo shook his head. "Straight women too. They even work with men. Mostly trans, but some cis."

She smiled. "Brave souls. Takes a special kind of guy to become an Amazon."

He laughed. "You still coming Friday?"

Melody nodded. "I called Peggy too. She's expecting us at three thirty Saturday for our first cooking lesson: Yeast rolls and mushroom gravy."

Tellumo's stomach growled. "Wow. I thought we'd start out boiling water. What do you want to do after?"

"Go to bed." She winked at him.

The look she gave him was a little unsettling. "I'm serious."

"Me too." She laughed. "We might leave Peggy's later than you think."

"Why?"

"Her business is booming too. A programmable sewing machine would save her a lot of time. She's got the money to buy one but is afraid she'd never figure out how to use it. I've been checking out embroidery software for her, and it looks easy enough. I think we could teach her."

Tellumo nodded. "I'll bring my laptop."

She furrowed her brow and looked him in the eye.

"With her own website, she could cut out the middleman and make more money," he explained.

His answer seemed to satisfy her. "Her own website, huh." She nodded. "Okay. You can bring your laptop, but no working on school stuff."

Tellumo frowned. He was hoping to make some headway with the layout for the *Salt Lick County Review*. "Okay, then you're not allowed to tweet, update your Facebook status, or post pictures on Instagram or Flickr."

She gasped. "Not even a video of the crucifix bouncing on the wall?"

He laughed. "We can talk about exceptions on a case-by-case basis."

"You drive a hard bargain, Mr. Magnamater, but I agree to your terms."

"Good. See you Friday?"

"Yeah. I'll pick you up at school again."

Tellumo checked the time, slid his phone into his pocket, and stood. If he went to the gym this late, he'd be up half the night—no matter how much valerian root and chamomile tea he drank when he got home. A nice, long bath sounded like a much better option.

DESPITE THE mediocre food, Oliver looked forward to eating at the Dinner Barn. The menu didn't offer much in the way of healthy options—the salads and vegetable plate had more calories than he consumed on the typical day at home. He ate healthy practically all the time. Having lived on his own cooking since before Christmas, however, he was ready for some strange.

As long as he didn't do it very often, splurging on something deep-fried with rich, creamy gravy wouldn't hurt him. Frying at home made too big of a mess, and the smell lingered for days. He'd been good for so long, he might even get the hot-fudge brownie sundae for dessert.

The Dinner Barn was packed. Oliver had to park his Taurus at the bank. He shoved his hands into the pockets of his jacket and headed for the entrance. His fedora kept his head warm but left his ears open to the chill wind. Had he known he'd have to walk so far, he'd have worn a scarf, gloves, and maybe earmuffs.

He scanned the crowded front porch but didn't see Janice.

"Harper, Collins, and Row—your tables are now ready. Please come to the hostess stand."

The crowd shifted, quickly filling the seats vacated by the family and two couples heading toward the entrance. Unlike several men, Oliver was too much of a gentleman to take a seat in the presence of so many women. Every few minutes, another round of names echoed from the speakers.

"I have tables ready for the Johnsons, the Masons, and the Crumbledowns. Please come to the hostess stand."

Crumbledown? Oliver moved toward the entrance. Janice was waiting for him at the hostess stand.

"I knew you wouldn't be late but didn't feel like standing out in the cold to wait for you." She smiled.

"Y'all wanna follow me," the hostess asked. Without waiting for a reply, she grabbed two menus and moved into the noisy dining room, stopping after a few feet to make sure they were following.

"I'm glad you put our name in," Oliver said. "I've been here for ten minutes and never even thought about it."

The hostess stopped. "Booth okay?"

"Perfect, thanks," Janice replied with a nod and a smile. She dropped her coat and purse on the vinyl seat and sat down.

Oliver removed and neatly folded his coat and placed it in the booth, setting the hat he doffed on top before taking a seat.

"Is Bill Pinkley still out there?" Janice opened her menu.

"The weather guy?" Oliver shook his head. "I didn't see him."

"They still haven't called his name. You sure? He was all bundled up with a silly red carnation in his hat."

"That's him?" Oliver snorted. "I never would have recognized him."

"He wasn't quite so bundled up when he first got here." She shook her head. "Poor guy has been lost since his wife died."

"Dorothy died?" The country-fried steak pictured in the menu made his mouth water. "I hadn't heard."

"Cancer." Janice sighed. "Pancreatic. By the time she found out, nothing could be done. She endured several rounds of chemo and radiation treatments, but nothing helped."

Oliver swallowed. "Letty just found out she has pancreatic cancer."

Janice reached across the table and placed her hand on his wrist. "Oh, Oliver. I'm so sorry. Did they catch it early?"

He shook his head. "No. She's decided to pass on the treatment."

Janice nodded. "Can't say I blame her. The first chemo treatment was the beginning of the end for Dot."

"Was she still teaching?"

Janice shook her head. "She took ill early in the summer and died sometime in July. We hired her replacement less than a week before school started—young guy from Cincinnati. Tellumo Magnamater."

"Seriously?"

"Yeah, that's his name. Unusual, isn't it?"

Oliver nodded. "What's he like?"

"Smart, capable, talented, easy on the eyes." She smiled. "The kids love him."

"I see," Oliver said. "So you like him?"

"I do." She nodded and closed her menu. "He's passionate about teaching."

"Unlike someone else you know…." He'd failed to ignite a passion for history in any of his students.

"Oh, Oliver." She smiled. "You were a much better teacher than you give yourself credit for. Why did you pick teaching as a profession anyway?"

"Path of least resistance and a personal interest in history." He sighed. "Definitely wasn't passion."

A waitress plunked two glasses of water on the table. "Y'all ready to order?"

After Janice ordered blackened catfish with steamed vegetables and rice, he thought about changing his order. Eating out was such a rare treat. To hell with what anyone else thought. "I'll have the country-fried steak with sawmill gravy, mashed potatoes, and green beans."

"Biscuits or cornbread?"

Who eats cornbread with gravy? Nobody he knew. "Biscuits, please."

She picked up the menus. "Alrighty, then. We'll have that out for ya in a jiffy."

An awkward silence fell over the table. Janice cleared her throat. "Oliver, the Teacher of the Year awards you racked up prove you didn't suck as a teacher." She looked him in the eye. "You're one of the few who ever managed to cover everything in the textbook—and you did it every year."

"Nobody told me covering everything was optional."

She laughed. "You and rules. You may have bored the hell out of your students—history isn't for everyone—but you never disrespected anyone or treated anyone unfairly."

"They hated me."

"No, they respected you and looked up to you."

"You missed the vulgar cartoons on the bathroom walls of me engaged in various sex acts with another man."

"That was you?" She smiled. "Could have sworn it was me." She placed her hand on his wrist. "Don't be so hard on yourself. You may not have been the best teacher your students ever had, but you're certainly one of the finest men they'll ever know."

No matter how many times Oliver swallowed, the lump in his throat wouldn't go away. He met her gaze. "Thanks, Janice." He paused and took a breath to regain his composure. "Coming from you, that means a lot."

Janice's opinion did mean a lot to him and always had. She was smart—some would say calculating—with an easy, affable way about her. Her high regard for Tellumo was a star in the golden boy's crown. Although friendly with everyone, she could count her friends on the fingers of one hand, and Oliver was one of them.

Janice's favor wasn't all that impressed him. He hadn't thought about what Tellumo might do for a living, but with a million chances, would never have guessed teaching. Choosing a low-paying career in education raised Oliver's esteem for the boy a notch or two.

Maybe Letty was right. Perhaps he had misjudged Tellumo. Keeping an open mind and giving him another chance was only fair.

Chapter Thirteen: Raining Cats and Dogs

THROUGH THE veil of rain pelting the windows, Tellumo and the students in his sixth-hour study hall watched a bent-up umbrella tumble across the schoolyard. Gusts of wind rippled the line of cedars edging the school grounds. The angry, dark clouds racing across the sky tricked streetlights and fixtures around the school's perimeter into thinking night had fallen.

The speaker mounted over the blackboard crackled, followed by Mr. Wyrick's voice. "May I have your attention, please?" He paused for a moment. "Because of the inclement weather and traffic problems arising from the long line of vehicles waiting to pick up students, the sheriff has asked us to close early."

Tellumo's class erupted into cheers and moved, en masse, toward the door. Tellumo glanced at the clock and saw they only had twenty more minutes. From the boisterous response echoing through the corridors and the loudspeaker, one would think they'd been given the day off.

"At this time, bus riders are released. Everyone else please remain seated."

As the chosen few left the room, groans filled the air. Tellumo stood and shouted to be heard above the commotion. "Okay, you heard Mr. Wyrick. Unless you ride the bus, take a seat."

The remaining two-thirds of his class grumbled and moped as they returned to their desks. Five minutes passed before Mr. Wyrick addressed the school again. "To keep the traffic congestion from getting any worse, at this time we're releasing everyone *except* students who drive to school."

More cheers than groans greeted his announcement as all but a handful of the remaining students left the room. Streetlights flickered and grew dim as a band of gray widened on the horizon. The winds had died down, but rain still fell in sheets. The telltale crackle again broke the silence. "Thank you for your patience. At this time, all—"

The bell announcing the end of another school day obscured his words.

"Again, all students are released at this time. Drive safely going home, and have a great weekend."

Tellumo stretched as the last remaining students filed out of the room, except for Dustin Delong, who stopped in front of Tellumo's desk and shifted his weight back and forth from one foot to the other. He had curly red hair, alabaster skin sprinkled with freckles, and startling blue eyes. "Hi, Dustin. What's up?"

"Uh, Mr. Magnamater, I was wondering if maybe you'd like to come to my gymnastics meet tomorrow. Lafayette—a big Lexington school—is coming to Fallisville, and I'm competing all-around for the first time." He blushed. "I mean, it's okay if you don't want to, but—"

"Am I interrupting something?" Melody stood at the door. "I'd have been here sooner, but the nasty weather slowed me down."

"Melody!" Tellumo was surprised to see her so soon. "Come on in." He waved her over. "Dustin was just telling me he's competing all-around for the first time in a big gymnastics meet tomorrow."

"Oh," Melody exclaimed. She hugged Tellumo and kissed his cheek. "I love gymnastics! What time is the meet?"

Dustin studied her like she'd sprouted a third eye. "Eleven o'clock."

Melody clasped her hands together and beamed. "We wouldn't miss it for the world!" She turned to Tellumo. "Unless you had other plans...."

Tellumo rose from his chair and met her teasing gaze. "Not until three thirty." Like she hadn't arranged for the cooking lessons with Peggy.

"The meet should be over by two at the latest," Dustin said, addressing the air between Tellumo and Melody.

"I guess it's settled, then." Tellumo smiled and nodded at Dustin. "We'll be there."

"Great!" His face lit up like he'd won the lottery. "I'll look for you." He turned to Melody and nodded. "Nice to meet you, ma'am."

"You too." She waved. "I'll be cheering for you tomorrow!"

"Thanks." He returned her wave, nodded at Tellumo, and then darted into the corridor. The sound of his shoes slapping the floor echoed for a moment and then faded away.

She smiled. "I'm guessing Dustin isn't the only student with the hots for you."

"For me?" He gaped at her. "What makes you think so?"

"My God, Tellumo, are you blind?" She laughed. "Did you see how his face fell when I kissed your cheek?"

"Then why did you say we'd go? I sure don't want to encourage him."

"Darling, that horse has left the barn." She patted his back. "Don't worry. Now that he thinks I'm your girlfriend, he won't be so forward again."

He looked at her. "How can you be so sure? You don't know him."

She threw her arms around him and laughed. "Trust me, I know. Bet he's the one who sent you the secret admirer valentine."

Tellumo's mouth fell open. Although Dustin wasn't on his list of suspects, he should have put two and two together as soon as Dustin had mentioned the gymnastics meet. "How did you know?"

"How did you not know?" She put her hands on her hips and shook her head. "If the adoring look in his eyes didn't clue you in, staying after class to invite you to watch him compete should have."

"I had no idea." Had Dustin been in one of the classes Tellumo taught, he might have noticed his interest earlier. Whether grading papers, updating lesson plans, or working on the literary magazine, Tellumo got more done in that last hour of the day than all the students in his study hall combined. Dustin could stare at him to his heart's content. Unless someone got too loud or otherwise attracted his notice, Tellumo rarely looked up from what he was doing.

"Made any plans for this evening?"

Tellumo shook his head. "Nope, other than kicking your butt at Mario Kart a few times. Anything in particular you want for dinner?"

She raised a finger to her pursed lips and furrowed her brow. "We'll probably end up eating our weight again at Peggy's tomorrow."

Tellumo nodded. "I hope so."

"Me too!" She laughed. "Let's stop at the store on the way to your place and get stuff for salad."

"Good idea." He grabbed his backpack from under the desk and pulled his coat from the hook on the back of the door. "Ready when you are."

HEAVY RAIN obscured the taillights of the car in front of him. Oliver pulled as far onto the shoulder as he could. Gravel crunched beneath the tires as he slowed, came to a stop, and flipped on his hazard lights. No matter how bad he had to pee, better to wait out the worst of the storm than to end up in an accident or stranded in a ditch.

Rain pounded the roof and cascaded down the windows, preventing him from seeing anything but the illuminated instrument panel and a Jiffy Lube sticker in the corner of the windshield indicating when his car was due for an oil change. Walls of water crashed against the Taurus as drivers lacking the good sense to pull over sailed past him. "Idiots!"

Had he known the horrific storm was coming, he'd have stayed home. The accuracy of Bill Pinkley's forecasts had nosedived since Oliver and Janice had seen the poor man shivering in the cold with a ragged carnation clutched in his gloved hands as they were leaving the Dinner Barn. He was clearly insane with grief and no longer had his head in the game. Where would Oliver go for forecasts and updates now? The Lexington and Cincinnati stations never even mentioned little Fallisville.

The radio wasn't much better for local weather information. Oliver scanned stations from one end of the dial to the other, again and again. Not a word about the downpour—except for maybe on one of the Hispanic stations. The eight words of Spanish he knew weren't enough to glean even a vague idea what he'd heard. Probably something about masculine enhancement products or egg donation centers. Aside from music, that's all he heard on any of the other stations.

He stomped the floorboard and whacked the steering wheel with his palms. "Dammit!" He had better things to do. Oliver preferred traveling from point A to point B as quickly and efficiently as possible. Sitting on the side of the road, clenching his knees together to hold it in, and waiting for the deluge to let up was getting him nowhere fast.

Travel was overrated. He'd skip the tedious journey, thank you very much. Driving to Dayton to visit Letty and Sid was about all the trip he could handle anymore. Forget about boarding a plane—he remembered when flying had been pleasant and enjoyable, in spacious cabins with wide seats and plenty of legroom. Until teleporting was possible, he wasn't going anywhere more than two or three hours by car from Fallisville.

He squinted and peered through the windshield but couldn't see beyond the overwhelmed wipers. Going to the gym early to free up his evening had backfired. Instead of more time to work on his book, he'd have less—a lot less, if the rain didn't let up soon.

Until the sudden onset of heavy rain beating against the gym's metal roof, the gathering clouds had escaped Oliver's notice. Had he been paying attention, he'd have cut short the new Friday workout Tellumo had given him and left when the gloom had induced the lights to come on in the parking lot. In his haste to get home, he'd ignored nature's call and left the gym without making a pit stop—a decision he'd since come to regret.

Tellumo was to blame. Had he not canceled their Friday workout appointment, Oliver would have gone to Fit as a Fiddle at his usual time and missed the storm. Instead of sitting in his car squeezing his knees together, he'd be home, writing—like he'd hoped to do with the rest of his day.

Wednesday's session had gone better than he'd expected. Tellumo's workout had kicked Oliver's butt. He wasn't about to be outdone, and had pushed himself harder than ever before. He'd gone through an entire tube of Bengay since then and still ached in places where he hadn't known muscles existed.

Tellumo's extensive knowledge had impressed Oliver. No wonder Janice liked Tellumo so much. He didn't just show Oliver what to do, he explained the rationale for the exercise, demonstrated proper technique, and highlighted variations to target different parts of the muscle. Oliver welcomed the constructive criticism about the way he'd been working out before his run-in with Tellumo.

Of course, Tellumo's appearance didn't hurt. Easy on the eyes was an understatement. Janice had never seen him at the gym. If Oliver could create the ideal man, he'd look an awful lot like Tellumo—minus the piercings and tattoos. Huge muscles were too much of a statement for Oliver, and he wasn't attracted to super skinny guys, no matter how fit they might be. A little body fat was a good thing, especially for cuddling.

Picturing a beautiful body in his mind's eye normally triggered a biological response, and would have had Oliver not had to pee so badly. The steady tattoo of raindrops striking the car tormented him and magnified his suffering. He couldn't escape the trickling, rushing, and splashing of thousands of gallons of water.

Wetting himself was too humiliating to contemplate. He'd never get the odor out of his upholstery and his car would smell like a nursing home. People would think he wore those old man diapers. There wasn't a thing wrong with his plumbing, not that he knew of, anyway. Whether everything still worked on demand was a mystery, but voluntary erections popped up all the time.

Despite his discomfort, Oliver couldn't stop thinking about his gorgeous workout partner. Between sets, they'd talked about living alone, cooking for one, and life in Fallisville. Tellumo wasn't just a pretty face on a beautiful body. The boy had brains and a charming way about him Oliver found hard to resist.

"Damn whippersnapper," he muttered.

His annoyance increased with the urgency of his need. If he didn't do something—and soon—he feared his bladder might explode. Kevin's beer-loving Aunt Shelley had died at a Vikings game when hers had burst while waiting in line for the bathroom at halftime. Oliver had never believed the story, but now, as he danced in his seat, he wasn't so sure.

A thorough search of the interior turned up no empty bottles, cups, or other containers for a makeshift urinal. No surprise. He was far too tidy to have left something behind, but he'd looked anyway. Getting out to check the supplies in his trunk wasn't necessary. He knew exactly what was there. The cat litter, blanket, nonperishable snacks, and a kit his mother had given him years ago for Christmas with jumper cables, hazard triangles, a can of foam tire sealant, and other emergency supplies offered no help.

With nary a shrub in sight, relieving himself on the side of the road with traffic whizzing by wasn't an option. He'd get arrested, and a thorough soaking in this weather would make him sick. He'd end up with pneumonia and die a miserable, lonely death in the Salt Lick County Jail.

Spending his final moments waiting for his bladder to explode wasn't an option. The anxiety would kill him first. Time to take control of his destiny.

Oliver put the Taurus into gear, checked his mirrors, and then eased back onto the road with his hazard lights blinking. Fear of hydroplaning and limited visibility kept him from going faster than thirty miles per hour. Oncoming headlights and pooling water rendered the yellow and white striping invisible, but the reflectors built into the pavement kept him in his lane.

His overfull bladder, staying on the road, and thoughts of Tellumo competed for his attention. The wake of vehicles going by him, whether moving in the opposite direction or passing him, buffeted his car and completely obscured his view of the road. Screw the people honking horns and flashing headlights behind him. They couldn't possibly be in a bigger hurry than he was.

Maybe he'd misjudged Tellumo. Letty and Janice seemed to think so. The age difference was an insurmountable obstacle to a serious relationship, but that didn't mean they couldn't be friends.

The rain had eased by the time he turned into Thoroughbred Acres. Traffic ceased to be a problem in the quiet residential neighborhood. He drove as fast as the curvy, narrow streets allowed, repeatedly pushing the button on his garage door opener starting a good block outside of the receiver's range.

He pulled into the garage, jumped out of his car, and ran to the kitchen door, slamming the button to close the garage as he entered the house. The telephone was ringing, but Oliver had a more urgent call to answer. Bent over with need, he hobbled to the bathroom, fumbling to unfasten his belt, the button on his pants, and the zipper as he beelined for the toilet.

Relief was immediate. Oliver sighed with pleasure as the cursed phone stopped ringing and the pressure in his bladder abated. He stood before the porcelain bowl for a long time. Not since the day or two before penicillin had cured him of the gonorrhea Steve had given him for his twenty-fifth birthday had urinating taken so long. Oliver had doubted Steve's dubious claim to have picked up the STD from a toilet seat, but feared losing him too much to say so and had kept his mouth shut.

Idiot.

In truth, he'd been more lucky than careful. His wildest and most reckless days had taken place before anyone had heard of AIDS or HIV, and birth control was the only reason to wear a rubber. Since then, he'd rarely used a condom because he hadn't had to. After the initial testing, unprotected sex in a monogamous relationship was safe—unless, of course, only half the couple was monogamous.

Oliver removed his clothes and climbed into the shower. The fragrant sandalwood soap calmed his nerves, but the gentle mist spritzing from the showerhead did nothing for the sore muscles in his chest and shoulders. A bath would have been a better choice, but the tub needed a good scouring first.

The distinctive ring of the princess phone on his bedside table startled him. Days might pass without a single call, and in less than an hour, he'd received two. The soap covering his body leered at the pathetic but persistent drizzle, yielding ground inch by slow inch. The phone stopped ringing long before the last of the lather went down the drain.

Maybe Tellumo's plans had fallen through and he was calling to see about working out together. Although he'd already worked out, he'd go back to the gym. If it was Tellumo calling—and that was a mighty big if.

Oliver dried off, moisturized, and slipped into his flannel shirt and house pants. Wondering who called was a game he no longer allowed himself to play. Thinking he'd missed a response to one of his letters from a federal or state agency, the governor of Kentucky, or maybe even the president of the United States drove him nuts. On the rare occasion when the phone did happen to ring again, his guesses were always wrong. Unless the caller tried again, he'd never know.

PEGGY COULDN'T wait for Melody and Tellumo to arrive. She needed the distraction. She'd not heard a word from Mr. Crumbly since before

Tuesday. Checking the computer every two minutes was driving her crazy and keeping her from accomplishing anything.

She'd waved when she'd seen him at the gym, but stopped short of introducing herself. As usual, he looked right through her. He always looked so angry! A week or two of her cooking would put a smile on his face, but until then, she'd leave him alone at the gym. Her workout attire wasn't exactly the most flattering outfit she owned anyway, and she still hadn't let Giorgio transform her with a makeover.

Patsy Curtsinger's Florida vacation kept her from missing work Wednesday morning. Lurleen had stopped by Tuesday evening with weirdo Martin Shankley, who'd been kind enough to jump her battery. Peggy was pretty sure he'd jumped Lurleen shortly thereafter, but she hadn't asked. If Lurleen wanted her to know, she'd tell her, though why on earth she'd keep anything from Peggy was beyond her.

She thought about e-mailing Mr. Crumbly, but nothing she typed sounded right. "Sorry I missed you, but I got out of work late, couldn't find anything to wear, and my battery died" sounded too much like "I had to wash my hair." Besides, she didn't want to send the wrong message. No point in him thinking she was desperate—even if she was.

The foul-mouthed fornicators next door had loaded up their noisy jalopy and driven off before lunch. They'd left the front porch light on, giving Peggy hope they wouldn't get home until after her guests were gone. The headphones Lurleen had recommended did the trick when she was by herself but would never do for company. Listening to her Statesmen Quartet's CD was far more enjoyable, and she hardly noticed the vibrating floor.

The daisy-covered VW—Vanessa, she'd learned—pulled up in front of the duplex. Tellumo stepped out of the passenger side, looking handsome in black slacks and a purple-and-yellow sweatshirt. Melody was similarly dressed.

"Y'all sure look cute in your matching outfits," Peggy said, grinning from ear to ear as she held the door open for them.

"Salt Lick County High School colors," Tellumo said. "We wore our purple and gold to a gymnastics meet this afternoon."

"Good to see you again!" Melody flung her arms around Peggy's shoulders and squeezed.

Thrilled by the warm reception, Peggy hugged her back. "Did you get caught in the storm driving down?"

Melody nodded. "Sure did." She shuddered. "Hydroplaning is scary. Vanessa almost kissed a guardrail, but we got here in one piece."

"Praise Jesus! I don't know when I've ever seen so much rain." Peggy ushered them into the kitchen. "Let's get the yeast rolls started, and then we'll visit, okay?" She supervised as Tellumo and Melody measured out the ingredients, tested the water temperature, and set the yeast to proof. The darling couple worked well as a team and clearly enjoyed being together. Her happiness for them trumped her envy.

In between steps, Melody shared what she'd learned about embroidery software. "Except for an embellishment here and there, your designs are all text."

Peggy nodded. "Hand-stitching lettering is time-consuming enough."

"Text is easy to program into the sewing machine," Tellumo said. "Working from scanned images or photographs is a lot more complicated."

"On the other hand," Melody said, "you can easily add images to text-only designs with a few mouse clicks. Want me to show you?"

Ten minutes later, Tellumo and Melody cooked while Peggy created files for each of her designs. The happy trio worked all afternoon. When shouted questions required more than a verbal response, Tellumo or Melody came to the spare bedroom or Peggy joined them in the kitchen.

She tried dozens of different fonts, playing with the size of the text and a wide range of special effects until she was happy. The clip art Melody had downloaded—hundreds of simple line drawings—enabled Peggy to dress things up with praying hands, doves in flight, angel wings, or stone tablets. Uploading the designs to the website Tellumo put together in a matter of minutes was a piece of cake. Charging more for the fancier designs was a no-brainer. Browsing through the images gave her dozens of ideas for new products too.

Melody came to the door with a wooden spoon in one hand and a baking pan in the other. She gave the metal pan a solid whack and struck a pose. "Dinner is prepared!"

Tellumo stood at the dining room table with a towel folded over his arm. "Allow me." He pulled out her chair.

Peggy took her seat, shifting as Tellumo pushed her closer to the table. She surveyed the spread before her and nodded. "Everything looks perfect."

Tellumo pulled out Melody's chair. She smiled and gave him a nervous look. "So far, so good."

Peggy gave thanks after Tellumo sat down, silently adding her gratitude for the neighbors' absence. After the roast beef, mushroom gravy, mashed potatoes, green beans, and yeast rolls had made their way around the table, she looked up to see Tellumo and Melody staring at her.

"Well…?" Melody said.

"How is it?" Tellumo gave her a worried look.

The way they finished each other's sentences was adorable. Peggy dragged a bite of roast beef through the gravy, raised her fork, and sniffed. "Smells delicious." The darling couple leaned forward and watched as Peggy chewed. The gravy was a little thin, and she'd have added another shake or two of salt and pepper, but all in all, they'd done well. She nodded. "I couldn't have done better myself."

Tellumo and Melody cheered, high-fived each other, and bumped fists. He leaned over and squeezed Peggy's wrist. "We couldn't have done it without you."

"Yeah." Melody nodded. "For sure, and I think maybe I could follow the recipes without your help now."

Tellumo nodded in solemn agreement. "You explain things really well." He smiled. "A natural-born teacher."

"Why, thank you!" Peggy glanced at the clock. To compensate for time lost to conversation, she'd decided to add fifteen minutes to her dinner hour. "I always wanted to be a home economics teacher."

"Do they even have them anymore?" Melody looked at Tellumo.

He nodded. "They call it family and consumer sciences." He chewed a moment and then turned to Peggy. "Why didn't you?"

Peggy poked at her mashed potatoes with her fork. "College really wasn't an option." Not without a high school diploma. She looked down at her plate and speared several green beans.

An awkward silence fell over the table. They ate wordlessly, accompanied by the clink of Peggy's good silver on the fancy china she'd mostly bought for herself over the years.

"You know…," Melody said, tilting her head as she looked at Tellumo, "for your mother's birthday dinner, instead of going to the Fallis House, we should cook something."

"Great idea, but my apartment isn't big enough." Tellumo smiled. "We'd have to eat on a blanket in the parking lot or something."

"You could have it here." Peggy beamed. "I'll even make the cake."

"Oh, no," Tellumo said. "I couldn't impose on you." He looked to Melody for support.

"Impose?" Peggy placed her hand over her heart. "I'd love to meet your parents!" She looked at the empty seats around the table. "And I've certainly got the room."

"Really, Peggy—"

"Nonsense!" She slapped the table with both hands. "I insist. When are they coming?"

"Last Saturday in March—three weeks from today."

Peggy got up and looked at the calendar she kept on the refrigerator. "It's a date." She wrote "Birthday Party" in the block and returned to her seat.

"I'm sure they'll love you," Melody said. She turned to Tellumo and smiled. "Don't you think, honey?"

"Sure!" Tellumo turned to Peggy. "It's just that, well… they're—"

"Vegetarians," Melody finished for him.

Peggy had heard of such creatures but wasn't sure she'd ever met one. She furrowed her brow. "They only eat vegetables?"

"Anything but beef, pork, or poultry," Melody replied. "We could find a good recipe for a main dish online."

"Sounds like a plan to me," Peggy said. She and Melody turned to Tellumo.

Tellumo raised his hands in surrender. "Okay." He sighed. "If you insist."

"I do." Peggy said with a quick nod. She pictured the scene. She'd sit at the head of the table, with handsome Tellumo and darling Melody to her right, and his equally attractive mom and dad on her left. Two lovely couples, and her—the widow Tucker—as necessary as a fifth wheel.

Peggy needed a date. As she thought about her options, another silence fell over the table. If she played her cards right, she could kill two birds with one dinner. She turned to Tellumo. "Have you made many friends since you moved here?"

He shook his head. "Not really—I've been too busy."

Melody poked his arm. "What about Oliver Crumbly?"

Peggy could have kissed her. She sopped up gravy with a roll and stuffed it into her mouth.

"I wouldn't exactly call us friends…."

"Working out together three times a week makes you friends," Melody said. "And from what you've said about him, he could use a friend or two."

Tellumo sighed. "He's mad at the world because he's all alone."

Peggy saw her opening. "Well, goodness sakes! Invite him to join us."

Melody clasped her hands together. "What a good idea!" She turned to Peggy. "Tellumo talks about him all the time, and I haven't had the pleasure of meeting him."

Tellumo shrugged. "I'll ask him, but don't be surprised if he says no."

He'd come. Peggy had yet to meet the man who'd turn down a free meal, especially when home cooking was involved. She'd dazzle him with her hospitality, culinary skills, and natural charm. The end of the month left plenty of time to find something nice to wear. Next week, she'd let Giorgio have his way with her too. Like the good book says, today is the first day of the rest of your life, and for Peggy, the future was filled with possibilities.

Chapter Fourteen: Regrets

OLIVER POKED at the pasta dish he'd fixed for his Sunday evening dinner with little enthusiasm. If he weren't so hungry, he'd toss the vile concoction. Coming up with an idea for something else to fix, however, appealed to him even less than eating the sickly sweet mess before him.

Frozen shrimp—cooked, deveined, and with tails removed—were a staple he kept on hand for quick and easy meals. Sometimes he added them to a green salad. More often, he stirred a can of diced tomatoes and a little seasoning into cooked pasta, added the shrimp, sprinkled mozzarella cheese across the top, and then popped the finished dish under the broiler for a few minutes. Bored with the same old same old, he'd tried something different. The creamy shrimp and mushroom pasta recipe he'd cut out of the newspaper called for half-and-half. Having none, Oliver had substituted a cup of sweetened condensed milk—a decision he'd since come to regret.

He grimaced and shuddered as the saccharine flavor hit his tongue and then swallowed. He'd choke down the rest and be done with it. Chasing each bite with a generous swig of wine helped some, leading him to consume three glasses rather than the one he usually had with dinner. The more he drank, the less the unusual taste bothered him.

As he was washing up the dishes, the telephone rang again. He grabbed the dish towel, dried his hands, and lifted the handset to his ear. "Hello?"

"She's gone, Oliver." Sid sobbed.

"What?" Oliver collapsed onto a chair.

"Letty's gone." A long pause followed, punctuated by the sound of Sid crying. "She complained about being short of breath after dinner last night and then started coughing up blood." He sniffed. "I took her to the emergency room, but there was nothing they could do."

"Oh my God, Sid." Tears streamed down Oliver's cheeks. He got up, pulled a paper towel off the roll, and dabbed his eyes. "I was planning to come up next weekend."

"She would have liked that." He sniffed. "Me too. We've been friends a long time."

"Oh, Sid." Oliver couldn't stop crying. He'd been certain he'd see her again. All he could think about were the things he wished he'd had the chance to tell her, like how much he loved her and what her friendship had meant to him over the years. But Sid needed his support right now, not the other way around. "I don't have to tell you how much in love with you she was."

"I've been a lucky man."

Oliver nodded. "Do they know what happened?"

"Pulmonary embolism." Sid's breath hitched. "In a way, I'm glad—at least she didn't suffer." Silence punctuated by sobs followed for a moment. "What am I going to do without her?"

The same question was going through Oliver's mind. He fought to maintain his composure. "Is anyone there with you?"

"Junior and his family. The rest of the boys should be here soon."

"Good." Sid Junior was the oldest of their four sons. "How are the boys?"

"Devastated," Sid replied. "We thought we'd have a few more months." He paused for a moment and blew his nose. "She'd lost weight and tired easily, but otherwise seemed to be doing okay—at least as well as expected."

"I'm so sorry." Oliver ran a hand through his thinning hair as regret washed over him. He should have gone to see her, called more often than once a week, written the letters he'd composed in his head recalling some of the more memorable events from their forty-plus years of friendship. "Have you made any arrangements yet?"

"Letty took care of the details a few days after we got the diagnosis." His voice quivered. "She made me promise not to drag things out. Visitation will be tomorrow night at the Newcomer Funeral Home with services Tuesday at the Tree of Life Unitarian Church."

Oliver grabbed a pen and jotted down the information. "I'll drive up tomorrow morning."

"Might be a little crowded, but you're welcome to stay here."

"Are Letty's brother and sisters coming?"

"Yes, but they're staying at a hotel."

Good idea. Being around kids was hard enough in the best of circumstances. "I'll get a room too."

"Call me when you get in town," Sid said. "Until we leave for the funeral home, we'll be here."

"Will do. Give the boys my love."

Oliver hung up the phone. Nobody could hear him wailing, not that he cared or could stop himself if he did care. Losing his parents hadn't hit him so hard. He'd known they'd die sooner or later and, after the way they'd responded when he'd come out, had grieved for the death of their relationship years before they passed on.

Letty and he were the same age. He couldn't remember a time when they hadn't been friends. She wasn't supposed to die before him and, unlike his parents, had always accepted him and loved him unconditionally. He pulled another paper towel from the roll, wiped the tears from his face, and blew his nose.

The telephone ringing startled him. He pulled himself together and answered the phone. "Hello," he croaked.

"Hi, Oliver. It's Tellumo." He paused for a moment. "Have I caught you at a bad time?"

Oliver's lip trembled. He wanted to reply, but the words couldn't get past the lump in his throat. All that escaped was a gut-wrenching sob.

"Are you okay?"

The question and the concern in Tellumo's voice triggered another breakdown. He bit his knuckle in a futile attempt to regain his composure.

"Oliver, what's wrong?"

"I can't talk right now." The phone slipped from his hands, fell with a crash, and slid across the floor. Oliver got up, retrieved the handset, and hung up. Then he sat back down and cried.

PEGGY COULDN'T believe how much progress filling back orders she'd made in a few hours. Without the fancy new programmable sewing machine she'd run down to the fabric store in Lexington to buy after church, stitching the finished products spread across the dining room table would have taken a week or more. Her only regret was not buying the miraculous device sooner.

She'd paid more than she'd planned to spend, but felt no remorse. The speed justified the extra two hundred dollars—more than six hundred stitches a minute—not to mention sixty spools of embroidery thread, prewound bobbins, a CD with thousands of designs, and a variety of attachments that came with her purchase. Judging from today's output, she'd recover the cost in no time.

Figuring out how to use the fancy contraption was easier than she'd expected. Turns out, the software Melody had installed wasn't necessary after all, but the time she'd invested creating designs on her computer hadn't been wasted. A USB port made transferring the files as easy as one, two, three.

Peggy smiled. Meeting Tellumo and Melody had changed her life. The help they'd provided to grow her business and make better use of technology was huge. Even bigger, however, was the impact on her frame of mind. Spending time with the fun-loving youngsters gave her something to look forward to and made her happy.

The darling couple's love for each other was obvious. The enviable friendship they shared boded well for a long and happy marriage. If Tellumo got on the stick and popped the question, a June wedding was still possible. She'd love to see them tie the knot in the garden at the Fallis House but suspected the marriage would take place in Cincinnati. Either way, assuming they'd invite her, she'd go. The thought of bearing witness to what she was certain would be a gorgeous ceremony brought a tear to her eye.

She picked up a potholder and studied the embroidery. The quality was every bit as good as what she did by hand. Better, really. She prided herself on the uniformity of her stitches, but the machine was more consistent, and the figure with outstretched arms she'd added really dressed things up.

Her stomach rumbled. The time had passed so quickly she'd forgotten to eat supper. She got up and checked her refrigerator. Opting to run to Lexington instead of grocery shopping like she usually did after Sunday morning services left her with few choices. Breakfast for dinner would do the trick.

She turned the oven on to preheat and pulled sausage, eggs, butter, and milk from the refrigerator, along with a box of Bisquick from the cabinet. Making biscuits from scratch took too long, and she didn't have any buttermilk. In a pinch, she could get by with toast, but gravy without biscuits was like a day without sunshine. Cleaning the cast-iron skillet she fried sausage in would be easier if she made gravy too.

After flipping the sausage patties, she popped the biscuits into the oven and set the timer for twenty minutes. She was about to wash up the mixing bowl when she heard a familiar chime on her computer. *Oliver?*

She hurried to the dining room table and saw a one-word message on the screen from HorseHungDude. "Horny?" Before she could block him, the chime sounded again and a picture of a penis next to a box of oats popped up. She shuddered. The gargantuan organ was as long as the cylindrical box and almost as wide. She offered a silent prayer of gratitude none of her husbands had been cursed with such an intimidating endowment and clicked on the box to make him and the horrifying image disappear.

The aroma of savory sausage filled the air, causing her stomach to growl. She transferred the patties to a paper-towel-covered plate to drain, sprinkled flour into the skillet, and poured the eggs she'd whisked with a little cream over the melted butter bubbling in a sauté pan. She added milk to the browned flour, stirring the gravy with one hand and eggs with the other until the timer indicating the biscuits were ready went off.

Although eating dinner only took twenty minutes, Peggy was too full to contemplate another bite. She washed the dishes, tidied up the kitchen, and was about to resume her fancywork when her phone rang. Peggy glanced at the screen but didn't recognize the number. "Hello?"

"Hi, Peggy. It's Tellumo."

What a pleasant surprise! "Well hello! I was just thinking about you. How are you this evening?"

"I'm good, thanks." He paused for a moment. "Listen, I hate to ask, but I really need a favor."

She beamed. After all he'd done for her, she'd do whatever she could to help. "I owe you at least one. What do you need?"

"I called Oliver to invite him to the birthday dinner—"

"Can he come?" She hadn't meant to cut him off, but her excitement got the better of her.

"Something is wrong. He hung up before I got a chance to ask. I was hoping you could pick me up so I could check on him."

"Of course!" Coming to Oliver's aid appealed to her as much as doing a favor for Tellumo. She glanced at the faux grandfather clock. "I'll be there in fifteen minutes."

"Thanks, Peggy." He gave her his address. "Just pull up out front. I'll watch for you."

She leaped from her chair and hurried to the bathroom to freshen up, discarding her robe and nightgown along the way. Her hair was a wreck and her makeup needed refreshing, but she didn't have time to doll herself up. She fluffed her hair with her fingers, touched up her lipstick, threw on some clothes, and hurried to her car.

ASKING PEGGY to pick him up bothered Tellumo less when an Internet search revealed Oliver lived around the corner from her. Rather than waiting outside, she could drop Tellumo off and go back home. When he was ready to leave, he could walk back to her duplex—unless Oliver wanted to drive him back to his apartment.

He'd never known anyone quite like Peggy. Unlike the women who'd surrounded him when he was growing up, she embraced religion, domesticity, and men. Her boundless enthusiasm, eternal optimism, and generous spirit impressed him as much as her naiveté, and the pseudo Bible quotes she tossed around amused him. The more he was around her, the more he liked her.

As a general rule, he avoided overtly religious people. Hearing them say he'd burn in hell for all eternity pretty much ended any chance of friendship. Peggy was different from other churchgoers he'd encountered. Not once had she ever used religion as a weapon. Still, he worried about how she'd react when she found out Tellumo had two mothers and Melody wasn't his girlfriend. Springing the news on her didn't feel right, but he hadn't found the nerve to tell her.

Peggy didn't talk about her past, but Tellumo got the impression she'd experienced more sadness and disappointment than joy. She deserved better. He'd never met anyone so willing to go out of their way to help other people. Rather than resenting his call, she'd dropped whatever she'd been doing to help him.

Going to see Oliver, uninvited and unannounced, was more troublesome. Oliver might not answer, and if he did, he might slam the door in Tellumo's face. Even so, he'd take his chances. Better to be rebuffed than to find out later checking on him would have made a difference.

Headlights swept the front of his apartment building as a car pulled into the parking lot. Tellumo recognized Peggy's Saturn and, after locking up his apartment, loped out to meet her. The car rolled to a stop, and Tellumo opened the door.

"I really appreciate you picking me up," he said as he slid onto the seat.

"Glad I could help," she said. "Where are we going?"

"Calumet Circle," Tellumo replied. "In Thoroughbred Acres."

"I know exactly where that is." She put the car in gear and headed for the parking lot entrance. "Any idea what's wrong?"

"He didn't say." Tellumo shook his head. "Said he couldn't talk."

"Oh dear," Peggy said. "I hope it's nothing serious." She glanced at Tellumo and then returned her gaze to the road. "Sweet of you to check on him."

Tellumo hoped Oliver felt the same way. "I had to do something. He sounded too upset to be alone." He looked both ways as Peggy pulled out of the parking lot and onto the road.

"Living by myself makes me nervous." She glanced at Tellumo. "If I fell and hit my head or something, I might lie on the floor for days before anyone found me."

Tellumo nodded. "I know what you mean. Don't you keep your phone with you?"

"I don't." Peggy laughed. "Can't believe I never thought of that. What a good idea!"

"Well," Tellumo said with a smile, "to tell you the truth, my smartphone always being within reach is less about safety than staying connected."

"Turning off my computer is hard enough. If I had a fancy phone like yours, I'd never get any sleep."

They rode along for a while without talking. Christian pop music played in the background. Tellumo broke the comfortable silence. "Hope I'm not keeping you from something. I know you have a lot of orders to fill."

"The only thing you're keeping me from is an empty house," Peggy replied. "Believe it or not, I'm almost caught up on all those orders. I ran down to Lexington after church today and bought a programmable sewing machine." She shot him a quick look. "It's amazing, and easier to use than I would have thought—at least so far."

"That's great!" He smiled. "And you figured out how to use it all by yourself?"

"Yes, but only because you and your girlfriend have taught me so much about using a computer."

Tellumo gulped. "Um…."

"Well, here we are." She pulled up in front of a ranch house. "I'll wait for you."

The moment had passed. Relief washed over him. "Thanks for offering, but you don't have to do that."

Concern furrowed her brow. "Are you sure? I don't mind."

"Positive." Tellumo opened the door and stepped onto the curb.

"How will you get home?"

"If Oliver won't take me, I'll call you." He smiled. "Keep your phone close by." He shut the car door and waved as Peggy drove off.

Chapter Fifteen: Revelations

PEGGY TURNED on her computer and stared at the screen. She had two orders for the few items she'd left up on Christian Bazaar, and more than a dozen directly from the web page Tellumo had created for her. To avoid the handling fees they charged, she'd wanted to take down all her listings from Christian Bazaar, but Melody had suggested leaving up a few of her most popular items with a link so potential customers could find the home page of Peggy's Fancywork.

The orders could wait. Tellumo's reaction when she'd referred to Melody as his girlfriend had surprised her. Rather than pleased, he'd looked pained. Lurleen's comment about his tattoo popped into her head. She needed to know if the pink triangle on his shoulder meant something.

She typed, "What does a pink triangle mean" into her browser and hit Enter. The first entry was something about Nazi symbols. Tellumo was far too nice to be a modern-day Nazi. She'd heard about them. Tellumo had long hair too. No way he was one of those skinheads.

The next two entries had to do with LGBT. Peggy had no idea what organization used the acronym. The first link offered no explanation. She clicked on the next and gasped when the web site for the Association of Lesbian, Gay, Bisexual, and Transgender Issues in Counseling of Alabama came up. She ruled out lesbian and transgender right away. By the time she finished reading, her hopes he was maybe bisexual had been dashed.

Poor Melody. No wonder she'd been fooled. Tellumo didn't seem homosexual. The muscular young man never lisped or acted girly and had shown no unusual interest in Broadway musicals. She picked up her phone, selected Lurleen's number, and pressed Call.

"Hey, Lurleen. It's Peggy. Got a minute?"

"Sure. Just watching *Tender Hearts* with Marvin. What's going on?"

"Well." Peggy chewed her lip for a moment, unsure how to broach the subject. "I looked up pink triangles on the Internet."

"Oh?" Lurleen paused. "What did you find out?"

"I'm pretty sure you know." She swallowed. "Tellumo is one of those homosexuals." She waited a moment for Lurleen's reaction but got none.

"I'm stunned. That poor girl…." She heard Lurleen whispering something but couldn't make out the words. Then…

"Poor girl? What makes you say that?"

"Good grief, Lurleen." Sometimes her cluelessness was exasperating. "Can't you put two and two together? She's about to marry him!"

"They got engaged?"

"No." Peggy shook her head. "But she's been looking at china patterns and spends the night with him all the time." She heard more whispering and then Marvin laughing.

"If I had to guess, I'd say she already knows."

"You really think so?" Peggy didn't see how such a thing was possible.

"I do. Young people don't care about that stuff these days. I bet they're best friends."

Peggy didn't know what to say. The idea had never occurred to her, but it made sense after she thought about it. She'd never seen them kiss, hold hands, or cuddle. They'd hugged her lots of times, but never each other. "Maybe you're right."

"Does him being gay matter to you?"

The question gave her pause. "The good book says—"

"Oh crap, Peggy. You like the boy, right?" Lurleen sounded downright angry.

"I'm not sure."

"Come on," Lurleen snapped. "He's all you've talked about since you met him."

She had a point. The truth was, Peggy did like Tellumo—a lot. Otherwise, she wouldn't be so upset. He and Melody had enriched her life beyond measure, and not just from the money Peggy's Fancywork was bringing in. "He seemed like such a good kid."

"Because he *is* a good kid, and from what I see, meeting him has been the best thing to happen to you in years."

"Maybe you're right."

"No maybe to it. He's still the same guy. Do you want him in your life or not?"

Peggy wiped a tear from her cheek. She hadn't seen as much of Lurleen since she'd been going out with Marvin. Without Tellumo and Melody, she'd be lonelier than ever. "I do."

"Then you need to get over your prejudice and accept the boy the way he is."

Prejudice? Peggy chafed at her remark but nodded anyway. "You're right. Thanks for the advice." They exchanged pleasantries for a few minutes before saying good-bye and ending the call.

Lurleen *was* right. Tellumo and Melody meant the world to her. Finding out Tellumo was homosexual and Melody wasn't his girlfriend shouldn't make any difference. They'd certainly never lied or attempted to mislead her. Their looming nuptials were entirely a figment of her imagination.

A chime sounded, and an instant message from LonelyNFallisville appeared on her screen. Her hand went to her throat, and she gasped.

Hi.

Hello! Are you okay? She hit Enter and waited for his response.

Better now. I was afraid you wouldn't respond. An oversized emoticon with a giant smile followed.

The smiley face surprised her. Tellumo said Oliver was too upset to talk. *Is Tellumo still with you?*

What's Tellumo?

Peggy's heart skipped a beat. LonelyNFallisville wasn't Oliver Crumbly. She thought for a moment about how to respond. *Never mind. I need to apologize for missing you at the Dinner Barn. My car battery died and I never got there.*

Really? I thought you weren't interested.

Throwing caution to the wind, Peggy replied. *I'm interested. You seem like a very nice man.*

Another big smiley face appeared, followed by a raised thumb, exploding fireworks, and several big red exclamation marks. *You just made my day.*

Peggy smiled. Whoever LonelyNFallisville was, he'd just made her day too. *Same here.* She thought for a moment and added, *I'm Peggy Tucker.*

Nice to meet you, Peggy. Bill Pinkley here.

Peggy gasped. *The Channel 13 weatherman?*

Yeah, that's me. Remember, the television adds ten pounds.

Peggy laughed. For the next hour, they chatted. Unlike before, she wasn't afraid to answer his questions and was surprised to discover they had so much in common. When he invited her to meet at the Dinner Barn Monday evening, she asked if he minded waiting until Thursday. Tuesday she'd shop for a new outfit and get the makeover Giorgio had promised. Wednesday she had prayer meeting. She was thrilled when he said he wouldn't mind at all.

EVEN WITHOUT the address, Tellumo would have known which home belonged to Oliver. Signs on either side of the lush lawn admonished passersby to pick up after their pets. The manicured, weed-free bluegrass stood in stark contrast to the dandelion- and henbit-infested yards of his neighbors.

He took a deep breath and headed toward the front door. Despite his anxiety about the surprise visit, Tellumo was impressed with Oliver's beautiful yard. Grape hyacinths lined the brick walkway curving across the lawn to the stoop. Well-tended flowerbeds in front of the evergreen foundation shrubbery sported monochrome clumps of what he thought might be crocus in yellow, white, and purple amid patches of emerging daffodil and tulip foliage. Fragrant pink and yellow hyacinths planted in pots on either side of the door greeted him as he stepped onto the porch.

He took another deep breath, pressed the doorbell with a trembling finger, and heard the chime sound inside. After a moment, the front door opened. Oliver, dressed in a worn flannel shirt and pajama bottoms, glared at him through the storm door. "What do you want?"

"Just making sure you're okay. You sounded pretty upset on the phone. I was afraid maybe you needed help."

Oliver glanced at the street and then turned to look at his driveway. "How'd you get here?"

"A friend dropped me off." Tellumo shoved his hands into his pockets. "Well, looks like you're fine, so guess I'll head home."

"Wait." Oliver opened the storm door and waved him inside. "You're here, so you may as well come in."

"Thanks." Tellumo stepped inside and looked around a spacious living room furnished with a large leather sectional, two lamp stands, and an oversized coffee table. Original artwork, a flat-screen television, and a pair of large mirrors occupied the walls beneath a vaulted ceiling. The absence of any clutter, bric-a-brac, or even family photographs lent an air of austere simplicity.

Oliver led the way to an eat-in kitchen. Several straight-backed chairs surrounded a table in front of a bay window overlooking the backyard.

"Can I get you something to drink?" Oliver asked. "I've got red or white wine, iced tea, and water, or I could make a pot of coffee."

"No, thanks, I'm good." Tellumo settled into the chair across from several magazines and a newspaper indicating where Oliver usually sat.

"Are you sure? I'm going to have a glass of wine—merlot."

"Okay." Tellumo nodded. "If you insist." Oliver moved about the kitchen with efficient familiarity. Tellumo took in a collection of orchids in the bay window, and outside, splashes of color the dusk prevented him from identifying. "You've really got a nice place."

"Thank you." Oliver placed a half-filled wineglass in front of him and dropped into his chair. They sat in silence for a moment, sipping wine. "I'm glad you came," Oliver said finally. A tear slid down his cheek and onto the table.

"I was worried about you." He studied Oliver's face. Tears fell like rain, but Oliver either didn't notice or didn't care. "Are you okay?"

Oliver responded with a gut-wrenching sob. "I'm sorry." He dabbed his face with a crumpled paper towel and took several deep breaths. Moments passed before he regained his composure. "My best friend died of cancer last night." The floodgates opened. Oliver put his head down on his forearms and wept.

Tellumo came around the table, dropped to his haunches beside him, and draped his arm across Oliver's shaking shoulders. "I'm so sorry." Losing a loved one was beyond Tellumo's experience—a small advantage, he supposed, to having young parents and no extended family. The thought of something happening to Melody or one of his mothers was upsetting enough. He couldn't imagine how he'd cope.

"I should have gone to Dayton to see her."

Tellumo patted his back. He didn't know what to say and was surprised when Oliver threw his arms around him and sobbed onto his shoulder. Tellumo shifted position, looped his other arm around him, and held him as he cried.

"I'm sorry." Oliver released him and wiped his eyes.

Tellumo stood. "It's okay. Really. Do you want to talk about her?" He watched Oliver's face but saw no reaction. "She must have really been special."

Oliver nodded. "Scarlett O'Mara Dawson was one in a million."

"Scarlett O'Mara?" Tellumo smiled and sat down. "Really?"

"Yes." The corners of Oliver's mouth lifted, but didn't quite make it to a grin. "Her mother loved *Gone with the Wind*. Everyone called her Letty."

"I already love her." Tellumo thought talking about her might help. "How long have you known her?"

"Always." Oliver's breath caught. He looked up at the ceiling for a moment and back to Tellumo. "We grew up together. I traded my Hot Wheels, Matchbox cars, and accessories for all her Barbie stuff when I was eight years old." He looked at Tellumo with red-rimmed eyes. "My father had a conniption fit, but Mom played Barbie with me. She always wanted a girl."

Tellumo nodded. "I can relate. They never said so, but I'm sure my mothers wanted a girl."

Oliver raised an eyebrow. "Mothers?"

"I'm the son of two lesbians." He reached across the table and took Oliver's hands. "Tell me more about Letty."

Oliver met his gaze and squeezed his hands but didn't let go. "What do you want to know?"

"I don't know—nothing in particular." Tellumo shrugged. "Anything you feel like sharing."

He let go of Tellumo's hands, picked up his wineglass, and studied the swirling contents for a moment before returning his gaze to Tellumo. "Well, she was the first person I kissed, outside of family, and she took credit for turning me gay."

"Turning you gay?" Tellumo laughed. "How'd she manage that?"

Oliver wiped a tear from his cheek and smiled. "She and her husband— they were dating at the time—took me to my first gay bar."

"How old were you?"

"A few months after my twenty-first birthday." He finished his wine. "Didn't have a clue I was gay until we hit the dance floor."

"Really?" Tellumo was surprised. "I've known since I was like six or something."

"Things were different back then." He stood up and moved to the counter. "More wine?"

"No, thanks," Tellumo replied. "Different how?"

"Nobody famous was openly gay." He filled his glass and returned to the table. "The only homosexuals anybody knew about were transsexuals—a word nobody used at the time—or dirty old men who hung out in bus stations and public restrooms." He shrugged. "I was neither of those; therefore, I wasn't gay."

"How did you figure out you were gay?"

"I'd always been attracted to men but thought I was just more honest than other guys." He laughed. "Seeing guys like myself was the nudge I needed to push me over the edge."

OLIVER'S ANNOYANCE with Tellumo for stopping by uninvited and unannounced faded faster than he would have predicted. His concern was sincere, and Oliver had to admit he was glad Tellumo had come by. Reminiscing about the good old days beat sitting alone getting shitfaced.

"Enough about me. Let's talk about you." Oliver looked into the handsome face. "What kind of name is Tellumo Magnamater?"

"I guess you'd say Roman-slash-feminist. Tellumo was a Roman divinity—the masculine counterpart to Tellus, the Roman goddess of the earth. Mag-NAM-ater is actually Magna Mater, a title used by several Roman goddesses. It means great mother in Latin."

"Oh, of course." Oliver thumped the side of his head with his palm. "The pronunciation threw me off."

"I usually say it derives from magnanimous, after a royal ancestor known for his generosity." He shrugged. "A little white lie I got by with because nobody takes Latin anymore." He met Oliver's gaze. "My family tree dead-ends with my mothers. To my knowledge, I have no grandparents, aunts, uncles, cousins...."

"I'm sorry." Oliver shook his head. "Only child?"

Tellumo nodded.

"Me too."

"Do you have other family?" Tellumo asked.

"I barely remember my grandparents—they died before I started school. My father passed away when I was forty-three, and Mother died three years ago. Unless they've died since the funerals, there are a few aunts, uncles, and cousins around, but I never knew them very well."

"At least you have some idea where you came from." Tellumo sighed. "Trish and Jules—my moms—have never said a word about any kin."

His sad expression touched Oliver. His own mixed European heritage was rather ordinary, but at least he had a good idea where he'd come from. He decided to change the subject. "I hear you teach English at Salt Lick County High," Oliver said, enjoying the look of surprise on Tellumo's face.

"I do." His brow furrowed. "How'd you know?"

"I taught history there for thirty years and get together with Janice Downey now and then. She mentioned you the last time we had dinner together."

"She did?" Tellumo's eyes widened.

Oliver nodded. "You've made quite an impression. We've been friends a long time, and I've never heard her speak so highly of another teacher." He smiled. "In case you're wondering, she doesn't know I know you." He shrugged. "Not that it matters." Other than not wanting Tellumo thinking he'd been the one to bring up his name.

"She's great," Tellumo said. "Everyone is, really."

"Between the low pay, the long hours, and government interference, good teachers are getting harder and harder to find. What made you go into teaching?"

Tellumo swirled his wine for a moment as he gathered his thoughts. "Growing up with two moms, men were a rare and exotic species I saw only from afar or on television." He met Oliver's gaze. "Until I got to school. The few male teachers I encountered made a big difference." He shrugged. "I think about all the single moms out there and hope maybe I can make a difference for their kids."

Oliver nodded and stroked his beard. As he wondered what kind of impression he'd made on kids like Tellumo, Janice's comments came back to him. He'd never thought about the absence of male role models, but knew many of his students, boys and girls alike, had little if any interaction with their fathers.

"I've been wanting to ask Janice's advice about something." He looked Oliver in the eye. "But you're probably in a better position to help."

"Oh?" Oliver raised an eyebrow. "What's the problem?"

"A guy in my study hall has a crush on me." Tellumo lowered his gaze to the table and studied his wineglass. "He slipped a Valentine's Day card into my backpack. For weeks, trying to figure out the identity of my secret admirer drove me crazy."

"I see." Oliver stroked his chin. "Well, first and foremost, make sure you're never alone together, and don't give him any extra attention or do anything to fuel the fire."

"Um." Tellumo blushed. "He invited me to his gymnastics meet."

Oliver frowned. "Did you go?"

Tellumo nodded. "I would have said no, but my friend Melody accepted his invitation." He smiled. "After she kissed me on the cheek and acted like we were a couple."

"Sounds like something Letty would do." Oliver smiled. "How's he been since then?"

"Quiet."

"Thanks to your friend, I don't think you have anything to worry about." He paused for a moment. "Why did you call me tonight?"

"Oh! I'm glad you asked." He shook his head and ran a hand through his hair. "Trish's birthday is two weeks from yesterday. Mel and I are cooking dinner at Peggy Tucker's house to celebrate, and she suggested we invite you to join us."

"Peggy Tucker?" Oliver scratched his head. "I don't think I know her."

"You've probably seen us talking at the gym. Older woman, a little overweight—"

"Oh, yes." Oliver laughed. "The woman who saved you from getting beat up in Boot Steppin' class."

Tellumo laughed. "That's her."

Oliver furrowed his brow. "I've never even met her. Wonder why she wants me to come?"

"I don't know, but I hope you will." He sighed. "Peggy is sweet as she can be…."

"But?"

"Well, she thinks Mel and I are lovers and has no idea I've got two moms instead of a mom and dad."

"Oh my." Oliver snickered. "I'd say no…."

Tellumo's face fell.

"But I'm curious to see how Peggy reacts and wouldn't mind meeting your mothers. Besides, I owe you one." He reached across the table, took Tellumo's hands in his, and looked him in the eye. "Thank you for coming over tonight."

"You're welcome." He smiled. "Have to admit, I was afraid you might slam the door in my face."

Oliver winced. "Janice will tell you I'm not half as mean as I look."

"I know." He met Oliver's gaze and winked. "Unless someone pisses you off—a distinct possibility given how I just showed up."

"I'm glad you did." He looked into Tellumo's piercing green eyes. He considered asking the handsome young man to come with him to Dayton for Letty's funeral but held his tongue. He couldn't ask Tellumo to take off from work. Besides, they barely knew each other.

Tellumo glanced at the clock over the stove and stood. "I can't believe it's almost ten o'clock." He stifled a yawn. "I have to catch the six-thirty bus or I'll be late for school."

"I forgot you don't have a car. Let me slip on some shoes and I'll run you home." He stood, picked up the wineglasses, and placed them in the sink to wash when he got back.

Chapter Sixteen: More Regrets

TELLUMO LET himself into his apartment when he got home from school and eyeballed the bed. He couldn't remember when he'd last stayed up much past nine when he had to work the next day. Morning had arrived a good two hours earlier than he'd have preferred.

Sleep had evaded him. Skipping his relaxing bath hadn't helped, but probably made little difference. He'd lain in bed staring at the ceiling and going over the time he'd spent with Oliver until well after midnight. Had it not been so late, he'd have called Melody back.

His cell phone buzzed in his pants pocket, startling him. He pulled out the device, checked to see who was calling, and touched the screen. "Hey, Melody."

Her anxious face peered back at him. "Where have you been? Did your battery die or something?"

"Sorry." He fell back onto the bed. "I was at Oliver's house. By the time I got home, it was too late to return your calls."

"Really?" She smiled and tilted her head. "Details, please."

"I called to invite him to Trish's birthday dinner. He was too upset to talk, so I called Peggy and asked if she'd pick me up and drop me off at his house."

"Is he okay?"

Tellumo nodded. "His best friend died suddenly." He shook his head. "Cancer."

"Died suddenly from cancer?"

"They thought she'd live at least a few more months. He was supposed to go to Dayton to see her this weekend and was beating himself up for not going sooner."

"Oh, man. That's too bad. How close were they?"

"Very." He wiped a tear from the corner of his eye. "Even closer than us. They grew up together, were college roommates—she even took him to his first gay bar."

"Wow. I can't imagine how upset I'd be if something happened to you—much less thirty years down the road." She shuddered. "How long were you there?"

Tellumo shrugged. "Three hours or so."

"What'd y'all do all that time?"

"Talked, drank wine, held hands…."

"Held hands?"

Tellumo nodded. "Yeah, after he cried on my shoulder. Getting him to talk about her helped. After an hour or so, he'd pulled himself together. By the time he brought me home, we'd sort of bonded."

"Did y'all kiss good night?"

"No. Neither of us had the nerve, but I think he wanted to as much as I did." He smiled. "The car had hardly come to a complete stop before I jumped out and thanked him for the ride home."

"Sorry you didn't kiss him?"

Tellumo shook his head. "No. Neither of us is going anywhere. May as well take our time. My only regret is not offering to go to the funeral with him. He's close to the husband too, but I doubt Oliver will get much time with him. He has four grown sons and a passel of grandkids."

"Poor Oliver. Did he ask you to go?"

"No. He knew I had to teach today. Oh!" Tellumo sat up. "You're not going to believe this. Before he retired, he taught history at Salt Lick County High and is good friends with Janice Downey, my department head. Small world, huh?"

"Well, it is Fallisville."

"There are plenty of towns a lot smaller than Fallisville. Don't forget, we have bus service."

"More like a bus."

"Two buses." He saw no need to clarify the second bus only ran for an hour in the morning and another hour in the afternoon. "Are you coming down this weekend?"

She shook her head. "No." A smile spread across her face. "I've got a date Saturday night."

"The cute guy who teaches fourth grade?"

"No. I swore off dating coworkers after things didn't work out with Danny."

"Danny?"

"You remember—the tall, blond guy in housewares when I worked at the department store."

"Oh, yeah. The guy who gave you the ultimatum about hanging out with me. So who's the lucky man?"

"Scott Williams." She smiled. "We ran into each other at the grocery store. Literally. I think maybe he crashed his cart into mine on purpose."

"Meeting guys at the grocery store really happens?" He laughed. "What did he have in his cart?"

"A lot of fresh fruit and vegetables, Greek yogurt, almond milk, and a big jug of protein powder." She fanned her face with her hand. "Dude really fills out his T-shirt."

"Nice." Tellumo fell back on the bed again. "Where you going?"

"Bogart's. He's got tickets for Peter Hook & The Light."

"Great venue for a concert. Is Peter Hook the New Order guy?"

"The very same. I've downloaded their last album." She shrugged. "It's pretty good. Should be fun."

"I hope you have a good time. You haven't gone out with anyone for ages."

"We teachers are a dull bunch." She smiled. "And I've gone on several dates since your last date. How's Peggy?"

"Same as ever. She ran down to Lexington and bought a programmable sewing machine." He smiled. "She's so cute. You should have seen how pleased she was to have figured out how to use it all by herself."

"I've been thinking." She pursed her lips. "You might want to fill her in on a few things."

"Me?" Tellumo stood up and walked into the kitchen. "Like what?"

"Well, she thinks we're going to get married, and that your mom and *dad* are vegetarians."

He opened the refrigerator and searched the shelves for something to eat. "And whose fault is that?"

"Peggy's." Melody shrugged. "We've never said anything to suggest we're dating, much less considering marriage."

"She does have a way of putting two and two together and coming up with eight or ten." He smiled and shook his head. "She means well."

"Yeah, I know. She's such a sweet lady—I hate to keep misleading her. At the very least, prepare her for your moms. You know how intense they can be."

Tellumo let out a long breath. "Yeah, you're right." He closed the refrigerator door and opened the freezer. "I'll talk to her this week."

"Any idea how she'll react?"

He grabbed a box of lasagna and shut the freezer. "Your guess is as good as mine."

Melody nodded. "Hard to say. She'll be surprised, and disappointed there's not going to be a wedding, but sooner or later, I think she'll come around."

"I sure hope so." He opened the box, popped the lasagna into the microwave, and tossed the empty package into the recycling bin.

"I'll let you go so you can eat your dinner." She held up crossed fingers. "Good luck talking to Peggy—let me know how it goes."

"Will do." He smiled. "Have a good week!"

As he ate his dinner, Tellumo thought about how best to break the news to Peggy. Her generation, especially if they were religious, wasn't known for its acceptance of homosexuality. On the other hand, knowing someone gay often made a difference. He didn't know how Peggy would react, but Melody was right. The time had come to clear up Peggy's misunderstandings.

EVERY SONG on the golden oldies stations Oliver preferred reminded him of Letty. Contemporary pop, talk radio, country-western, and classical music wore on his nerves. He turned off the radio and drove back to Fallisville with nothing but the sound of passing traffic to distract him from his thoughts.

The silence offered no consolation. Driving with the windows down failed to lift his spirits. His gloomy mood stood in stark contrast to the beautiful spring day.

By the time he merged onto I-75 South, sorrow and loss had been pushed aside by self-pity and a profound loneliness he couldn't shake. He'd been an outsider at visitation and the lovely, well-attended funeral. Accepting condolences from neighbors, coworkers, and relatives left Sid and his sons little time for Oliver. Sitting alone at the funeral and standing around the funeral home by himself at visitation had been enough. He'd opted to return home instead of joining the funeral procession for the graveside service and had skipped the wake at Letty's sister Suellen's house afterward.

If only he'd asked Tellumo to join him. A substitute could have covered his classes. Accompanying a friend to the funeral of a lifelong friend was perhaps a questionable reason to miss work, but Janice would have understood.

Traffic slowed on I-275 around Cincinnati. He stayed behind a panel truck for Amazon Home Repair most of the way around. "Tired of waiting for a man to do the job? Call the Amazons." Despite his melancholy, the slogan made him smile.

He dreaded going home to his empty house. The solitude he'd enjoyed since Kevin's departure no longer appealed to him. Before Tellumo's unexpected visit, the only fingers to have pushed his doorbell belonged to Jehovah's Witnesses, delivery drivers, or kids in the neighborhood wanting him to buy something for a fundraiser. Were anything to happen to him, how long would newspapers pile up in his driveway before someone checked to see if he was okay? Days? Weeks? Months?

Overwhelming sadness fell over him. He had only himself to blame for his loneliness. Aside from the increasingly rare get-togethers with Janice, the only time he left the house was to go to the gym, the grocery store, the barbershop, or a doctor's office—none of which, except for outings with Janice, involved much in the way of social interaction.

When had he become an antisocial, crotchety old man? Throughout high school and college, Oliver had been a social butterfly. Instead of writing complaint letters, he'd penned long missives to his out-of-town friends. His telephone had rung off the hook whenever he was home, which wasn't very often. If he wasn't running around with Sid and Letty, he was out with friends seeing a movie, shopping at the mall, or dancing at a gay bar.

Staying single would have helped. With each new relationship, he closed himself off a little more. Trust was the issue. More specifically, the absence of trust. After his breakup with Steve, he hadn't wanted to let Angelo, James, Tim, or Kevin out of his sight for fear they too would cheat on him. The self-fulfilling prophecy left him bitter and destroyed his faith in mankind.

He didn't trust himself anymore. Sex had guided Oliver's mate selection process. His dick was his divining rod. He'd believed a hard cock was proof of something more than desire, with disastrous results—not once or twice, but five times.

Meeting Tellumo was the best thing to happen to Oliver since he'd retired from Salt Lick County High. Perhaps since he'd moved to Fallisville. During Tellumo's unexpected visit, Oliver's lingering preconceived notions about the young man had been shot down like clay pigeons at a trap shoot. He couldn't have been more wrong about him if he'd tried.

Tellumo had handled Oliver's grief with an easy aplomb. Rather than causing him embarrassment, crying on Tellumo's shoulder had worked like a salve on his broken heart. Tellumo's encouraging him to talk about Letty had shifted Oliver's focus from what he'd lost to the gift her friendship had been throughout his life. Holding hands had brought surprising comfort and helped Oliver to feel less alone with his grief.

Holding Tellumo's hands had also been one of the most intimate experiences of his life. He'd wanted to kiss him, but feared screwing things up between them. Rather than disappointed, he'd been relieved when Tellumo had jumped from the car like it was on fire when Oliver had dropped him off at his apartment.

Even if he'd made a move, Oliver suspected Tellumo wouldn't have let things go any further than they had. His interest in Oliver was as obvious as his enviable restraint. The look in his eyes, the way he'd caressed the palms of Oliver's hands, and the time Tellumo had spent consoling him pointed to more than a casual friendship.

Despite an age difference of more than three decades, Tellumo had called the shots. Had Oliver been in charge, they'd have ended up in his bed. Rather than anger about not getting his way, Oliver was relieved and more than a little excited. Rushing things hadn't worked out very well in the past. Perhaps moving slowly would result in a better outcome.

Oliver glanced at his watch as he veered onto the ramp for the Fallisville exit. School was about to let out. Rather than turning into Thoroughbred Acres, he continued toward Salt Lick County High. He could use a dinner companion, and Janice would enjoy a surprise visit.

PEGGY HURRIED out of the driver's license office right on time for a change. Thanks to the new battery she'd purchased, her car roared to life when she turned the key. Giorgio had been booked solid for Tuesday, but had promised to fit her in Wednesday. She made it to Holy Snips with time to spare before her appointment.

The receptionist said Giorgio would be with her soon. Peggy settled into a comfortable chair with black leather upholstery and picked up a tattered issue of *People* magazine. Since Earl's passing, she'd allowed subscriptions to the *Fallisville Gazette* and several magazines to run out. Peggy's Fancywork kept her too busy to watch much television. She couldn't remember the last time she'd watched her soap operas or the news.

She'd flipped through about half the magazine when Giorgio came out of the back. The first thing she noticed was the pink triangle emblazoned across the front of the black T-shirt he wore with a wide pink belt around his waist she thought to be vinyl. His yoga pants ended midcalf, exposing hairless ankles and pink high heels.

"Look at you!" His heels clicked on the tile floor as he approached her. "Miss Thing, you look amazing!"

Peggy's face grew hot. Giorgio was homosexual too. Earl would have said queer as a three-dollar bill. How could she have been so blind? She stood and gave him a weak smile. "Thanks, Giorgio."

"Let's get you shampooed so I can make you even more beautiful." He turned toward the back. "Derrious, be a dear and wash Miss Peggy, would you?"

Derrious came around the corner and smiled at Giorgio. "Be happy to." He had on the same T-shirt as Giorgio with black jeans and pink high-top tennis shoes. "Let me get you a smock." He disappeared, returning a moment later holding a lavender smock he helped her into. "Come on back."

She followed him to the washbasins and lowered herself into the chair. "Is Ernesto off today?"

Derrious frowned. "He doesn't work here anymore."

"Oh, I see." She thought for a moment as Derrious wetted her hair. "Did he get another job?"

"I don't know." Derrious shrugged as he lathered her up. "Nobody has seen him since he got fired."

"Fired?" Peggy gasped. She was about to ask how Giorgio could fire his own son, but stopped herself. "What happened?"

He leaned down and whispered. "Giorgio caught him in bed with another man."

"Oh." She didn't know what else to say. Her face heated up again as she recalled her assumptions about Ernesto and Derrious. "Well, in that case I'm glad he's gone."

"Um-hmm, me too." He rinsed the Halo shampoo from her hair and worked in a dollop of Angel Wing conditioner. "He'd been cheating on him for years. Everybody knew but Giorgio."

Not everybody. She didn't say anything, but thoughts raced through her head. Unlike Tellumo, the homosexuals working at Holy Snips fit the stereotype—and still she'd been clueless. Would knowing have made any difference?

Before she'd found out about Tellumo, the answer would have been yes. Like the good book says, God made Adam and Eve, not Adam and Steve. She didn't know Ernesto or Derrious very well. Writing them off would have been easy.

Giorgio, however, was different. As with Tellumo, she adored Giorgio so much she'd refused to see what was obvious to her now—and to anyone else who saw him in his high-heeled shoes, with or without the pink triangle on his shirt.

Derrious raised the chair back and wrapped her head in a towel. "I can't wait to see what you look like when Giorgio finishes with you." He offered his arm and helped her up from the chair. "He's been talking about your makeover for months."

"He has?"

Derrious nodded. "Don't tell him I told you, but you're one of his favorite clients."

"I am?"

He nodded again. "You remind him of his mother." He led her over to Giorgio's chair. "She's ready for you, Papi."

Giorgio turned her around so she couldn't see herself in the mirror. He hummed as he worked, pausing now and then to step back to assess his progress. By the time he'd finished cutting, the floor around her was covered with hair.

She didn't want to betray Derrious's confidence, but curiosity got the best of her. "Are you close to your mother?"

Giorgio stopped what he was doing, and his face grew sad. "No. She objects to my lifestyle. We haven't spoken to each other in years."

"Oh." She patted his arm. "I'm so sorry. I'd be proud to have a son like you." She paused for a moment. "Does she live around here?"

Giorgio nodded. "I see her out and about sometimes." He wiped a tear from his cheek. "She acts like I don't exist."

What kind of mother would ignore her son—especially one as full of life and charming as Giorgio? "What's her name?"

He hesitated. For a moment, Peggy thought he wasn't going to answer.

"Gladys Honeycutt." A tear slid down his cheek. "My birth name is George Martin, but I liked Giorgio Mancini better, so I changed it. She divorced my father years ago."

Now that she knew, she could see the resemblance between him and the gossipy head of the altar society. "Where's he?" Peggy couldn't remember when she'd ever been so angry and couldn't wait until she saw that gossipy Gladys again.

"He moved to Florida after the divorce. We stayed in touch until he passed away about ten years ago."

An hour later, Peggy left the shop charged up and feeling like a million bucks. Giorgio had lightened her hair several shades and added highlights. She adored the short, layered cut, and was surprised how much younger she looked with bangs. Her only regret was not taking him up on the makeover offer sooner.

Finding out about Giorgio's treatment by his mother had clarified her feelings about homosexuals. Nobody deserved to be treated so poorly by anyone, much less a parent. She couldn't fathom how a mother could be so cold and unfeeling.

She slid into her car and headed for church. If she hurried, she'd get there before prayer meeting ended. Gladys always hung around afterward, spreading gossip and ugly rumors. Peggy intended to give Gladys a piece of her mind.

Gravel flew as she pulled into the parking lot. She leaped from her car, slammed the door shut, and hurried down the steps to the basement, where refreshments were served after prayer meeting. She made her way to where Gladys was holding court around the coffeepot.

"Peggy Tucker," Gladys exclaimed. "We were just talking about you." She took in Peggy's new hairdo. "Your hair looks darling! Where'd you get it done?"

The women she'd been talking to turned to Peggy and admired her new do. "I'm glad you asked." She was, too. She paused as the women waited for her response. "Little shop on the other side of town where the best hairdresser in Fallisville works."

"Who's that?" Ida Campbell asked.

"Giorgio Mancini." She turned to Gladys. "You know him, Gladys, don't you?"

Gladys blanched. "I don't think so."

"Oh, I think you do." Peggy glared at her. "He's the son you've pretended doesn't exist for the last twenty years."

The women around Gladys gasped.

"I don't know what you're talking about."

"Yes you do, you sorry excuse for a human being." Peggy was furious. "How you could turn on your own flesh and blood is beyond me." She eyed the women standing openmouthed around Gladys. "I'm talking about Giorgio Mancini. He's homosexual, so she hasn't had anything to do with him since he was sixteen years old."

"The Bible says—"

"Don't you go throwing verses at me, woman. God is about love, and you've shown damn little of it for a fine young man I'd be proud to call my son."

Ida turned to Gladys. "Is Giorgio your son?"

The rest of the women watched as Gladys stared at the floor without saying anything.

"Peggy's right," Ida said. "He's the kindest, sweetest man in Fallisville. I've been going to him for years."

After a moment, Gladys nodded. "He is."

A disproving murmur erupted. Ida and the other women shook their heads.

Peggy folded her arms across her chest and glared at Gladys. "You've delighted in spreading gossip about anyone and everyone for years—a far worse sin in my book than loving someone of the same sex." She stabbed the air in front of Gladys's face with her index finger. "I suggest you call him, invite him to your house for dinner, and if he's kind enough to accept your invitation—and he's too good a person not to—then you get down on your knees and beg him to forgive you for being such a cold, heartless bitch."

Without waiting for a response, Peggy turned and went back the way she'd come. Her hands were shaking so much she could barely get the key in the ignition. No doubt, repercussions would follow her outburst, but Peggy no longer cared what other people thought—especially small-minded people like Gladys Honeycutt.

Chapter Seventeen: A Chance Encounter

TELLUMO WALKED out of Salt Lick County High School Friday afternoon sorry to see the week come to an end. Despite the gorgeous weather, the prospect of another lonely weekend depressed him. If he had a car, he'd make a spontaneous trip to Cincinnati for the weekend. All he had to do was call and Jules would come pick him up.

But no, he had papers to grade. Grocery shopping to do. Dirty clothes to wash. Lesson plans to go over. He stifled a yawn and headed for the bus stop.

A cool breeze and warm sunlight felt good against his skin. Rather than waiting for the bus, Tellumo decided an invigorating walk home would do him good. He removed his sports coat, hefted his backpack into place, and then hooked a thumb in the collar and slung the coat over his shoulder.

He was in no hurry to get home to his empty apartment. Oliver was still in Dayton and wouldn't be working out with him. Other than the gym and the grocery store, Tellumo had no place he had to be until school started Monday morning. Nope. He shoved his free hand into his pants pocket. No place at all.

He kicked a rock down the sidewalk and, as he neared where it had stopped, adjusted his pace to kick it again. Oliver occupied his thoughts more with each passing day. Tellumo wasn't obsessed so much as intrigued. The more he learned about Oliver, the more he wanted to know.

Physical attraction was definitely a factor. He could fall into those dark brown eyes and never come out again. Keeping his hands off of Oliver when they were together required serious effort. Thoughts of caressing his bearded cheek with the back of his hand, stroking his forearms, or fingering the hair at his throat distracted him and interfered with his ability to focus on Oliver's words.

That the man Tellumo had admired from afar and lusted after for so many months was not the dominant and aggressive alpha male he'd imagined was a pleasant surprise. Oliver certainly looked the part, but beneath the crusty shell was a sweet, vulnerable man. Tellumo suspected he'd been hurt too often and by too many people to let down his guard.

Oliver's disdain for the younger generation set him apart from the older men who'd pursued Tellumo in Cincinnati. They'd seen him as a conquest—a prize to be won. Some wanted to lord over him like he was a sex slave/personal servant. Others wanted someone to coddle and spoil in annoyingly patronizing ways. Whether incapable or unwilling, none had wanted an equal partnership, and thanks to his mothers, he'd settle for nothing less.

Chasing younger men wasn't Oliver's game. He clearly had no desire to be anyone's daddy or time to waste on boys. He was all business, all the time. Had he not gotten pinned beneath that barbell, Tellumo suspected he might still be admiring Oliver from afar.

Since they'd met, Tellumo had broken through Oliver's contempt for anyone under thirty years old. The two of them weren't exactly peers, but the deference wasn't one-sided. Oliver had forgotten more than Tellumo knew about a lot of things, but had little knowledge of exercise, nutrition, technology, and contemporary gay culture. The respect, attentiveness, and willingness to learn Oliver showed during their workout session and his vulnerability the night Tellumo had stopped by uninvited were as encouraging as they were endearing.

He kicked the rock again. It stopped in the middle of a driveway. Before Tellumo could kick it another time, an old Taurus pulled in and stopped. Oliver's kind, handsome face smiled from the driver's side.

"Can I give you a ride?"

"Sure!" Tellumo ran around to the passenger side, opened the door, and tossed his coat and backpack into the backseat. "You're back early." He slid in and closed the door. "Are you okay?"

Oliver nodded. "Being a stranger at my best friend's funeral got old." He put the car in gear and backed out onto the street. "Hungry?"

All of a sudden, he was. "What did you have in mind?"

"It's such a gorgeous day. How about tossing a few steaks on the grill?" He winced. "I forgot. Your moms are vegetarians."

"Yeah, they're also lesbians, but that doesn't make me one."

Oliver laughed—an unfamiliar sound Tellumo found very much to his liking. Oliver's grief had pulled at his heartstrings. Once you got to know him, Grumpy Oliver was kind of cute. Happy Oliver was downright irresistible.

"Mind running to the store with me?" Oliver asked.

"Not at all," Tellumo replied.

"Good." Oliver turned up the radio. "I haven't heard this song since I was your age." He nodded in time to the music and lip-synced the words as he drove.

Tellumo couldn't help but smile. Oliver's seat dancing was as unexpected as his sudden but very welcome appearance at Salt Lick County High School. "Have you been home yet?"

Oliver shook his head. "No." He shot a quick glance at Tellumo. "I was going to drop in on Janice, but then I saw you kicking that rock down the sidewalk, looking all sad and forlorn."

Tellumo laughed. "I might have been feeling a little sorry for myself. I'm glad you stopped." He was also glad he'd decided to walk home instead of riding the bus. Otherwise, he wouldn't be sitting in Oliver's car headed to the store to pick up fixings for a steak dinner.

"Why the pity party?"

The concern Tellumo heard in his voice kept him from getting defensive. "Melody's visits were the first time I've done something fun since I moved to Fallisville."

Oliver nodded. "Occupational hazard." He pulled into a parking place in front of the store and shut off the engine. "Staying too busy for a life outside of work is an easy thing for teachers to do."

"Hard not to," Tellumo said.

"Yeah." Oliver opened his door. "The future is at stake."

Tellumo studied his face. He couldn't tell if Oliver was being sarcastic or serious.

"A mind is a terrible thing to waste and all that." He shut the door and dropped his keys into his pocket. "That's what they want you to think." He gestured toward the grocery entrance. "Shall we?"

Tellumo nodded and then fell in beside Oliver. "Teaching *is* a big responsibility."

"Absolutely." Oliver nodded. Then he shrugged. "My advice to any new teacher would be the same. It's all about balance. A life away from school keeps you from getting stale and makes you a better teacher."

Jules and Melody had told him more or less the same thing. The universe was trying to tell Tellumo something. Perhaps the time had come to listen.

STOPPING TO check on Tellumo when he'd seen him kicking the rock down the street had been a good idea. Having extended the invitation, Oliver fully expected and was prepared to do all the cooking. Tellumo insisted on helping, and had picked up ingredients for a delicious roasted broccoli salad and dessert—chocolate fudge brownies with vanilla ice cream. Oliver bought steaks, bread, and a bottle of red wine.

Tellumo had been right. Having him wash the pots and pans was faster and more efficient than drying. He didn't need to know where anything went to wash, and if he'd dried, Oliver having to tell him where to put something would have interrupted the conversation.

"I haven't eaten so much since Peggy cooked dinner for me and Melody," Tellumo said. "What did you put on those steaks before you grilled them?"

"I'd tell you," Oliver replied. "But then I'd have to kill you." In truth, he didn't remember what he'd tossed into the rub, and was glad the improvised mix had turned out so well. He hung the dish towel on the oven door to dry as Tellumo rinsed out the sink.

"You should package that stuff and sell it," Tellumo said. He dried his hands with the towel Oliver offered him.

Their eyes met. Oliver resisted an overwhelming urge to throw his arms around Tellumo, pull him close, and kiss him. He didn't think Tellumo would mind, but he wasn't certain and would be humiliated if he kissed him and was wrong.

"Back to the deck?" Oliver asked.

Tellumo nodded. "Let me get my coat out of your car."

"No need." He opened a closet, pulled his old Kentucky sweatshirt from the shelf, and handed it to Tellumo. The garment was several years older than Tellumo, a fact Oliver refrained from sharing. "Might be a little big."

"Thanks." Tellumo slid the sweatshirt over his head and pulled the overlong sleeves up to his elbows.

"Another glass of wine?" Oliver asked.

"No." Tellumo shook his head. "Two glasses is my limit." He grabbed a glass from the cabinet and filled it with ice. "Water is fine for me. Want some?"

Oliver nodded. "Thanks. Two glasses is my limit too." Of course, Oliver had been a good ten years older than Tellumo was now before he'd learned that lesson. He took the glass of ice water Tellumo handed him and led the way to the deck.

Tellumo settled onto a loveseat glider, and Oliver sat beside him in his rocking chair. Neither of them said a word, the comfortable silence interrupted by a boisterous gathering of frogs serenading one another.

"What did you do to keep teaching from taking over your life?" Tellumo asked finally.

"Nothing on purpose." Oliver sipped his water and collected his thoughts. "For most of my career, taking care of someone who wasn't able to take care of themselves did the trick."

"You mean like foster kids or people with disabilities?" Tellumo asked.

Oliver laughed and shook his head. "Nothing nearly so noble. My exes. All five of them." He looked Tellumo in the eye. "I've never admitted that to anyone before, not even Letty."

"Ouch. I'm sorry." Tellumo smiled. "At least you can laugh now."

He could. The news surprised him. "I guess I can." He paused for a moment. "I did have a plan…."

"To do what?" Tellumo asked.

Oliver told him about the book he'd always wanted to write, the research he'd done, and the letters he'd collected over the decades.

"I'd love to take a look at those letters sometime."

"Are you serious?" None of his exes had ever shown the least bit of interest in Oliver's letters or his plans to write a book.

Tellumo nodded. "I don't know much about gay history." His face reddened. "Hadn't really thought about it and don't remember the subject ever coming up in any of my history classes."

"I had the same experience. It's the reason for all the letters." Oliver stood. "Come on. I'll show you."

Tellumo stood and took Oliver's hand in his. The gesture surprised Oliver and quickened his pulse. He led Tellumo through the house into the spare bedroom, turned on the light, and opened the closet.

"Oh my God!" Tellumo exclaimed. "I thought you meant like a shoebox full of letters."

"Before I changed to plastic storage containers, I had about a dozen shoeboxes full of letters." He paused and squinted at the ceiling. "That was probably ten years ago." He pulled out the container with the oldest letters. "I file them by date. These are approaching forty years old, with many sharing stories about things that happened decades before the letter was written."

Tellumo stared at the container with a dazed expression. "Abso-fucking-lutely amazing!" He blanched. "Sorry. This is incredible. How far along are you with the book?"

Oliver sighed. "It's 90 percent done in my head. I just need to type it all up." He pointed to the reliable IBM Selectric typewriter he'd paid a small fortune to buy so he could type his own master's thesis.

"With the letters organized by date, how do you find the content you want when you need it?"

"I keep digging until I find the letter I want." Oliver shrugged. "I tried keeping an index for a while, but I got behind and then gave up."

Tellumo shook his head. "I know you're no fan of technology—"

"You got that right." Oliver nodded.

"You have a treasure trove of material here, untapped because there's just too much to wrap your head around."

"But—"

"Don't get defensive." Tellumo smiled. "I want to help you."

Oliver took a deep breath and blew it out. "Sorry. I can go from zero to total bitch in a heartbeat." He smiled. "Customer service reps all over town tremble when they see me coming."

Tellumo laughed. "Listen, Oliver. There's something I have to know."

Oliver met his gaze, but couldn't read his expression.

"It's bothered me all night."

Oliver racked his brain. Had he done something to offend him? "What?"

Tellumo held his gaze. The corners of his lips turned up. "Would you mind if I kissed you?"

Oliver's heart leaped into his throat and his face got hot. He tried to conceal his shock but didn't think he'd succeeded. "Mind?" He leaned toward Tellumo. "I've been resisting the urge to kiss you since you got in my car this afternoon."

Their lips met. The storage container fell to the ground, spilling forty-year-old letters around their feet as Oliver wrapped his arms around Tellumo, who returned his embrace and languid kiss with equal fervor. Time stopped, and Oliver's world narrowed, excluding all but the overwhelming sensations emanating from his mouth, curling his toes and raising the hair on his neck.

Tellumo's hands on his chest gently pushed him away as he broke the kiss. "We need to stop." Tellumo smiled. "Or we'll ruin your letters."

Oliver kissed him again. "I don't care."

Tellumo laughed and pushed him away. "Well, I do."

"My bedroom is right across the hall…."

"Oh, believe me, I know." Tellumo took Oliver's hands in his. "For months, I've thought about kissing you." He kissed Oliver again. "And it's even better than I imagined."

Oliver pulled him close and kissed him again. Demanding and urgent. Tellumo responded passionately, then pushed him away again, panting. "I don't want to cloud the memory of our first kiss with a bunch of other firsts. I'd kinda like to savor this for a while." He kissed Oliver again. "Okay?"

Oliver didn't know what to say. Fear of showing emotion in his voice kept him silent. He nodded. "Okay."

"Good." Tellumo picked up the storage container. "Let's clean these up, and then you probably should take me home." He kissed Oliver one more time.

Damn! Oliver couldn't get enough of Tellumo's kisses. Back in the day, his refusal to jump in the sack would have been a deal breaker. Look what that had gotten him. "Okay, boss."

Chapter Eighteen: True Confessions

OLIVER PULLED up in front of Janice's house. He thought about honking and waiting for her to come out, but decided ringing the doorbell was the right thing to do. He put the car into park, but before he could turn the key, Janice came out in a sleek black dress and high heels.

He leaned across the seat and opened the door for her. "Don't you look nice!"

"Thanks, you're looking good too. Can't remember the last time I saw you wearing a tie." She slid into the seat and pulled the door closed. "I haven't been to Fallis House in ages. What's the occasion?"

Oliver shrugged as he put the Taurus in gear. "Nothing special." He glanced over his shoulder and merged into traffic. "Thought a glass of wine with dinner might be nice."

"You'll get no argument from me." She sighed. "Drinking alone at home makes me feel like a lush."

He nodded. "I know what you mean. Calling my nightly glass of wine a prescription for good health helps."

"You handle living alone a lot better than I do." She shook her head. "I'd retire, but without work to keep me busy, I'd go nuts."

Oliver was more of a loner than Janice but wasn't sure he agreed with her assessment about his ability to handle a solitary existence. "Hear much from your kids?"

"Not as much as I'd like. Matt calls every few weeks. Jenny calls once or twice a month and sends e-mail messages now and then with pictures of my grandkids." She shook her head. "I should have put my foot down after the divorce and made them stay with me, but they wanted to live with Dirk, and I thought letting them go where they wanted rather than forcing them to stay with me was the wiser course of action."

"I'm sorry." Dirk's desire for a divorce after fifteen years of marriage had blindsided Janice. He'd resented the time she gave to her job and had always wanted her to stay home with the kids.

"Water under the bridge now." She swiped under her eye with a knuckle. "How was Letty's funeral?"

"The service was beautiful, but the overall experience was depressing." He glanced at her briefly. "Nothing like a funeral to highlight the difference between family and old friends."

"I'm sorry." She smoothed her dress out over her thighs. "I feel the same way about weddings. Too many people for more than a few words with anyone in the family."

Oliver pulled into a parking space close to the entrance of the Fallis House. "Well, here we are." He got out and walked around the car to open the door for Janice.

"Thank you," She stood and looked out over the garden. "Not much to see yet."

"Too early. We'll have to come back a month or so from now when the peonies and tulips are blooming."

She smiled. "It's a date."

They headed up the stone walkway to the entrance of the nineteenth-century mansion. The hostess greeted them at the door in period costume and led them to a table for two in what was once the front parlor. Candles in glass sleeves topped the tables, and gas logs burned in the fireplace beneath a mantle adorned with greenery clipped from hollies and other evergreen shrubs.

Oliver studied the menu. "What looks good to you?"

"Everything." Janice smiled. "But I'm leaning toward the lamb chops with roasted white asparagus and sunchokes, and potato au gratin. What about you?"

"I can't decide between the scallop-and-crabmeat-stuffed sole with wild rice and shredded brussels sprouts or the sage-rubbed seared calves' liver with mashed yams and sautéed cabbage."

"Both sound delicious, but go with the calves' liver or we'll never agree on a bottle of wine."

Oliver laughed. "Okay, calves' liver it is."

A tuxedoed waiter not much younger than Oliver materialized beside the table to take their order, reappearing moments later with the bottle of wine Janice had selected.

"To old friends." Oliver raised his glass.

Janice winced as she touched her glass to his. "Make that to dear friends. The older I get, the more sensitive I am about my age."

They sipped their wine in silence for a few minutes. Stephen Foster tunes emanating from a piano elsewhere in the old house mixed with the quiet conversations of the diners occupying tables across the parlor.

Janice interrupted the comfortable silence. "What's up? I can tell you want to talk about something. Out with it."

Oliver grinned. "You know me too well." He cleared his throat. "Seems I've developed feelings for a younger man."

"Oh?" Janice raised an eyebrow. "Anyone I know?"

He nodded. "As a matter of fact, yes." He took a sip of wine and met her gaze. "Tellumo Magnamater."

She picked up the bottle the waiter had left on the table. "More?"

Oliver nodded. "Yes, thanks."

She filled their glasses and then met his gaze. "Thirtysomething years is a pretty big age difference."

"Yeah, I know." He glanced down to adjust the napkin in his lap and then at Janice. He studied her face for some sign of what she was thinking. "Call me a foolish old man."

She shook her head. "I don't think so. Crotchety, headstrong, and too trusting, yes, but never foolish." She ran her finger along the edge of her glass. "Does he know?"

Oliver nodded. "I'd say he does."

"How long have you known him?"

"A month or two. We met at the gym and have been working out together."

"I see."

"He called right after Sid let me know Letty had passed. I was too upset to talk, so he came over to check on me."

She nodded. "I'm not surprised. He's a very caring young man."

"I stopped by school on my way home from the funeral. I was going to surprise you, but I saw him walking and gave him a ride home."

"And…?"

"Well, we ended up cooking dinner together and talking. We kissed a few times. I didn't take him home until after ten o'clock."

"Are you asking for my permission?"

Oliver shrugged. "In a way. Is the age difference too much?"

She reached across the table and placed her hand on his wrist. "Age is just a number, right?"

Oliver nodded. "So they say. And the boy—no, Tellumo—is mature for his age."

"That he is. My advice? Take your time and see how things go." She smiled. "What have you got to lose?"

PEGGY COULDN'T make up her mind what to wear to meet Bill Pinkley. All three outfits she'd purchased Tuesday after work were two sizes smaller than anything in her closet. She'd even splurged on a pair of black shoes with three-inch stiletto heels, rather than the five-inch versions Giorgio preferred.

She picked up her ringing telephone and glanced at the screen. "Hello, Lurleen. How are you?"

"I'm fine." She paused. "I heard about what you did after prayer meeting last night. Why didn't you tell me? Everyone in town is talking about it."

Peggy's face grew hot. "Really?"

"Cold, heartless bitch?"

"I—"

"Truer words would have been hard to find." Lurleen chuckled. "I just wish I'd been there to see the look on Gladys's face. Ida said you were wonderful. After you left, Gladys resigned from the altar society and ran out of the church."

"Really?" Peggy didn't know what else to say. "I've been waiting for Pastor Brown to call to tell me I've been kicked out of the church."

"Nope. Matter of fact, Ida said they unanimously agreed you should be the new head of the altar society." She paused for a moment. "I'm proud to call you my best friend, Peggy."

Peggy was speechless.

"Can't wait to see your new hairdo. Ida says you look like a million bucks. Said the short style knocks twenty years off your age."

Peggy glanced at her reflection and smiled. "We'll have to get together for dinner again soon."

"I'd like that," Lurleen said. "Well, I won't keep you. Just wanted to call to say how proud I am of you."

"Thanks, Lurleen. I couldn't have done it without that little push from you."

"You've got a good heart, Peggy. I knew you'd come around. See you at church Sunday?"

"See you there." Peggy smiled. "The head of the altar society never misses Sunday services."

Peggy flipped her phone shut. Repercussions from her confrontation with Gladys were nothing like she'd expected. She'd still put an extra twenty dollars in the collection basket for all the cussing she'd done of late, but she was pleased Lurleen thought she'd done the right thing.

Head of the altar society? She'd have to call Ida to see if everything was ready for Sunday services. With Easter just around the corner, her work was cut out for her. Good thing she'd bought the programmable sewing machine or she'd never have the time for her altar society duties.

She examined the outfits on her bed again and opted for the black-and-white striped slacks and a black, V-neck, long-sleeved T-shirt. The horizontal stripes were interesting and more stylish than anything she'd worn since high school. She pushed the sleeves up to just below her elbow like the salesclerk at Happy Lady Boutique had shown her, stepped into her heels, and checked herself out in the full-length mirror on the back of her bedroom door.

She struck a pose and addressed her reflection. "Miss Thing, you look amazing!" The expression made her giggle. She wasn't sure what Miss Thing meant but had to admit she did look pretty amazing. She dropped her phone into her purse, retrieved her keys from the kitchen counter where she'd left them, and headed for her car, being careful not to twist her ankles.

The Dinner Barn was as busy as ever. She found a parking place and, after again checking her reflection in the rearview mirror, touched up her lipstick before getting out of the car. Although she was a few minutes early, she saw Bill Pinkley sitting in one of the big rocking chairs on the front porch, waiting for *her*. She smoothed her blouse down over her slacks, took a deep breath to calm her nerves, and made her way toward him.

As she neared, her heart skipped a beat. He was even more handsome in person. She smiled when she was a few feet away and extended her hand. "Hi, Bill. I'm Peggy Tucker."

He jumped from his chair, grasped her hand in both of his, and smiled. "It's a pleasure to finally meet you." He let go of her hand and stepped back. "You are an incredibly beautiful woman."

Her cheeks grew hot. "Why, thank you."

He offered her his elbow. "Shall we go inside?"

She slid her hand beneath his arm and nodded. People smiled and waved as they passed, some calling out greetings or thanking him for the beautiful day. She was surprised to see Ernesto in a Dinner Barn uniform at the hostess stand. He didn't seem to recognize her.

"Hello, Mr. Pinkley." He pulled two menus from the rack and moved toward the dining room. "Follow me, please."

As they made their way through the dining room, Bill waved and smiled at half a dozen customers who called out his name as they passed. Ernesto stopped at a table for two by the window, and Bill pulled her chair out for her.

"Thank you," Peggy said as he pushed her closer to the table.

He sat down across from her and gave her a sheepish grin. "Sorry about that."

"About what?"

"All the attention." He leaned forward and whispered, "All that smiling and nodding makes my cheeks hurt and gives me a pain in my neck, but it's part of the job."

She laughed. "I don't mind." In truth, the attention made her feel like a celebrity herself.

The waitress set two glasses of water on the table with a couple of straws. "Hi, Mr. Pinkley. The usual?"

He nodded and looked at Peggy. "Unsweetened tea with a splash of sweet. What would you like?"

"Oh, just water is fine for me."

He nodded. "Care for an appetizer?"

Peggy shook her head. "No, thanks." She'd decided not to worry about her dinner hour tonight. In fact, she'd been too busy to cook enough food for the full hour for a couple of weeks. Despite going off the diet, she'd continued to lose weight.

The waitress returned a moment later with Bill's custom blend of iced tea. She turned to Peggy. "Ready to order?"

"I'd like the steak and shrimp salad, please—with italian dressing."

"Yes ma'am." She made a note on her pad. "What about you?"

"I'll have the same, only with honey mustard dressing."

"Great! I'll go ahead and put your order in."

"Thank you," Bill said. He looked across the table at Peggy. "Since Snowmageddon, our chats have been the highlight of my boring life." He smiled. "You're such a kind and gracious woman. Now that I've seen you, for the life of me I can't imagine why you're still single."

Peggy's cheeks grew hot again. She smiled and met his gaze as she racked her brain for an honest but clever response. "I've been saving myself for a nice man like you." She picked up her straw, slipped the paper wrapping off, and stuck the straw into her water.

Bill raised his iced tea. "To new beginnings."

Peggy clicked her plastic tumbler against his and met his gaze. "Yes, to new beginnings."

TELLUMO WAS as eager for the end of the school day as the students in his study hall. He didn't need to check the clock. The clap of closing books and the rustle of backpacks let him know the bell would soon ring.

A pleasant breeze rattled the blinds and drew his attention to the windows he'd opened after lunch. Fluffy white clouds paraded across an azure sky, casting shadows on the rolling hills of bluegrass beyond the cedars edging the school grounds. He hoped the lovely weather persisted into the coming week for spring break.

The bell rang, launching the students from their desks with a clamor of screeching chair legs, footsteps, and excited conversations. Tellumo watched as his classroom emptied and was relieved to see Dustin Delong greeted by a striking young man who'd come to the door to meet him. They made a handsome couple and were obviously quite smitten with one another.

Tellumo closed the windows, slung his backpack over his shoulder, and made his way down the deserted hallway and out of the building. The bus stood idle with the door open, waiting for him to board. Tellumo waved him on. "Go ahead, Jack. I'm visiting a friend who lives nearby this afternoon."

"Okay, Tellumo. See you in the morning?"

He wasn't sure. "I think so." Jack was so conscientious and such a nice guy, Tellumo suspected he might knock on his apartment door if he wasn't at the bus stop in the morning. "Don't count on it, though. I might get a ride in."

Jack gave him a knowing look and smiled. "All right. Have a good evening." He pulled the lever closing the door and drove off.

Oliver had offered to pick him up, but Tellumo had insisted on walking. Oliver's house was maybe a mile and a half from school. After skipping the gym Tuesday and again today, he could use the exercise, and the fresh air would do him good.

The weekend he'd been dreading had quickly turned into one he would never forget. The memory of Oliver's sweet kisses sustained and tormented him. Monday's workout had been charged with sexual tension. Stopping the kissing had been hard enough. Any more and Tellumo didn't think he'd be able to resist.

Oliver's crusty exterior was like scar tissue, protecting him from further harm. He'd opened up while they prepared dinner, sharing ribald tales of his salad days and horror stories about his ex-boyfriends. Tellumo couldn't remember when he'd laughed so much. Yet beneath the humor lurked disappointment, heartbreak, and self-loathing for having fallen for a string of losers.

Before Tellumo got halfway up the curved sidewalk, Oliver opened the door and stepped onto the stoop to greet him. "Couldn't ask for a nicer day. Enjoy the walk?"

Tellumo nodded. "I sure did." He noticed the sunburn on Oliver's nose and forehead. "Looks like you've been outside today."

"Spent a few hours pulling weeds and sprucing up the flower beds." He smiled. "Planting time is just around the corner."

"Take me on a tour," Tellumo said. "By the time we finished fixing dinner the other night, it was too dark outside to see much."

"Happy to show you around." Oliver held the door open for him. "Come inside and grab a glass of wine first."

Tellumo dropped his backpack by the door and followed Oliver into the kitchen. "Wow! Smells great. What's cooking?"

"Spaghetti and meatballs." Oliver smiled. "You should probably reserve judgment until you've had a chance to taste it." He poured wine into a couple of glasses. "I have a gift for screwing up the simplest recipes."

"Well, if it tastes half as good as it smells...."

He handed Tellumo a glass. "Ready for the tour?"

Tellumo nodded. For the next thirty minutes, he followed Oliver along a cobblestone path winding through his yard and listened as he talked about the various shrubs, trees, and perennial flowers he'd amassed over the years. The clumps of foliage all looked pretty much the same to him, but Oliver knew the scientific names, blooming season, and other details about each one. His passion was obvious, and aside from grumbling about a neighbor's cat using his raised beds for a litter box and rabbits feasting on his bellflowers, his crustiness disappeared.

After the tour, Tellumo sat in a comfortable chair on the patio sipping wine. Oliver came out of the house, placed a plate of cheese and crackers on a small table between them, and sat down. "Dinner won't be ready for another hour."

"I love this view," Tellumo said.

Oliver nodded. "Having a horse farm for my backdoor neighbor was the reason I bought this house. The sun coming up over the hill is beautiful, especially this time of year when the Bradford pears are blooming."

"Oh, I can imagine." Tellumo wondered if he'd find out for himself one day.

They sat quietly for a few moments, the comfortable silence interrupted by the occasional birdsong and the ever-present hum of honeybees flying around the pear trees. Then Oliver turned to Tellumo. "You've talked me into getting a computer, a scanner, and maybe even one of those smartphones."

"I did?" Tellumo smiled. He'd explained how technology could help Oliver finish his book while they'd worked out.

Oliver grabbed a piece of cheese and a cracker. "Think I'm too old to learn how to use them?"

"Hmmm." Tellumo furrowed his brow and stroked his chin. "You are awfully old, and a smartphone is a big step up from rotary dial telephones." He smiled. "But with the right teacher—someone patient and willing to invest the time—I think you could learn."

Oliver's face fell. "Would the place where I'd buy them from give me that kind of help?"

Tellumo nodded. "For a price. The library offers classes sometimes too."

"Oh. I see." Oliver frowned and looked out over the garden.

"Or I could teach you."

His face lit up. "You'd do that? I was afraid you wouldn't have time."

Tellumo met his gaze. "For you, I'll make time."

Oliver met his gaze. "I don't know what to say."

Tellumo got up, walked over to him, and dropped to his haunches until their faces were inches apart. "I've wanted to meet you for months. Everything about the way you look pushes all my buttons, in a good way."

He leaned in and pressed his lips against Oliver's. When Oliver's wine glass fell to the patio and shattered, Tellumo broke the kiss and smiled.

"Physical attraction is a nice start," Tellumo said. "But I'm more interested in what's on the inside." He shrugged. "I've been attracted to a lot of assholes in the past."

"Me too." Oliver kissed the tip of Tellumo's nose and then smiled. "Does that mean you're a top?"

Tellumo chuckled. "Guess we'll have to find out, won't we?" He stood, took Oliver's hand, and helped him up. "Sorry about the glass."

"I've got more." He smiled and kissed Tellumo again. "Are you hungry?"

Tellumo nodded. "Starved." He smiled. "But maybe we should eat something first."

Chapter Nineteen: Dinnertime

PEGGY COULDN'T remember having ever been so happy. Since Thursday, she'd seen Bill every day. He'd even insisted on accompanying her to church Sunday morning.

Seeing the looks on the faces of the other women when they walked in together had tickled her as pink as the new dress she'd worn. Pastor Brown included an announcement in the bulletin about her elevation to head of the Trinity Baptist Church altar society. After services, half the congregation had swarmed around her to offer congratulations, to compliment her new look, and to meet the smiling celebrity who stood by her side.

Gladys hadn't skipped church, but the sight of her, dejected and defeated, slinking out before services ended had saddened Peggy. She wasn't one to hold a grudge. After the dust settled, she'd swing by the Honeycutt residence with a plate of her special cinnamon buns.

When the oven timer buzzed, she checked the strawberry cake for doneness and then removed two nine-inch pans from the oven. She placed them on a wire rack to cool and measured out the ingredients for the strawberry frosting, placing her pastry bag over the food coloring so she'd remember to fill it before tinting the rest. Her piping skills left much to be desired, but she thought she could manage, "Happy Birthday, Trish!" and a little ornamentation.

Melody had phoned the night before to discuss ideas for the menu. Lurleen was right. Melody knew all about Tellumo, who'd been her best friend for years. She had no intention of marrying anyone anytime soon, but had recently gone out with a young man she'd run into at the grocery store and was looking forward to a third date with him after her visit to Fallisville.

Peggy had confessed her confusion about the identity of LonelyNFallisville and how awkward Oliver coming to dinner would be. Confessing the truth to Bill or Oliver was too embarrassing. Melody had encouraged her to invite Bill to the birthday dinner. Turned out Oliver was also gay and had been spending a lot of time with Tellumo.

Finding out Tellumo was gay had come as a shock. Anger about Gladys's treatment of Giorgio had overshadowed the revelation about the gay men at Holy Snips. Peggy had been too relieved when Melody told her about Oliver to feel shocked. He seemed a little old for Tellumo, but who was she to judge?

When her telephone rang, Peggy glanced at the clock and then flipped open the device. "Hello?"

"Miss Peggy?"

"Giorgio! What a pleasant surprise!" She couldn't imagine why he'd call except to see how she liked the makeover. "I can't thank you enough for the new hairstyle. I love it!"

"Thank you. I'm glad you like it." He paused for a moment. "Thank you for talking to my mother."

Peggy's face grew hot. "How did you hear about that?"

"She called a few days ago and invited me over for lunch today."

Peggy almost dropped her phone. "She did?"

"Yes, ma'am. I don't know what you said to her…."

Peggy breathed a sigh of relief.

"But whatever you said sure hit home. She's wanted to see me for a while, but so much time had passed, she didn't have the nerve."

"How'd it go?"

"Pretty good—maybe a little awkward. She apologized for the way she's treated me all these years and promised to make up for lost time."

"Oh, Giorgio! I'm so glad."

"Me too." He paused for a moment. "She wants me to bring Derrious over for dinner after church tomorrow."

Peggy started to ask if he'd told her Derrious was black, but didn't. She hoped Gladys handled the interracial thing better than she had the gay thing. "That's wonderful!"

"I don't know why she couldn't ask you herself, but she wanted me to invite you and Bill Pinkley to join us."

If he didn't know, Peggy wasn't going to tell him. "Oh, we'd love to come if we didn't already have plans. Bill has some kind of surprise lined up after church." Declining the invitation increased the need for Peggy to stop by with a tray of cinnamon buns. "Rain check?"

"Sure," Giorgio said.

The doorbell rang. Peggy looked out the window and saw Bill's Buick parked behind her Saturn. "I've got to run. Talk to you soon!"

She flipped her phone shut and hurried to the door. Bill stood on her front porch with a vase of pink roses in one hand and a wrapped gift in the other. He smiled. "Hello, beautiful."

Peggy blushed as she held the door open for him. "Come on in, handsome."

He stepped inside and kissed her on the cheek. "The flowers are for you, and the gift is for Tellumo's mother." He winked. "It's a weather radio."

"How sweet of you!" She took the vase from him and sniffed before setting them in the middle of the dining room table. "I love the smell of roses." She pointed toward the coffee table where her gift waited. "You can put your present there."

"Anything I can do to help you get ready?"

Peggy glanced at the grandfather clock. "No, I don't think so." She walked into the kitchen. "Have a seat and relax while I frost the cake. Can I get you something to drink?"

"No thanks." He pulled a chair from the dining room table into the kitchen and sat down. "I'll just drink in your beauty." He smiled. "When are Melody and Tellumo supposed to get here?"

"You sweet-talker, you!" Peggy's cheeks grew hot. "Any minute now. I can't wait for you to meet them!"

"Me either. They sound like great kids." He paused for a moment. "What's the dad's name?"

Peggy looked up from the bowl of frosting and frowned. "I don't know." She smiled. "Guess we'll find out soon enough."

TELLUMO CLOSED the trunk and hopped into Melody's Volkswagen. The big celebration was mere hours away. They'd wrapped their presents for Trish the night before, finalized the menu for her birthday dinner, and made a list of items to buy at the grocery store.

"Hope we didn't forget anything," Tellumo said as he fastened his seatbelt.

Melody started the car and backed out of the parking space. "We got everything on the list." She glanced at Tellumo before pulling into traffic. "You're as nervous as a cat in a room full of rocking chairs."

"Yeah." He took a deep breath. "I'll tell Peggy about my moms before they get here."

"She took the news about you and Oliver well—much better than I would have expected, thanks to her new boyfriend."

"How'd they meet?"

Melody giggled. "Instant messaging. For weeks, she thought she was talking to Oliver. That's why she invited him to the dinner. Can you believe it?"

Tellumo smiled. "She's something else, isn't she?"

"Definitely. Not at all what you'd expect." She smiled. "Like the good book says, you can't judge a book by its cover."

"Her facts might be messed up, but her heart's in the right place." He pushed his hair back over his forehead. "Since she knows about me and Oliver, I feel better about her meeting Jules and Trish."

"But…?"

"I'm worried what Trish and Jules will think when they find out about me and Oliver."

"What's to find out?" She reached over and patted his knee. "As long as you don't hold hands or make out or something, he's just a friend."

"Yeah, a friend I invited to Trish's birthday party." He wiped his sweaty palms across his jeans. "Besides, I've never been able to keep anything from them—they can read me like a book."

"You didn't invite him. Peggy did. If they knew how earnest he was, and how adamant he is about taking things slow, they'd be less likely to worry."

"I hope they don't pick up on anything." His brow furrowed. "I'm not ready for that conversation yet."

"What if they do suspect? They're not going to cause a scene. I haven't heard them rail against the patriarchy for a long time."

"True." Tellumo tried to recall the last time he'd heard one of them rant about something a man had done. Surely there'd been something since his middle school principal had brought back uniforms with only skirts for girls.

"Being successful businesswomen has mellowed them out, don't you think?"

"Maybe." Tellumo stroked his chin. "When they started Amazon Home Repair, they were only going to do jobs for women, but decided refusing to serve half the population would be bad for business."

"You said they use contractors who are men now. Sounds like they've outgrown the radical views of their past."

"Even if they've come to love men, I'm their son. They won't be thrilled I'm dating someone older than they are."

"Then don't tell them. Outside of the gym, you've only been together a few times anyway. Besides, with so much going on, I don't think they'll give Oliver a second thought."

Tellumo wasn't so sure. "I hope you're right."

After Melody parked behind a red Buick Regal, Tellumo walked around to the back of the Volkswagen and opened the trunk. When Peggy emerged from the duplex with a distinguished-looking man by her side, he almost didn't recognize her. "You look absolutely amazing!"

"Thank you!" She smiled. "I want you to meet—"

"Bill Pinkley." He held out his hand. "You must be Tellumo. Let me help you with those bags."

"Thanks." Tellumo pumped his hand and then turned to Melody. "This is my friend Melody Abshire."

"Nice to meet you." She squeezed his hand, then hugged Peggy. "I love your hair!"

"Aren't you sweet!" She took Melody's hand. "Can you boys handle the groceries without our help?"

Bill smiled. "I think so." He reached into the trunk and grabbed several bags. "You got the rest?"

Tellumo nodded. "I hope we have enough food for everyone."

"Looks like enough to feed an army."

They carried the groceries to the kitchen. Peggy and Melody were washing dishes and wearing aprons with "Bless this Food and Drink" embroidered on the front. Tellumo saw the cake sitting on the counter by the refrigerator. "Wow! Did you make that beautiful cake?"

Peggy nodded. "I'm glad you like it. I can bake, but decorating isn't really my thing. I need to take a class or something."

"I disagree," Melody said. "It's too pretty to eat."

"Looks like something you'd see in a food magazine," Tellumo said. "What kind is it?"

"Strawberry cake with strawberry frosting." Peggy dried her hands on her apron. "What's for dinner?"

Melody looked at Tellumo. "We changed our minds half a dozen times."

Tellumo nodded. "We finally settled on tossed salad with italian dressing, eggplant parmesan over whole-wheat penne, sautéed broccolini, and garlic bread."

Peggy inspected the ingredients they'd purchased. "Fresh tomatoes would have been better, but they're no good this time of year, so the canned will work just fine." She frowned. "I'm not a big fan of frozen bread." She studied the foil packaging. "I suppose this will be okay."

"What can I do to help?" Bill asked.

"Nothing." Tellumo looked at Melody. "We've got this, right?"

Melody nodded. "I think so. Y'all go watch television or something."

"Yeah," Tellumo said. "Leave the cooking to us. We'll yell if we need your help."

"We'll be in the spare bedroom." Peggy smiled. "Bill is helping me catch up on orders."

He nodded. "Peggy does all the embroidery. I'm in charge of shipping and handling."

"Oh." Peggy turned to Tellumo. "What's your father's name? I'm embroidering everyone's name on linen napkins."

Tellumo gulped. "Well, to tell you the truth, I don't really know."

Peggy gave him a confused look. "You don't know?"

Tellumo nodded. He struggled to find the right words, but came up empty-handed.

"He's got two moms," Melody said. "Jules and Trish."

Bill's eyes grew wide, but he didn't say anything.

"Oh, I see." Peggy furrowed her brow. "Which one's your mother?"

"They never told me," Tellumo replied. "They were afraid if I knew, I'd treat my natural mom differently."

Peggy nodded. "Oh, okay. How do you spell Jules?"

"J-U-L-E-S," Tellumo replied.

OLIVER HAD no idea making sangria could be so complicated and expensive. The recipe Tellumo had given him called for seventeen different ingredients. To finish, he'd made three trips to the store.

Given his poor track record with omissions and substitutions, Oliver had taken special care to follow the recipe. He'd premeasured all the ingredients, lined them up on the kitchen counter, and double-checked to make sure he hadn't left anything out. Instead of skipping the orange liqueur and coconut-flavored rum as Tellumo had suggested, he'd run to the liquor store at the last minute rather than taking a chance on screwing things up.

Fearing twelve servings might not be enough, he'd doubled the recipe. Finding a container big enough to hold the mixture and small enough to fit in his refrigerator had required the third and final trip to the store. To get the twenty-quart storage container to fit, he'd removed most of the contents of the refrigerator so he could reposition the shelves.

He'd been disappointed by the flavor of the spoonful he'd sampled before placing the mixture in the refrigerator. A second sampling while he'd waited for his coffee to brew tasted much better. The flavors had blended overnight.

Getting the sangria into his car posed another challenge. The plastic container fit fine inside the trunk, but without a way to keep it from sliding around, he feared what might happen along the way. In the end, he placed the container in the passenger seat and secured it with the seatbelt.

Oliver drove with care, making sure not to accelerate or turn corners too fast. The sangria still sloshed around, but the seatbelt kept the container from shifting position. Seeing no place to park, Oliver drove past 716 Hummingbird Lane, turned around, and pulled up on the opposite side of the street from his destination at exactly five o'clock.

A boxer watching him from a picture window barked furiously as he got out of the car. When Oliver came around the Taurus to retrieve the sangria, the dog went berserk. Oliver feared the glass separating him from the angry beast would break.

He carried the big container up the steps. Before he could knock, a woman he suspected was Peggy's younger sister opened the door. "You must be Oliver," she said, extending her hand. "I'm Peggy Tucker."

Oliver shifted the container onto his hip and shook her hand. "Pleasure to meet you." He couldn't believe how different she looked from the woman he'd seen at the gym. "Thanks so much for inviting me." He nodded at the container. "I brought some sangria—Tellumo said it's a family favorite."

She smiled. "How thoughtful of you! We'll have to make room in the refrigerator." She waved him inside. "This is Bill Pinkley."

Bill nodded, and Oliver shifted the container onto his hip again to shake his hand. "Oliver Crumbly. Meeting you is a pleasure. I'm a huge fan!"

"Thank you," Bill said. "Always nice to meet a viewer. What do you do?"

"I'm a retired teacher." He decided not to mention having worked with Dot.

Bill nodded. "A noble profession. Here, let me take that to the refrigerator." He took the sangria from Oliver and retreated to the kitchen.

Oliver smelled a mixture of garlic, a perfume he didn't recognize, and vintage potpourri. Organ music played softly in the background. A staggering quantity of religious memorabilia covered the walls, shelves, and tabletops. Tellumo came into the living room, followed by a pretty young girl with short red hair and big blue eyes.

"You must be Melody." Oliver smiled and offered his hand. "Glad to finally meet you."

Instead of taking his hand, she surprised him with a hug. "The feeling is mutual." She stepped back and looked him over. "Tellumo never mentioned how handsome you are."

Oliver's cheeks grew hot. "Nor how pretty you are."

She folded her arms across her chest and stuck out her lower lip. "He didn't?"

Tellumo looked from one to the other and shrugged. "Well, now you know."

Melody laughed. "Tellumo is the master of understatement."

"I'd rather you be pleasantly surprised than disappointed." He glanced out the window to the street. "My moms are here."

Oliver followed his gaze and saw a panel truck with Amazon Home Repair emblazoned on the side parking behind his Taurus. "I've seen that logo before."

"They're all over Cincinnati," Melody said. "Tellumo's moms own the company."

Bill laughed. "Love the slogan."

Oliver watched as two women got out of the van and headed for the front door. He could see why Tellumo didn't know which one was his natural mother. They looked enough alike to be sisters. The driver, wearing khaki pants and a long-sleeved oxford-cloth shirt, was thinner and a tad taller. The other woman wore a long dress Oliver would describe as bohemian in style. She wore glasses, had longer hair, and carried a bouquet of flowers.

Peggy came out of the kitchen carrying a crystal tray of hors d'oeuvres. "I can't wait to meet them."

Tellumo greeted his mothers at the door. "Oliver, Bill, Peggy—this is Trish, the birthday girl."

"Hi everyone." The flower-bearing woman smiled and waved before coming into the living room. "Nice to meet you all."

The second woman came through the door. "And this is Jules."

A loud crash drew everyone's attention to Peggy. She was trembling and as pale as a ghost. Hors d'oeuvres and shattered glass surrounded her.

Melody hurried over to her. "Are you okay?"

"I'm fine." Peggy nodded. "I don't know what came over me." She bent down to clean up the mess.

"I'll get it," Melody said. "Go sit down a minute." She hurried into the kitchen, returning a moment later with a trash can and some paper towels.

Bill held Peggy's elbow as she made her way for the sofa. "I'm so embarrassed," Peggy said.

"No need to apologize." Trish stepped over to the sofa. "Thanks so much for hosting a party for me." She held out the flowers. "These are for you."

"Thank you." Peggy smiled. "Let me get a vase." She started to get up, but Bill pulled her back onto the sofa.

"Let me," Bill said. "Where are they?"

"Under the sink."

"Don't get up," Tellumo said. "I'll get it." He went into the kitchen.

After a moment, Oliver heard water running. He stepped over to Tellumo's mothers and shook hands with Jules. "Oliver Crumbly. Nice to meet you."

"You too." Jules nodded and pumped his hand once.

Tellumo returned with a vase of water and took the flowers from Trish.

"Happy Birthday." Oliver extended his hand to Trish.

She smiled and took his hand in hers. "Thank you so much. Nice to meet you."

Tellumo placed the vase of flowers on the coffee table. "Anyone care for a glass of sangria?"

Chapter Twenty: Nothing but the Truth

AFTER A glass of sangria, Tellumo relaxed. Thanks in no small part to Peggy's gracious hospitality, Bill's seemingly endless supply of amusing anecdotes, and Oliver's sangria, things were going better than he'd expected. When the grandfather clock chimed six times, he and Melody excused themselves and retreated to the kitchen for final preparations.

Tellumo picked up the bread he'd sliced and stuffed with garlic butter earlier and slid the sheet pan it was on into the oven. "Well, what do you think?"

"So far, so good." Melody poured olive oil into a skillet and turned on the burner. "Everyone's having a good time." She smiled. "Jules seemed a little uptight at first, but the sangria loosened her up a bit."

"Yeah. Can you believe how Trish and Oliver hit it off?" Tellumo shook his head. "I never knew she was such a history buff." He retrieved the salad from the refrigerator and drizzled the greens with italian dressing.

"Jules and Bill buddying up is a bigger surprise." Melody stirred minced garlic into the skillet. "But then, he's so charming."

Tellumo nodded. "Everyone in Fallisville loves him." He furrowed his brow. "What do you think happened to Peggy?"

"Something to do with Jules. She took one look at her and turned white as a sheet."

He pulled the salad fork and spoon from the drawer and tossed the greens to distribute the dressing. "Wonder why? She wasn't the least bit shocked when she found out I had two moms."

"How much longer on the bread?"

He glanced at the timer. "About five minutes."

She dumped the broccolini they'd cut and washed earlier into the skillet. "Whatever it was, she recovered quick enough."

"Yeah. Hang on." He carried the salad into the dining room, placed it on the table, and returned to the kitchen. "Did you notice the way Peggy keeps looking at Jules?"

Melody stirred the broccolini with a wooden spoon. "Not really." She shrugged. "Might be the contrast. You'd be hard pressed to find two people more different than Jules and Peggy."

"That's true." Tellumo heard a crash from the other side of the duplex through the kitchen wall, followed by loud swearing from an angry male voice. "Uh-oh." He couldn't help but smile. "Sounds like the neighbors are fighting again."

Melody groaned. "Peggy will die of embarrassment if they go at it while we're eating again." She turned off the burner, dumped the broccolini into a serving dish, and carried it to the table.

When the oven timer went off, Tellumo removed the bread, slid both loaves into a basket, and covered it with a linen napkin embroidered with "Our Daily Bread." He set the basket on the table and then pulled a simmering casserole dish from the oven, placing it on a hot pad between the salad and bread. "Is this everything?"

Melody nodded. "I think so." She turned around and faced the living room. "All right everyone, time to eat!"

Peggy rose from the couch and moved to the head of the table. "Everything looks wonderful!" She smiled. "Trish, as the guest of honor, you sit here." She pointed to a chair at the foot of the table. "Jules, you're here next to her, and then Bill." She pointed to the other side of the table. "Melody, you're here next to me, with Tellumo and Oliver between you and Trish."

"Anyone need a refill?" Oliver moved around the table with a pitcher of sangria as everyone took their seats.

Oliver sat down beside Tellumo and gave his thigh a quick squeeze. Tellumo shot his mothers a glance, but neither seemed to have noticed. A woman's angry voice hurling obscenities came through the wall.

Peggy cleared her throat. "Let's bow our heads and give thanks for the wonderful food and drink and the company of friends." She closed her eyes and lowered her head for a moment. The room fell silent except for the organ music coming from speakers in the living room.

"You dirty rotten bastard! I wouldn't fuck you if you were the last man on earth!"

Peggy blanched. Bill glanced at her and then picked up his sangria and raised his glass. "I'd like to propose a toast to the guest of honor." He turned to Trish as everyone raised a glass. "Cheers to your birthday and may the best days of your life be yet to come."

Glasses clinked around the table amidst a chorus of "Cheers!"

"Don't touch me you pig-faced son of a bitch!"

Peggy turned crimson. Jules and Trish glanced at the wall and then to each other. Oliver kicked Tellumo under the table, and Melody nudged him with her thigh.

Oliver picked up the salad bowl and handed it to Trish. "Salad?"

"Thank you." She set the bowl between her and Jules and then filled their salad bowls.

"Goddammit, bitch, get over here!"

Bill picked up the basket, pulled back the linen, and offered it to Peggy. "Bread?"

She gave him a thin smile as she pulled out an end piece. "Thank you."

A loud crash shook the crucifix hanging on the wall between the two apartments. "Leave me alone, fuckwad!"

Jules dropped her napkin onto her plate and stood. "I can't sit here and listen to this anymore." Tellumo could see she was angry. "I'm going next door."

Bill jumped up and followed her. Oliver glanced at Tellumo, then stood up and hurried to catch up.

Trish turned to Tellumo. "Are you just going to sit there?"

He thought about telling her what would happen next, but decided against it. Besides, with Jules intervening, he wasn't sure what might happen. He dropped his napkin onto his plate and hurried outside.

Jules pounded on the door. "Open up or I'm calling the police!"

OLIVER WAITED behind Jules with Bill and Tellumo for someone to answer. He didn't know what he'd do if things got out of hand. If push came to shove, self-preservation had always motivated him to pick flight over fight.

Standing on the porch waiting for no telling what to happen scared him. He wiped his sweating palms across his pants and hoped his racing pulse wasn't a precursor to a heart attack. He kept telling himself there was safety in numbers, unless, of course, the occupant had a gun.

Jules pounded on the door again. "Open the door by the time I count to ten or we'll break it down." She turned to the men behind her. "Won't we?"

Oliver gulped. Bill wiped his forehead with a linen napkin. Tellumo stepped up to stand beside his mother as the deadbolt clicked and the door opened. A thin-faced woman with pale green eyes and stringy blonde hair stared at them. "What do you want?"

Jules stepped closer. "Are you okay? We heard you shouting from next door. Sounded like you were in trouble."

"Mind your own fucking business."

Before she could shut the door, Jules rammed her foot in the opening.

A male voice came from behind the blonde. "What the fuck's going on, Daisy?"

She looked back over her shoulder. "Bunch of do-gooders trying to protect me from you."

He laughed. "Tell 'em to fuck off and get your ass back here. I'm horny as fuck now."

Daisy peered through the crack. "You heard him. Fuck off."

Jules reached through the opening and grabbed her by the collar with both hands. "Listen up, you crazy bitch." She pulled her close and looked her in the eye. "If you want to stay with that asshole, I can't stop you, but—"

"Hey, who you calling an asshole?"

Tellumo moved closer to the door. Oliver didn't know what to do, but decided to bluff. He drew himself up to his full height, puffed out his chest, and clenched his fist. Bill had his cell phone out and looked ready to call the police.

"You." Jules released Daisy. She fell back a few steps and the door swung open, revealing a scrawny, long-haired man in dingy white boxer shorts behind her. Jules folded her arms across her chest and glared at the two of them.

The boyfriend seemed to have a change of heart. "Sorry, lady. I'd never hurt her. Talking rough gets us all worked up."

Daisy took his hand in hers and nodded. "He's telling the truth, ma'am. Johnny has never hit me or roughed me up. We just like to playact."

Jules shook her head. "What you do in the privacy of your home is your business, but you need to keep it down. Your stupid little game is interfering with our enjoyment of a quiet dinner together."

Daisy looked at Johnny. "We're sorry. Messing with the lady next door is half the fun."

Johnny hung his head. "Yeah, we're sorry. We didn't mean nothing by it."

Bill shoved his phone into his pocket and stepped up beside Jules. "Listen here, Johnny. The lady next door, Peggy Tucker, is one of the kindest, sweetest women I've ever met."

Daisy studied Bill's face. "Oh my God! You're the weatherman on Channel 13!"

Bill nodded and then stabbed the air in front of the shocked young man. "She better not hear another peep out of you ever again. Understand?"

Johnny nodded. "Yes, sir, Mr. Pinkley." He draped his arm over Daisy's shoulder. "Tell Ms. Tucker we're sorry."

"Yeah," Daisy said. "It won't happen again." She paused. "Hold on a second, will you?"

Bill shrugged and turned to Jules, who nodded her consent. Oliver gave Tellumo a worried look.

Daisy returned a moment later with a pen and a small red-bound book. "Will you sign my autograph book?"

After Bill complied with her request, the four of them returned to the other side of the duplex. Peggy, Trish, and Melody had watched the proceedings from Peggy's front door. "Oh Bill!" Peggy threw her arms around his neck and kissed him. "You're the sweetest man I've ever known."

Bill smiled. "Just looking out for my lady."

Peggy turned to Jules. "Thank you, Jules." She took a deep breath. "We need to have a little talk."

PEGGY WRUNG her hands together and tried to collect her thoughts. She'd known the second she laid eyes on Jules, but wasn't entirely sure and had watched her all evening. The more she saw, the more certain she'd become. Seeing her all fired up had removed any doubt.

"Let's take a walk," Peggy said. She glanced back at the porch and saw everyone watching them. "Y'all go on and eat. We'll be back in a bit."

Jules fell in beside her. "What's up?"

"Thanks for saying something to my foul-mouthed neighbors. They've tormented me with their antics for more than a year now."

"Jerks." Jules patted Peggy on the back. "You won't have to listen to them any longer."

Peggy took another deep breath. She still wasn't sure how to proceed, but decided to start at the beginning. "Where did you grow up?"

"In Covington, across the river from Cincinnati." She shoved her hands into her pockets. "Why do you ask?"

Peggy slid her hand under Jules's arm. "Bear with me for a few minutes, can you?" Peggy met her gaze. "Answer a few more of my questions and then I'll answer yours."

Jules shrugged. "Sure."

"When's your birthday?"

"August twenty-third. I'm two years older than Trish."

Peggy did the math in her head and nodded. "Were you adopted?"

Jules stopped and turned to her. "I was raised by half a dozen different foster families. Nobody wanted me."

Peggy wiped a tear from her eye. "I'm so sorry."

Jules studied her face. "How did you know?"

Peggy took her hand in hers and looked into her eyes. "When I was sixteen, the young man I was dating got me pregnant." Tears cascaded down her cheeks, but she didn't want to let go of Jules's hands.

"I was in love, but instead of asking me to marry him, he wanted me to have an abortion." She shook her head. "My parents wanted an abortion too." She wiped the tears from her cheeks with the back of her hand.

They walked in silence. After a moment, Jules spoke. "What did you do?"

"I went to the Catholic hospital and talked to one of the nuns. She told me about a home for unwed mothers in Covington." She looked up at Jules. "Sister Julianne made all the arrangements for me. She even bought my bus ticket."

Jules stared at her.

"On August 23, I gave birth to a beautiful baby girl. I named her Julianne."

Jules gasped. "How did you know I was your baby?"

Peggy smiled. "You're the spitting image of your father."

"Is he still alive?"

"No." Peggy shook her head. "He got killed in the Vietnam War."

"What about your parents? Are they still alive?"

"No. They died years ago." She took Jules's hands in hers again. "They were ashamed of me. What other people would think was more important to them than you or me. To punish them for keeping me from my daughter, I moved to Fallisville and never saw them again."

"God," Jules said. "What an incredibly brave young woman you were."

"I wasn't brave." She shrugged. "I did what I had to do. I've never told a soul." She smiled. "Telling someone after all these years is a huge relief."

She studied Peggy's face. "Did you have any other children?"

Peggy shook her head. "No. Miscarried a few times. You're my only child." She squeezed her hand. "I've thought about you every day, wondered if you had a happy childhood, how you turned out, if you had any kids of your own."

Jules nodded. "I've thought a lot about you too. I was angry because you didn't love me enough to keep me." She threw her arms around Peggy and held her tight. "All this time I've been so wrong about you."

"Hearing about your childhood breaks my heart." Tears streamed down Peggy's cheeks. "I was sure you'd be adopted by a nice family who would take better care of you than I could."

Jules stepped back and took Peggy's hands in hers. "I worked through my anger issues with a good therapist. She had me make a list of all the things I'd say to you if we ever met."

Peggy winced. "Go ahead. Get it out of your system. I deserve it."

"None of that matters anymore." Jules shrugged. "Yeah, my childhood wasn't normal or happy. In the end, I turned out okay, and I wouldn't be the person I am today without those experiences, good and bad."

"You turned out a lot better than okay," Peggy said. "You're successful, beautiful, and have a wonderful family who loves you." She met her daughter's gaze. "I have one more question for you."

"What?"

"Is Tellumo your son?"

Jules bit her lip. "I promised Trish I'd never tell him."

"He's not asking. I am."

Jules hesitated for a long moment and then nodded. "Yeah. His father was a friend of ours—a gay man who died of AIDS when Tellumo was four years old."

"I'm so sorry," Peggy said. "Do you think finding out you're his natural mother would change how he feels about either one of you?"

Jules shook her head. "No. Trish and Tellumo have a great relationship—always have."

"I see." She paused for a moment. "Your secret is safe with me, but I'm not sure it's a secret worth keeping."

"Thanks, Mom." She smiled. "I'll talk to Trish tonight."

Peggy hooked her arm in Jules's elbow. "Well, I guess we should head back. I don't know about Trish, but I'll never forget her fortieth birthday."

"Me either," Jules said. "I got a mom."

Peggy smiled. "I got a daughter and a grandson."

Chapter Twenty-one: New Beginnings

DESPITE HIS splitting headache, Oliver woke up Sunday morning with a smile on his face. Trish's birthday party had turned into quite the celebration. He couldn't remember when he'd last had so much fun.

His bedroom door opened and Tellumo walked in, carrying a tray and wearing Oliver's boxer shorts. "Good morning, sleepyhead." As he neared, the sun streaming through the window hit him like a spotlight, highlighting his well-muscled chest, broad shoulders, and chiseled abs.

"Good morning." Oliver threw back the covers, sat up in bed, and stretched. He took in the sight of the gorgeous young man and met his gaze. "Has anyone ever told you how beautiful you are?"

"Not when they were sober." Tellumo smiled and set the tray on the bedside table. "How are you feeling?" He leaned down and kissed him.

Oliver tasted coffee and bacon on his breath. "A little rough, but I'll live. Thanks for driving me home."

"Like I had a choice." He laughed. "You're kind of cute when you're trashed."

"I'm glad you think so." Oliver suspected he was stretching the truth but wasn't about to disagree. "How long have you been up?"

Tellumo glanced at the clock. "Couple of hours. I wanted to see the sun come up over your garden. You were right. The sun rising behind the pear trees is beautiful."

"You should have woken me up!"

"I tried." He reached over and mussed Oliver's hair. "Anyone ever tell you you're kind of growly in the morning?"

"Just until I've had my coffee." He eyeballed the bedside table.

"Here you go." Tellumo grabbed a steaming cup of coffee for him off the tray. "I made scrambled eggs, bacon, and toast too."

"Smells great." Oliver took a sip of the hot coffee. "Nobody's ever made breakfast in bed for me before."

"Why am I not surprised?" Tellumo grinned as he sat down beside him and kissed him again. "Your predilection for picking losers is well established."

"Smartass." Oliver smiled. "How did I end up with a winner like you?"

"I picked you, remember?" He stroked the fur on Oliver's chest with the back of his hand. "You had it in for my entire generation."

Oliver kissed the pink triangle on Tellumo's shoulder. "I stand corrected."

Tellumo picked up the plate and a fork from the tray. "Hungry?"

Oliver nodded. "Starving."

"I'm not surprised." Tellumo placed eggs and bacon on a piece of toast and folded it in half. "Open wide."

"Yes, sir." Oliver opened his mouth and took a big bite. He chewed for a moment and then swallowed. "I usually don't feel like eating until I've been up a few hours." He chuckled. "Somehow, I worked up quite an appetite after dinner."

"We need to work on your endurance." Tellumo fed him the rest of the sandwich. "You zonked out before midnight."

"Did I?" Oliver scratched his head. "I don't remember."

"Must have been the sangria."

"I blame all the carbs. Peggy's cake was delicious." He furrowed his brow. "Should you check on your moms?"

"I called them while I was cooking breakfast." He smiled. "Have to admit, I'm a little surprised they like you so much."

Oliver frowned. "What makes you say that? I thought we really hit it off."

"You did." He pushed his hair back over his forehead. "Nothing personal. I grew up believing older white men were the enemy."

"Watching the news often makes me feel the same way."

Tellumo nodded. "I know what you mean. Still, I'm relieved. Liking you is easy enough. Given the age difference, I thought they might object to us being together."

"Trish told me she was glad to see you so happy." He smiled. "They've worried you'd grow old here in little Fallisville without ever meeting anyone."

"They've worried about my love life for years. Dating has never been that important to me."

"Wish I could say the same." Oliver sighed. "For years, I thought being single was the worst thing that could happen to a person."

Tellumo shrugged. "I had other priorities."

"Well, for whatever reason, I'm glad they approve. Think they snooped around your apartment?"

Tellumo shrugged again. "Probably, but there's nothing I wouldn't want them to see." He fed Oliver the last bite of sandwich. "I talked to Melody too." He laughed. "After Bill went home, she and Peggy stayed up talking half the night."

"Peggy and Jules sure were chummy after their little walk. Any idea what that's about?"

"Not a clue." Tellumo furrowed his brow. "Something is up, though. Jules wanted to be alone with Trish last night—and I don't think it was the sangria."

"Think we'll find out at brunch?"

Tellumo shrugged again. "Did you notice how disappointed Bill looked when Peggy invited everyone to join them? I think he had something more intimate in mind."

"Peggy must have said something to him when they were cleaning up the kitchen." Oliver sipped his coffee. "He seemed downright excited about us getting together again." He glanced at the clock again. "What time are we supposed to be at Fallis House?"

"Eleven thirty."

Oliver tossed back the rest of his coffee. "Guess I need to get up from here and help you clean up the kitchen."

Tellumo took the empty mug from him, set it on the tray, and pushed him back into the bed. "It'll wait."

PEGGY PULLED back the covers and jumped out of bed. She'd hardly slept a wink all night but didn't feel the least bit tired. After Bill left, she'd chatted with Melody for a couple of hours and then lay in bed thinking about her daughter and grandson.

She slipped into her robe and slippers and tiptoed past the spare bedroom where Melody slept to the kitchen. Imagining her daughter had been adopted into a loving family had kept her from feeling so guilty about giving her up. Learning she hadn't had upset Peggy and caused her to rethink the decision she'd made more than forty years earlier. How different might things have turned out—for both of them—had she kept the baby?

At the time Peggy had had few options. Rodney Brubaker had ruled out marriage, and abortion was too horrifying to consider. Dropping out of school to have the baby had made her life difficult enough. Throwing a child into the mix certainly wouldn't have made things any easier.

Like the good book says, things always worked out for the best. Jules had reacted to the news with sympathy and understanding. She'd survived whatever hardships she may have endured, and grown up to become a successful woman with a partner who loved her and a beautiful son. Truth be told, she'd fared quite a bit better than had Peggy.

She made a pot of coffee, unloaded the dishwasher, and put up the dishes she and Bill had hand-washed and left to dry. Thinking about him made her smile. Prompted by his disappointment about her spontaneous decision to invite everyone to join them at the Fallis House and her fear the truth could come out at any moment, she'd told him about her conversation with Jules.

Melody came into the kitchen rubbing sleep from her eyes. "Good morning!"

Peggy hugged her. "Coffee's ready. Did you sleep well?"

"Until Tellumo woke me up at the crack of dawn." She smiled as she filled a mug with coffee. "He had to show me the sun coming up over Oliver's garden."

Peggy poured herself half a cup of coffee, added a heaping spoon of sugar, and stirred in enough milk to fill the cup. "Oliver is a lot nicer than he looks."

Melody nodded and leaned back against the counter. "Especially after a couple of pitchers of sangria." She sipped her coffee for a moment. "Heard from Bill?"

"Not yet." Peggy glanced at the clock. "He'll be here around eleven to pick us up."

"I'll follow you so I can head back to Cincinnati after brunch."

Peggy sighed. "I have to admit I'm a little disappointed you're not marrying Tellumo."

"Oh? Why's that?"

"Don't get me wrong. I'm happy for him and Oliver, but I kind of got used to the idea of the two of you together." She put her arm over Melody's shoulder. "I was looking forward to cooking dinner for the two of you a few times a month, getting together for special occasions, babysitting your children...."

"We still can." Melody hugged her. "Except for babysitting our children." She smiled. "We'll see what happens. The more I come to Fallisville, the more I like it."

Peggy's phone rang. "Oh, I bet this is Bill." She pulled the phone from her robe pocket and flipped it open. "Hello?"

"Hey, Mom. Are y'all up?"

Peggy smiled. "Yes, darling. We are."

"If it's okay, Trish and I wanted to stop by before brunch."

"Of course it's okay!" She glanced at the clock. "When?"

"We'll be there within the hour." She paused. "I'm calling Tellumo to see if he and Oliver can join us."

"Good. See you soon!" Peggy closed her phone and turned to Melody. "Miss Thing, we need to get a move on!"

WHEN OLIVER turned onto Hummingbird Lane, Tellumo saw Bill's Buick and Vanessa, his moms' van, parked in front of Peggy's duplex. "Wow. Everyone's here already. Wonder what's going on?"

Oliver shook his head. "Guess we'll find out soon." He pulled up behind the van, shifted into park, and removed the key from the ignition. "Ready?"

Tellumo nodded. "Yeah." He got out of the car and waited on the sidewalk for Oliver to join him. "I feel like a kid again, waiting for Jules to punish me."

"What makes you think you're in trouble?"

"Not knowing what she's going to say or do." He shuddered. "Brings back old memories."

Oliver laughed. "I don't think she'd have called everyone together to punish you."

Tellumo nodded. "Yeah, I guess you're right." He took Oliver's hand and headed for the porch.

Peggy greeted them at the door, grinning from ear to ear. "Come in!" She hugged them both and kissed Tellumo on the cheek. "Take a seat."

Jules got up from the recliner and stood beside Peggy. Trish, Melody, and Bill were seated on the couch. Melody looked at him and gave a quick shrug. She didn't know what was up either.

Oliver dropped into the rocking chair, and Tellumo settled into the recliner. Jules and Peggy stood in the middle of the room and looked at each other. Peggy nodded at Jules, who looked around the room and cleared her throat.

"Thanks for coming with such short notice."

Tellumo had never seen her so nervous.

She cleared her throat again. "Yesterday I found out something I've wanted to know my whole life." She glanced at Trish, who smiled and gave her a nod of encouragement. Then she turned to Tellumo. "Finding out made a big difference, not just for me, but for you too."

Tellumo's heart jumped into his throat. He tried to swallow but his mouth was too dry.

Jules smiled when Peggy put her arm around her waist, and then draped her arm over Peggy's shoulder. "This kind, generous, and beautiful woman is the reason we're here." She looked at Tellumo again. "More than forty years ago, she faced a tough decision. Instead of doing what everyone wanted her to do, she made the ultimate sacrifice…."

Tellumo had seen Trish cry before, but never Jules. The emotion in her voice brought a tear to his eye. Oliver and Melody stared at Jules, transfixed.

"She quit school, left her friends and family, and boarded a bus for Covington." Jules paused to pull a tissue from the box Peggy offered her and wiped her eyes. "A few months later, she gave birth to a little girl she named Julianne, after a kind-hearted nun who told her about the home for unwed mothers and bought her a bus ticket to get there."

Trish got up to stand beside her. The lump in Tellumo's throat expanded as the tears slid down his cheek. "Peggy is your mother?"

Jules nodded. "Yes, and your grandmother."

Melody gasped. "You're Tellumo's natural mother?"

Trish nodded. "She is. I wanted to keep it a secret." She turned to Tellumo. "I was afraid you'd love me less if you knew. Finding out made such a difference for Jules." She smiled and hugged her again. "She's at peace now. We decided you had a right to know the truth and deserved a loving grandmother."

Tellumo went to his mothers and grandmother and hugged them. The four of them held each other for a long moment, sobbing and whispering words of love to each other. When they finally broke apart, Tellumo saw Melody, Oliver, and Bill dabbing their eyes with tissues.

"Wow." Tellumo wiped his eyes with the sleeve of his shirt. "I sure didn't see this coming."

"That makes two of us." Peggy hugged him close. "We've got a lot of catching up to do."

"I told you something about Peggy reminded me of Jules when I first met her," Melody said.

Tellumo nodded. "You did." He turned to his grandmother. "On some level, I think I knew." He smiled. "Why else would I hang out with a middle-aged straight woman?"

"My good friend Lurleen says you and Melody are the best thing to happen to me in ages." She smiled. "When I called her this morning to let her know I wasn't going to be at church, she knew for the head of the altar society to miss Sunday morning services something big was up. She'll die when I tell her the whole story."

"Tellumo's father was a close friend who died from complications from AIDS." Jules looked at Oliver. "For some reason, you remind us of him."

Trish nodded. "He'd look a lot like you if he was still alive. He taught high school history too." She shrugged. "So what if you're old enough to be Tellumo's grandfather." She smiled. "There's something karmic about the two of you being together."

Bill stood up and looked at his watch. "Well, folks, I hate to break up this little party, but we have an eleven-thirty reservation at the Fallis House."

Tellumo walked over to Oliver and kissed his cheek. "Hear that, gramps?"

Oliver put his arms around him and hugged. "Sure did, whippersnapper."

Stay tuned for an excerpt from

Until Thanksgiving

A Holiday Tales Novel

By Michael Rupured

JOSH FREEMAN left the Bar Complex well before last call. Except for the hustlers that prowled the streets behind Lexington's one and only gay bar, nobody noticed him leaving. A rough-looking kid in a tank top and jeans sized him up and walked toward him.

"Looking for some company?"

"No, thanks." Josh kept walking. The gravel crunching under his Justin Ropers didn't cover the laughter the boy got from the other hustlers. Josh wasn't hard up enough to pay for sex. Yet. The cold shoulders at the bar had been bad enough.

He unlocked his red Toyota Celica. Gay life in Lexington, Kentucky, had changed. The bar crowd that evening was nothing like the good old days, when the place overflowed with good-looking, readily available men—before AIDS and the siren call of gay meccas like Atlanta, San Francisco, and New York. That school was out for the summer didn't help. The class of '97 had moved on, and the class of 2001 hadn't yet come to town.

Going to the Bar had been a mistake. Josh hadn't talked to anyone and nobody had talked to him. He wasn't surprised. Unless he needed help crossing the street or had fallen and couldn't get up, the college boys shaking their stuff on the dance floor had no cause to talk to him.

He started the car and headed to Jerry's Restaurant for a late-night snack, smoking the rest of the joint he'd left in the ashtray. Smoking pot kept him from feeling so lonely. These days, he smoked so much he didn't really feel anything.

"Table for one?" asked the waitress, chomping her gum and tugging on a severely strained bra strap.

"Table for one" sounded like a life sentence. Absent enough money to justify the sugar daddy label, he had slim to no chance of finding another lover.

"Here ya go, darlin'." The waitress plunked down a food-stained menu and a glass of water. "Can I get ya some coffee or something to drink?"

"Water is fine, thanks."

"Ready to order or do ya need a few minutes?"

"I can order. I'd like a J-Boy plate."

"Sure. I'll be right back out with that for ya, darlin'."

A tiny spark of hope still glimmered, enough to get Josh off the couch earlier that evening and into the shower. By ten o'clock, he'd whipped his hair into a look, fingered through some gel, squeezed into his best jeans, and donned a Polo golf shirt for a solo night out on the town.

The waitress returned with his food, interrupting his thoughts. She set the burger, coleslaw, and mountain of crinkle-cut fries down in front of him. "Ya gonna save some room for hot fudge cake?"

Josh was tempted to say yes. He could eat whatever he wanted now. What difference would it make if he got big as a house?

"No, thanks. I'll be doing good to eat this."

"Well, just let me know if ya change your mind." She left the check on the table and headed to the hostess stand to seat a group of punk rockers that had just arrived.

Josh glanced at his watch and noticed it was after one o'clock. The bars had closed, and a line waiting for tables had formed just inside the door. He wolfed down the rest of the burger, finished off the slaw, and made a noticeable dent in the mountain of fries. After leaving two bucks on the table for the waitress, he picked up the check, settled with the cashier, and returned to his car.

The J-Boy plate had filled him up, but left him feeling just as empty as before. Instead of going home where he belonged, Josh headed for the bookstore.

He parked under the trees at the very back of the parking lot, smoking a cigarette and watching guys coming and going through the bookstore's rear entrance. A steady stream of cars cruised slowly through the parking lot. Now and then the cars paired up, driver's side to driver's side, for quick conversations. If the drivers connected, a two-car convoy headed to a secret rendezvous for a hookup. More often, both cars returned to the parade circling the bookstore in search of a hot encounter.

After seventeen years with Ben Dixon, Josh was single. It wasn't his fault. He'd done everything right. The idea of cheating never even occurred to him. As far as Josh was concerned, once you decided to move in together, death was the only way out.

He thought Ben agreed. In a way, he did. Ben didn't want the relationship to end, either. Not the relationship with Josh or the relationship Ben had on the side with his coworker, twenty-five-year-old David Hicks. That Josh considered David to be a good friend added insult to injury. In one fell swoop, he'd lost two of the most important people in his life.

Oh well, Ben is history. No more lies. No more worrying about what's going on behind my back.

But the absence of gnawing paranoia was a small comfort in the face of reality. Josh knew his best chance for finding the love of his life was now behind him. Downhill was the only direction left for a single, middle-aged gay man.

He locked his car and made for the rear door of the bookstore. When he crossed the threshold, the scent of Pine-Sol punched him in the nose. There wasn't enough cleanser in the world to cover the smell of all the sex that went on in the cubicles making up the dim back half of the store. The brightly lit front of the establishment featured dirty magazines, an eclectic collection of pornographic videos for sale or rent, and a wall of dongs, dildos, and other sex-related paraphernalia.

A dozen small cubicles with coin-operated video players featured an assortment of porn. Scattered throughout the dark maze connecting all the cubicles lurked maybe a dozen horned-up men. Some were married and popped into the booths for the blowjobs their wives refused to deliver. Most of the rest were there to oblige. The way they leered made Josh uncomfortable.

Never a lurker, Josh stepped into a cubicle and dropped some quarters in the slot to watch some gay porn. On the screen, an obviously bored African-American plowed the ass of a homely white dude who tried to act like it hurt. Neither performer was likely to win any acting awards. Josh pushed the button and the scene changed to a blond frat-boy type blowing a hairy, muscular white guy.

Fearing what he might sit in, Josh ignored the wooden bench seat and remained standing. The black plywood walls of the booth were riddled with holes of various sizes, none part of the original construction. Smaller holes allowed for spying on the action in the neighboring cubicle. Larger openings served more illicit purposes. Every few years, the police raided the place and the owner would board up all the holes. New holes reappeared in days.

Watching the action on the little screen gave Josh a hard-on. When a finger appeared through a baseball-sized opening on the right side of the booth, beckoning, he figured what the heck. Getting off was getting off. He went over, lowered his pants to his knees, and stuck his cock through the hole into the warm, wet mouth waiting on the other side.

Josh concentrated on the video, imagining the frat boy sucking his dick instead of one of the leering men he'd seen outside the cubicle. He dropped more quarters in the slot, then focused on the video and the mouth milking him through the glory hole. Soon Josh was pounding the wall with his hips. The sound attracted bystanders to the holes in surrounding cubicles to see what the noise was all about.

Josh felt the beginning of his climax tingling in his balls and groaned. The hot mouth working urgently on his throbbing cock quickly produced the desired result. On still trembling legs, Josh zipped up his pants and headed home to his empty bed.

• 2 •

THE DOORBELL'S steady ding, ding, ding woke Josh from a sound sleep. He stumbled out of bed and tripped over an assortment of pizza boxes, dirty clothes, old newspapers, and empty cans on his way to the front door. He saw his friend Linda Delgado through the peephole and opened the door.

"I've been ringing your doorbell forever. You up?"

"Does it look like I'm up?" Squinting from the bright sunlight, Josh looked at his arm and then remembered his watch still sat on his bedside table. "What the hell time is it, anyway?"

"Way past time for your sorry ass to still be in bed. You were supposed to meet me at the pool two hours ago."

He rubbed his eyes. "You could have called."

Linda put her hands on her hips and glared. "I did. Three times."

Josh looked over and saw the red blinking light on his answering machine. "Oh. Sorry." He ran his hands up over his eyes and through his hair, pulling the bangs back, then letting go and shaking his head. "Guess I was sleeping pretty heavy. I went downtown last night and was a little late getting home."

"Late getting home? Did you get lucky? Is he still here?"

Josh decided not to mention the anonymous blowjob to his one and only friend. Women really didn't understand about casual, anonymous sex. "No, I didn't get lucky. Nobody even looked at me twice, much less talked to me."

"Poor Joshy. Everyone probably thought you were too busy enjoying your little pity party to bother with anyone else."

Josh shook his head. "Linda, sometimes you're a real bitch."

"As your best friend, it's my job. If I don't tell your hunky ass the truth, who will?" She looked past him. "Are we just going to stand here on the porch all day and talk?"

Josh yawned and stepped back, opening the door wider so Linda could come in. "Sorry. I'm still about half asleep."

Linda pushed her way past Josh into the condo. She took three steps, then turned back to Josh. "Jesus Christ! What the hell is that smell?"

Josh sniffed the air. "What smell? I don't smell anything."

"It smells like a crack house in here, or maybe a dumpster." She covered her mouth and nose with her hand and talked between her fingers. "Damn, Josh! When was the last time you took out the trash?"

"Uh. I dunno. Sometime before Ben moved out."

"That was more than three weeks ago. Can't you smell it?"

Josh sniffed again and shrugged. "Not really. Maybe a little when I first come in. You get used to it."

Pinching her nose and holding her hand over her mouth as she kicked through trash and clutter, Linda made her way into the living room. On the coffee table, empty cans and glasses surrounded an ashtray overflowing with cigarette butts and the tail ends of an uncountable number of joints. Linda kicked a bunch of dirty clothes and old newspapers off the sofa and onto the floor to clear a place to sit.

She looked slowly around the living room, her eyes jumping from mess to bigger mess as she took it all in. "So this is what three weeks of wallowing in self-pity looks like."

Josh cleared himself a spot on the sofa, knocking over a half empty glass of what might have been milk as he sat down. "I guess so." He picked a small pipe from the table. "You mind if I catch a little buzz before we hit the pool?"

Linda sighed. "Sure. Why not?" She glanced around the room again. "I may even have to join you."

He was more than a little surprised. Since divorcing a guy with a deep affection for cocaine who everyone thought could easily have passed for Josh's brother, Linda rarely got high. Josh retrieved the jewelry chest his mother had given him for his twelfth birthday, and after knocking a bunch of cans to the floor, cleared a spot for it on the coffee table. He opened the chest and took out a nearly empty bag of pot to replenish his pipe.

"Guess I've been smoking a lot since Ben left."

Linda glanced around at the filthy, cluttered condo. "No shit. Too bad getting high doesn't inspire you to go on a cleaning binge."

"Ben usually did all the cleaning." Josh filled the pipe and offered it to Linda.

Linda hesitated. "When in a frat house, do as the frat boys do." She took the pipe, fired it up, inhaled deeply, and held her breath before returning it to Josh. "Are you going to tell me about your night downtown?"

Josh took a big hit and then exhaled. "There's really nothing to tell. I had a couple of drinks, took in the drag show for a while, then watched a bunch of people I don't care to know dancing to music I'd never heard before. It was a good time."

He looked at Linda. Two years younger than Josh, she was still beautiful, with short raven hair, olive skin that quickly tanned a dark brown, and dazzling blue eyes. Their mothers had been best friends. They'd grown up together, and Josh could tell she knew there was more to his story. She looked at him and cocked her head. "Did you run into Benjie and David?"

Josh shook his head. "No. They weren't there." He relit the bowl and took another hit.

"That's good." She reached across and pulled his chin around so she could see his eyes. "You know you're going to run into them sooner or later, don't you?"

Josh returned his attention to the pipe. "Not if I can help it. David knows Ben has trouble keeping it zipped. The Bar is the last place they'd be."

He loaded the bowl again and handed it to Linda. Having outgrown the youthful crowd of regulars, he and Ben had long ago quit going to the Bar Complex. In truth, the decision to avoid the place had been less about the young crowd than Ben's wandering eye.

Linda snorted. "If David was that smart, you and Ben would still be together."

"Yeah, and if I was smart, we would never have hooked up." In hindsight, Josh should have seen it coming. Ben had left his previous lover to be with Josh. If they'd do it for you, it was only a matter of time before they'd do it to you.

"Do you miss him?"

Josh looked at her. "I don't know, maybe. Part of me is glad he's gone. It's like a big weight has been lifted from my shoulders." He shrugged and looked at the floor. "Maybe I should become a monk. Then I could put all this celibacy to good use."

Linda laughed. "You're not really the celibate type." When he didn't laugh, she slid closer to him and wrapped an arm around his waist. "Thought any more about that job offer?"

Josh draped his arm across her shoulder and rested his chin on her head. "Not really."

Walker, Cochran, and Lowe, the law firm where he worked, had offered him a promotion to national director of communications. The catch was he'd have to transfer to the Washington, DC, branch of the firm. Ben had been opposed to the move, but what he thought didn't matter anymore.

Linda leaned her head into his neck. "Why not go? It's a great opportunity for you, and there's no better time than now to get the hell out of Dodge." She sat up, pushing him away. "You should go."

Josh looked into her eyes. He couldn't remember a time when she hadn't been part of his life, and he loved her like the sister he never had. More than her words, the concern for his well-being he saw on her face told him she was serious.

But he couldn't imagine life without her, especially now that his love life was over. If he couldn't have a lover, at least he had Linda. Being single without her to keep him company was just unimaginable. He set the pipe in the ashtray and stood up.

"Come on. It's a beautiful day outside. Let's not waste it in here chitchatting about work."

Linda laughed and shook her head. "If you insist."

"I do. Let me jump into some trunks."

Josh returned a few minutes later in navy-blue swim trunks, a white T-shirt, and flip-flops. "Ready?"

"I was ready two hours ago," Linda smirked.

A Holiday Tales Novel

Terrence Bottom wants to change the world. A prelaw student at Columbia University majoring in political science, his interests range from opposing the draft and the war in Vietnam, to civil rights for gays, to anything to do with Cameron McKenzie. Terrence notices the rugged blond hanging around the Stonewall Inn, but the handsome man—and rumored Mafia hustler—rebuffs his smiles and winks.

Cameron McKenzie dropped out of college and left tiny Paris, Kentucky after the death of the grandmother who raised him, dreaming of an acting career on Broadway. Although he claims to be straight, he becomes a prostitute to make ends meet. Now the Mafia is using him to entrap men for extortion schemes, he is in way over his head, and he can't see a way out—at least not a way that doesn't involve a swim to the bottom of the Hudson in a pair of cement flippers.

Cameron is left with a choice: endanger both their lives by telling Terrence everything or walk away from the only man he ever loved. The Mafia hustler and the student activist want to find a way to stay together, but first they need to find a way to stay alive.

www.dreamspinnerpress.com

MICHAEL RUPURED grew up in Lexington, Kentucky, the thoroughbred horse capital of the world. In 1998, he moved to Athens, Georgia, home of the B-52s, R.E.M., Widespread Panic, and countless garage bands aspiring to make it big. He's an avid fan of SEC sports—especially Georgia football, Kentucky basketball, and women's gymnastics. Michael's personal involvement in sports consists of running, working out at the gym, and playing with his longhaired Chihuahuas, Tico and Toodles. In addition to "writing stories true enough for government work," he's on the faculty of the College of Family and Consumer Sciences at the University of Georgia. He's received numerous awards for financial education programs he's developed over the last thirty years for youths and low-income families and served in a variety of leadership roles at the state and national level. In 2015, he was named Postsecondary Educator of the Year by the Georgia Association of Teachers of Family and Consumer Sciences and the Georgia Association for Career and Technical Education. He joined the Athens Writers Workshop in 2010 and has since published three novels: *Until Thanksgiving* in 2012, *After Christmas Eve* in 2013 (rereleasing as *No Good Deed* in 2016), *Happy Independence Day*—a Rainbow Award runner up for historical fiction in 2014—and *Whippersnapper* in 2016.

Blog: ruptured.com

Twitter: @crotchetyman
Facebook: www.facebook.com/AuthorMichaelRupured
E-mail: mrupured@gmail.com